# MORGETTE
## AND THE
# SHADOW BOMBER

**Center Point
Large Print**

**This Large Print Book carries the
Seal of Approval of N.A.V.H.**

# MORGETTE
## AND THE
# SHADOW BOMBER

## G. G. BOYER

Center Point Publishing
Thorndike, Maine

This Center Point Large Print edition
is published in the year 2005 by arrangement with
Golden West Literary Agency.

Copyright © 2003 by Glenn G. Boyer.

All rights reserved.

The text of this Large Print edition is unabridged. In other aspects, this book may vary from the original edition. Printed in Thailand. Set in 16-point Times New Roman type.

ISBN 1-58547-520-3

Library of Congress Cataloging-in-Publication Data

Boyer, Glenn G.
　Morgette and the shadow bomber / G. G. Boyer.--Center Point large print ed.
　　p. cm.
　　ISBN 1-58547-520-3 (lib. bdg. : alk. paper)
　　1. Morgette, Dolf (Fictitious character)--Fiction. 2. Mines and mineral resources--Fiction. 3. Bombings--Fiction. 4. Idaho--Fiction. 5. Large type books. I. Title.

PS3552.O8926M59 2004
813'.54--dc22

2004013400

# Prologue

The explosion blew out all the front windows in Matt Morgette's house plus a substantial number all over the neighborhood. A powerful dynamite charge had been set off, apparently by an electrical device controlled by a bomber watching at a safe distance.

The newspaper story covered the known details:

> Just before daybreak today a powerful bomb exploded immediately inside the front gate of the old Wheat mansion, now owned by Matt Morgette, prominent local rancher. Morgette does not regularly reside there and was not home at the time. It is thought that the target was Morgette's father-in-law, Will Alexander, who is living there temporarily. He is the majority stockholder in the New Ajax Mine, and is here in connection with the recent labor troubles. This is the third in what is obviously a series of bombings directed at the mines, such as have taken place elsewhere in the state due to attempts of the unions to organize the miners. Up till this time the local bombings have been directed only at mine property. This is the first aimed at a mine owner.
>
> It is a mystery why Alexander should be the first mine owner targeted, since he has met the demands of the union and his is the only mine not out on strike. In any case, the charge went off prematurely for some reason, which saved Alexander's life. It is probable that he was being watched from a dis-

tance, and the bomb was obviously designed for electrical detonation, to avoid catching some unintended victim. Alexander says he leaves his house every morning at the same time to go down to the company office.

Pieces of the infernal machine scattered as far as a block away and reveal the construction of the thing to be similar to others used elsewhere throughout the state by professional bombers employed by unknown parties.

Chief Mike Hanratty is investigating the crime and has several suspects under surveillance.

Hanratty sat, feet propped up on his desk, smoking a cigar. He threw down the paper after reading the article and said to Will Alexander: "It sounds good anyhow. If the bastards think you're looking down their rain pipe, they sometimes lay off a while till you have time to trip them up. Just like I did it on the old Barbary Coast. Everyone in Frisco thought you suspected them after you leaked a story like that one. Hal Green down at the paper planted it for me, but I actually don't have suspect one."

Will laughed. His permanent home was still in San Francisco, so he knew things hadn't changed there since Hanratty left. "Not quite as hopeless as Frisco up here," he said, "though the population has probably doubled since I was here last . . . must be ten thousand people now."

Ed Kirby, Hanratty's secretary, said—"Eleven thousand, two hundred, and twelve on the last census."—

and impressed Will with both his knowledge and the fact that he spoke without pausing while he pecked at his typewriter with his two index fingers.

Will was further surprised since it was the first time he'd ever heard Kirby interrupt a conversation. "Thanks," he said. Kirby grunted an acknowledgment, never taking his eyes off the keys.

"Ed knows everything," Hanratty said. "It's the main reason I hired him. Of course, typed letters make us look fancy."

Will wondered what the other reasons were since Kirby looked more like a minister than a cop, especially the thick eyeglasses, but he didn't ask. He returned to the subject of the recent bombing. "I was lucky. I wonder why the damned bomb went off prematurely? It looks like an amateur job . . . or maybe it was designed to go off when I opened the gate, and the gate blew open and spoiled the guy's plan. There was a stiff wind in the a.m."

Hanratty sent smoke at the ceiling, and said: "Maybe. It looks to me like somebody was watching to make sure they got the right party. You know I found a lot of wire that might have set the bomb off with a battery and let the guy that did it stay a long way out of the blast. In that case, maybe he didn't really want to get you, or he would have. Maybe somebody wants to scare you."

"Why even scare me?" Will asked, missing the point, and looking puzzled. "I'm the only one that agreed to an eight-hour day and four-dollar shift. The union's got no beef against me."

"True. But how about your friends that own the other

mines . . . especially Bradley's outfit? They're mad at you, and maybe trying to get you to go along with them and cut wages."

Bradley was the local manager of the other big mine, the Magnate, and spoke generally for the absentee owners of several smaller mines.

"I never thought of that."

"Best start. It would explain why the thing went off ahead of time. To scare you. Unless somebody hired the world's worst bomber. I'd expect a note of some kind if I were you, suggesting that you play ball, probably signed by 'a well-meaning friend'."

Dolf Morgette got his first word of the bombing from the above newspaper clipping that his son, Junior, mailed to Alaska along with a letter.

Junior wrote: *We always seem to manage a little excitement for your visits home. See enclosed clipping. At least us ranchers are having a peaceful time of it since your last visit.*

That left a lot unsaid. He might have written: *because of* your last visit. Dolf had a record going back more than a dozen years of administering the kind of poison that the Pinebluff area sometimes begged for to keep the human skunk population at a tolerable level. The job had been somewhat like the Hydra, as Dolf had found to his sorrow—lop off one head and two grew in its place. He'd even spent five years of a life term in prison where he'd been railroaded for a self-defense shooting. After his pardon, he'd exposed the plot that had sent him to jail, and had to kill its principal perpetrator.

In the months and years following his last visit to Pinebluff three years before, the remains of a number of prominent horse thieves and cattle rustlers had been found in remote spots. Those found early on were still recognizable, hanging by their necks on the means of their demise. The rest were bones, scattered on the ground beneath a noose dangling from a tree above them. Others that had been caught and incarcerated had been sent on free vacations behind bars. Suspicions were directed in the proper quarter regarding the mysterious hangings, but it wasn't considered healthy to mention them directly to Dolf.

The first of several bodies was discovered before Dolf returned to Alaska, but only one person had had the guts—or lack of sense—to bring the matter up directly to him. She was Pinebluff's leading busybody and conscience, Artemisia Allenby, who had confronted Dolf on the street and delivered her speech: "I guess your gang had something to do with those disgraceful lynchings."

He'd replied: "I'm afraid you're blaming the wrong parties, Missus Allenby."

She'd sniffed: "I don't believe it! You've been in the middle of all the trouble in this community as long as I can remember."

He had smiled calmly down at her. "Yes, ma'am, and never started any of it . . . only finished it. And what I just said was, my gang didn't have a hand in those hangings. I did every one of them all by myself."

Then he had tipped his hat and walked away, suppressing a grin with difficulty. Artemisia had looked after the tall retreating figure, mouth agape, wondering how a lone man could hang somebody, to say nothing of hanging a dozen or more. Such a reputation was one of the reasons he'd moved to Alaska. Another was a profitable gold mine there.

He lived there with his wife, Margaret, daughter of the famous Chief Henry. The whole country knew who the chief was, after the braves under his leadership had whipped half the U.S. Army in a historic thousand-mile flight of his tribe more than a decade before.

Dolf and Margaret led an idyllic existence most of the time in Alaska, raising their son, Henry, who was five, *going on fifteen*, a real handful of energy and curiosity. They also had adopted an Indian daughter, Little Maggie, just past four. She was Henry's complete opposite. Dolf's grandmother, Mum, had followed them to the Last Frontier, as had Dolf's best friend, Doc Hennessey.

Dolf and Margaret were almost packed to make a trip back to Pinebluff for an impending double birth in the family, the wives of Dolf's son, Junior, and brother, Matt, who were expecting within a week of one another. They were in the final stages of preparation when the clipping regarding the bombing arrived in Junior's letter. Dolf read it to Margaret and Doc, who was having coffee with them as he did almost every morning. When Dolf finished the article, he looked at them for a reaction.

"Sounds about normal for the old home town," Doc said.

Margaret's Indian warning system was setting off alarm bells. She knew Dolf would suspect what she was thinking and that he was watching her, although she avoided looking directly at him. She tried to appear unconcerned, sipped her coffee, and didn't say anything. Dolf prompted her: "What do you think, honey?"

She managed a properly impassive face, finally saying: "If it wouldn't break Father's heart, I'd say . . . let's stay home. It sounds to me like the kind of trouble people always get you mixed up in to rake their chestnuts for them."

Dolf had been thinking the same, but knew Chief Henry doted on their son and wanted to meet the adopted daughter he'd never seen. He shrugged. "The kids can learn a lot spending a summer with your father, especially Henry."

Mum came over just then from her next-door cabin and took her accustomed chair at the kitchen table. "Let's get this show on the road. I'm packed," she said.

"The boat'll wait," Doc said. "I won it in a poker game last night."

She gave him a hard look. "I wouldn't put it past you, but, at your age, you'd look a lot worse if you was up all night."

Doc eyed her amiably. "I won it early and went to bed and slept the deep, peaceful sleep of the just."

"I almost believe you," Mum said.

Margaret poured her a cup of coffee, and passed her a fritter.

"Better believe it," Doc said. "It's gospel."

"On what kind of cards?" Mum asked. "And who was dealin'?"

"Not me," Doc replied. "And on a lousy three jacks. Can you imagine a damn' fool bluffing his boat away on cards that wouldn't lay over three jacks?"

"Yeah," Mum said. "In Alaska I can. And I can imagine you bettin' that high on a lousy three jacks. What were you two drinkin'?"

"Water, in my case," Doc said. "And I can read old Cap Whatsis like a book, drinkin' or not. Besides, what if I did lose? I'm rich. I own a gold mine."

"What were you bettin' ag'in' him?"

"My mine."

Mum knew Doc was kidding, but nonetheless said: "A dang' fool and his money are soon parted." As she said it, she was stuffing a big bite of fritter in her mouth, and, after chewing a while, she observed: "Oom, these are good, Margaret."

Dolf smiled at his crew of good-natured lunatics. All of them, even the women, had killed someone in a pinch, and he knew they were capable of doing it again. Yet, none of them had a single mean bone in his or her body. He shrugged inwardly, thinking: *Come to think of it, I've killed my share and, as far as I know, don't have a real enemy in the world.*

Then he remembered why. He'd had to kill them all. It was why his face had made the covers of both *Leslie's Weekly* and the *Police Gazette* a couple of times apiece. His face was almost as familiar as Buffalo Bill's, and he was recognized almost everywhere he traveled as a result, even though he tried to travel incognito, usually under the name Morgan. He thought of that and made excuses to himself for having killed: *Every damn' one of 'em I croaked needed it bad, and was askin' for it. Besides, after I got the hang of it, you might say they committed suicide.*

He had a well-earned reputation as the quickest and best shot on the frontier. It was a reputation that would ensnare him in the brewing trouble at Pinebluff whether he liked it or not, since his weakness was siding his family and friends. Will Alexander, apparently now the target of a bomber, was as good a friend as he had, next to Doc.

The Morgette cavalcade detrained at Pinebluff from the facetiously nicknamed *Northern Bullet*, looking like a happy family just home from a sightseeing trip to the big city. The *Bullet* was only three hours late, about average, and the parties waiting for them, knowing it would be, had just arrived. Dolf saw his son, Junior, and brother, Matt, before the train stopped, and waved at them. Behind them stood Will Alexander, smiling. He'd half expected to see Chief Henry.

## Chapter One

Matt and Junior crowded up, grabbed Dolf as he stepped off the train, and a typical Morgette waltzing and bear-hugging reunion followed. Mum watched this from the steps and said: "Doc, help me down, so's I can git into the wrestlin' match."

"Holy cow!" Matt yelped as she hugged him. "You're strong as an ox."

She pulled away, grabbed Junior, and administered a dose of the same.

"Been choppin' wood," she said. "An' haulin' water from the river, to say nothin' of workin' my own claim." She looked around. "Where're your women? Gettin' too fat to be seen out?"

"You guessed it," Matt said. "Speakin' for mine, Diana begged off by saying . . . 'I can't let Dolf see me like this!'" He looked disgustedly at his older brother. "I told her if she was fit for me to look at, Casanova here would probably be able to stand it."

Margaret was standing out of the way, watching, shy as ever around her paleface relations, much as she loved them all. She kept Henry and Little Maggie out of the initial mêlée. Junior noticed and grabbed her, with the kids still hanging onto her hands, and gave her a squeeze. "Hi, Ma," he said. "Welcome home."

There was a general laugh, since he was almost as old as his step-ma, this diminutive second wife of his father. Next, Junior grabbed Henry, hoisted him in the air, and got a kick and pummeling by sturdy little fists for his effort. Henry wasn't used to so many rowdy Morgettes yet.

"Hey, Pa!" Junior yelled. "Tell this here wildcat little brother of mine I got paddling rights if he gets too uppity."

"You ain't my brother!" Henry yelled, scowling at him.

"Durned well am," Junior said. "Ask your ma and pa."

Little Maggie had taken refuge behind her mother and was peeking out. "I'll get her later," Junior said. "She looks like she might cry if I don't baby her up first."

While that sideshow was in progress, a general handshaking was taking place between Will Alexander, Dolf, and Doc. Matt came over and pumped Doc's hand. He said: "The ladies'll be glad to see Skookum Doc. Yer their *fave-o-rite* midwife."

"Haven't lost my touch," Doc said. "Lots of practice up North as soon as the dusky ladies found out I delivered babies cheap, like free if they didn't have any money, and most *klootches* don't."

"By the way, where are the ladies hiding?" Dolf asked. "And how about Clemmy, Will? Did she come with you?"

"Yep. She's got the two fat, bashful ones up at Matt's, gettin' ready a real spread for you folks. Gave 'em an excuse to stay out of sight. We got the front fence fixed, by the way, and filled the hole. I guess you heard about the little calling card someone left me."

Dolf nodded, looking sober. "Run in any suspects yet?"

"Nary a clue. A local character claims he saw a suspicious-looking stranger scooting out of the neighborhood about fifteen minutes before the big bang."

"Hank H.," Matt said. "You remember him, I guess. Still works down at Dawson's livery. He was on his way to work."

Dolf remembered Hank H., reputedly the village dimwit, and he figured that was why Will had qualified Hank's testimony as "claims he saw", as though he thought Hank was daft.

"Don't sell Hank short," Dolf cautioned. "I got lots out of him when it counted, and he's just as smart as he *has* to be."

Behind the new railroad depot, waiting to haul the party home, was the same big surrey Dolf had rented three years before to carry his son's and brother's wedding party to the train for their honeymoon trip. It had been thirty miles to the railroad junction then; the new mining boom had finally brought the rails into town. The *Bullet* now ran daily, but not any more predictably, despite what its timetable proclaimed.

While the boys loaded baggage, Dolf looked around and saw a city where he'd first known only a moose pasture which had been supplanted by a village that started as an irregular sprinkling of miner's cabins, and later, boasted one dusty main street—when it wasn't muddy—with a few businesses scattered along it. Looking down the same main street now from where it dead-ended into the depot, he saw several blocks of two- and three-story brick buildings. Horse-drawn vehicles and pedestrians were busy as ants as far down as he could see. It reminded him that he hated cities, even little ones. To Maggie, holding onto his arm for reassurance, he said, low-voiced: "I can hardly wait to get out to your pa's reservation."

She squeezed his arm. "Me, too. I suppose we'll have to stay tonight or we'll hurt your family's feelings."

He shrugged. "Maybe a couple of nights. Mum'll need help settling back into her house."

"I'll stay and help with that. . . ." She didn't have to say the rest. After that she'd run for it, if need be—head for the empty spaces and solitude they both loved.

Listening, little Henry asked: "When do I see Chief Grandpa?" He could dimly remember leading Chief Henry, wherever he needed him, by taking one thumb and tugging. "I want a pony, too. And, Pa, can I ride your horse?"

Dolf had left his stallion, Wowakan, behind. Alaska was no place for a horse, although plenty of people brought them there.

"Maybe," Dolf put off Henry. "We'll see, when the time comes."

That meant after he'd ridden him down first, and after he was sure his son could handle hot-blooded horses, to say nothing of studs. Lots of ranch and Indian kids not much older than Henry learned to manage a horse like Wowakan, or at least survive the attempt, as well as grown men. After that Dolf knew there'd be a fight if he tried to keep the kid off the big horse he'd heard so much about. *He'll have to take his lumps*, Dolf thought, *just like the rest of us did. It's the only way to really learn, and kids' bones don't break like old folks'.*

Henry had heard so much talk about both his grandfather and Wowakan that they were a sort of magic brew mixed up together in his mind. Little Maggie wasn't so sure about any of it—but was elated at the prospect of some excitement when she could watch her brother get into his usual mischief. She wasn't too sure what a chief was, but realized it was somebody important, so was anxious at least to look at her grandfather.

"I want to go out to the reservation *now!*" Henry said. "Why do we have to wait?"

Before he answered his son, Dolf handed Little Maggie up to her mother, then swung Henry up into the surrey and held him between his knees with his hands on his shoulders, looking him in the eyes. "It's like this, Son, sometimes *us men* have to learn to wait. I want to see Wowakan and Chief Grandpa as much as you do."

"OK, Pa. If we have to." He scrambled up on the seat and looked over the passing scene. He turned and checked to see that their hound, Jim Too, was trotting along where he was supposed to be, behind the surrey. They'd taken Jim Too's traveling crate out of the baggage car, let him out, and got a reproachful look, as though to say: "That was a hell of a shabby trick to pull on a member of the family." Now he followed, ignoring everything but his duty to stay with his people.

Will drove the surrey up the main drag to show off the expanded town. "Getting to be some burg," he said.

The sight of the congestion and what it implied did something to Dolf's stomach that didn't please him. He'd liked it better when it had been a moose pasture. Sight of the Wheat mansion brought back bittersweet memories. Years before, he'd finally nerved himself to march down there to tell Victoria Wheat he loved her. As he had drawn near, lamplight reflected on the verandah had revealed Victoria kissing Alby Gould good bye, a typical contradictory feminine gesture after telling Alby she wasn't in love with him. Dolf, who knew Alby was courting her, misinterpreted this gesture, since he knew Alby was her class and was acutely reminded that he wasn't. It was a mistake that had changed his entire life. He'd turned back, packed, and pulled out of Pinebluff for good. When he finally learned his tragic mistake from her letter, he was married to Margaret. Later Victoria was engaged to Alby, and they were soon married. He reflected on that, thinking: *It was probably all for the best. Margaret and I are the same kind. Tough.* He loved his little wife dearly and loved their kids. He would not have traded places with any man.

All the same he could never forget that Victoria had told him, when they met years later: "For every woman, there's that *one* man, and you'll always be that *one* for me." He'd often wondered what his life would have been like as Victoria's husband. Would they be living here in the Wheat mansion, with him making a respectable living as an attorney, which he'd qualified to be while he was in the penitentiary? The law was a thriving profession in mining communities where everyone was always suing everyone else over property rights.

The two expecting Morgette wives had been watching for the arrival of the surrey and trooped out onto the verandah, led by Clemmy. She left the others and tripped down to the gate.

"Dolf Morgette," she said, "don't you ever age like the rest of us?"

He grinned. "You look like you're holding up pretty fair yourself."

She ignored everyone else, put her arms around Dolf's neck, and kissed him hard on his lips. Then she remembered that Dolf's wife was watching and said: "At my age I'm entitled to a motherly kiss."

Margaret didn't think it was that motherly, mainly because, whatever Clemmy's age, she kept it, as Dolf said, "pretty fair". She was sometimes mistaken for her daughter Diana's older sister. Just then Diana yelled: "Hey, Mom, don't hog him!" She made her way a trifle slowly down the steps and came to join them. She impulsively embraced Dolf, kissing him even more fervently than her mother had. Margaret had long had suspicions about how well Dolf and Diana had known each other when he was in San Francisco on a manhunt a few years before, mistakenly believing that she and their son had drowned in Alaska. The newspapers had had Dolf and the Alexander heiress engaged. Watching them now, Margaret felt even more left out than she had at the depot. Diana was a very lovely woman; her advanced pregnancy made her awkward, but gave her face the radiant glow common to happily expectant mothers.

Margaret tried hard, but not entirely successfully, to argue down her jealousy with the thought: *Dolf would never do anything to hurt me. This is just the way he affects women and this isn't the first time I've seen it . . . and the simple, innocent man doesn't even know it.*

Catherine Green Morgette had married Dolf's son, Junior, on the pragmatic basis of settling for one Morgette, if she couldn't get the one she really wanted. Her greeting was more restrained than the other women's, a light kiss, but her eyes briefly revealed memories and lost hopes that more than matched the others, which she quickly masked, but not before Margaret noted her reaction.

Margaret knew and liked her best of all the other women and realized that of the might-have-been-wives in Dolf's past, she would have been the most suitable companion: a horsewoman from the toes up, one who could work cattle, shoot straight, and had chopped her share of wood, hauled water, got in hay, and done everything else attached to ranching and living close to the land.

They all went inside with much gabbing, and in a short while Catherine's father, Hal, arrived. He shook Dolf's hand warmly.

"Sorry to be late. The *Independent* is a daily now, and I have to mind the store."

He had more than the store to mind. He was also the new lieutenant governor and had to see to political fence mending. His past loyal championship of working miners, farmers, small ranchers, and the down and out had brought him a statewide reputation for heart that pulled in a lot of votes for the ticket and put his party in the governor's mansion.

After a noisy, convivial meal, Hal drew Dolf aside.

"You heard about our labor trouble, I suppose. Especially Will's wake-up call."

Dolf nodded.

"The miners are still out on strike. Some with families are getting mighty desperate. Who can blame them? People do a lot of things they'd never do otherwise when they're hungry, some sick to boot. Some undernourished kid dies almost every day. The lid's apt to blow off anytime."

Will overheard Hal, and said: "It's all damn' greed at the root of it. Big outside money doesn't understand like the old mine owners who lived here did. They send in a bunch of managers trained in a college back East, who don't give a damn about anything but making some money and going back where they came from. The sooner the better, except another one shows up in their place. It's penny wise and pound foolish to fight over fifty cents a day, or even a dollar. The amount they've lost already would pay the miners for a good two years. Besides, there's plenty of profit without gouging on wages."

Dolf almost laughed at Will's vehement condemnation of big outside money. The biggest outside money in the district was Will's—except maybe for Alby Gould, who was into a lot of things besides mining. The difference was that Will had never forgotten he'd once been dirt poor and had to scrabble for a living, not that Alby had any less sympathy for the poor, despite having been born with a gold spoon in his mouth.

Hal said: "Now they're really asking for trouble by bringing in scab labor. Local men are going to fight them. If they do, we'll have to bring in the militia. Maybe U.S. troops. I intend to oppose that, but the governor will overrule me. It's a real mess, and it's going to get worse before it gets better."

Dolf didn't see where it was his business except as a

concerned citizen, although he sympathized deeply with the many hungry workers and their families. At least, it wasn't the sort of situation he was apt to be drawn into. If mob war started here as it had in other spots in the nation, there was no way that even a man with his reputation could separate the opposing forces. Hal was right, the militia would come in, and there would be no winners in the end.

A racket outside broke up the conversation. Henry ran out, and yelled back from outside the door: "It's Chief Grandpa!" He wasn't sure that's what the strange cavalcade in the street was, but made the right guess.

Little Maggie ran to a front window and saw her brother scoot down the walk to the tall chief who was decked out in his most formal garb, war bonnet and all. Chief Henry stood on his dignity in public and looked down at his grandson with a face as unemotional as chiseled stone. Outside the fence, a warrior held his painted and feather-bedecked Appaloosa horse, and a score of others sat their horses, silently watching. Young Henry, rather than being confused or disappointed, grabbed his grandfather around his legs and hugged him. It was too much for the old man, who pried him loose, swung him up so he could look him over, then beamed widely and searched his English vocabulary for just the right words. He said: "Hi, kid."

Henry, in his grandfather's tongue, said: "You're supposed to say . . . '*Hau*'! Ma read it to me out of a book."

Margaret had allowed the two a private greeting and was now near enough to overhear her son. Little Maggie was inside with Mum, unwilling to go with her mother to meet this awesome person who was her grandfather.

Regarding Henry's brash admonition, Margaret said: "He's right, Father." She had a hard time suppressing a laugh.

The chief's twenty-man bodyguard, still mounted, was astounded to see the dignified old man break down in a hearty laugh before a bunch of palefaces and, much like a paleface, hug his daughter in public. The braves exchanged puzzled glances, shrugged, and joined in the laugh.

"It is good to see my daughter and grandson," the chief said. "Where is that mighty warrior, Dolf Morgette, and the other child?"

Dolf had been keeping inside to avoid cramping a very private family reunion but now came out to greet his father-in-law formally. Margaret had seen to young Henry's fluency in her tribal tongue and always included Dolf in their daily lessons, when he was home, which was why Dolf had no trouble conversing with the chief in his own language.

"It is good to see you, Father," he said. "We didn't expect you or we would have laid on a feast with much eating and smoking."

Chief Henry discharged his bodyguard with a wave of his hand, only the horse holder remaining. Inside, the chief spied Little Maggie, peeking at him from behind a chair. He said nothing, realizing that she was shy. He sat down and pretended to ignore her. To Margaret he said: "Does the little girl speak our tongue?"

"Of course."

"Ah, that is good. I have a special pony for her, and clothes, and things to play with. Even a puppy. It's a shame she's too shy to come and talk to her grandfather. Maybe sometime she will 'brave up' like her brother and let me swing her up in the air."

Young Henry said: "Aw. She's only a girl." His tone of voice indicated plainly that he thought it was an inferior state from which there was little hope of advancement.

Little Maggie stuck her tongue out at him, and came over to her grandfather and stood beside his leg in determination but at a terrible price. "You can pick me up and swing me if you want to," she said.

Chief Henry beamed at her and gently picked her up and let her down fast so she got butterflies in her tummy. She giggled. Her father and Doc often did the same thing with her.

"You smell like smoke," she told him.

He looked her over carefully, and said: "You don't smell like anything yet. But you will after I sit with you by a fire in my lodge and tell you old-time stories of *our* people."

Over coffee and pie, the chief and Dolf decided that, since the old man was in town, he might as well escort Margaret and Henry to his camp the following morning. Margaret, who'd been listening, was obviously pleased, but asked Dolf: "When will you be coming out?"

"Soon," he said. "I'll help Mum get her things ordered up and visit a few old friends and hotfoot right out. Give me a couple of days." Then he whispered in her ear: "And keep that young hellion off Wowakan."

While that was in progress, Little Maggie whispered to her brother behind her hand: "Grandpa eats pretty good with a fork, for an Indian, doesn't he?" She had seen plenty of them in Alaska who didn't and saw nothing derogatory about her observation.

Her brother was thinking the same thing and nodded in agreement.

## Chapter Two

Dolf was sure that Mike Hanratty was the ideal chief of police for Pinebluff, or any Western hell-on-wheels sort of town. He'd cut his eyeteeth as a cop on the Barbary Coast in San Francisco and retired as precinct captain on a private pension accumulated by graft, a procedure so common in major American cities as to render it legal by *prima facie* tolerance. When Mike retired to his native Boston and lost that retirement nest egg to a young tart who ran out on him, he took it like the amiable, homicidal Irishman that he was and said: "If I got the two back, I'd use the money to endow an insane asylum to retire in, and use the tart to feed fish out in the bay."

Undeterred, Mike then had applied the well-known principle that "absence makes the heart grow fonder", and offered San Francisco's underworld boss, Chris Buckley, a deal: he would remain *absent* for $200 a month, subscribed to by all the crooks apt to go to Folsom Penitentiary if he came back and, figuratively, started digging up bodies. As a result of enthusiastic response to his offer, Mike really didn't need his job as chief of police of Pinebluff, except as a basis of accumulating another annuity. Dolf knew how Mike would do that, too—by accepting a monthly donation from every fallen lady, gambler, joss house, carny man, and vendor in town.

This was the man Dolf wanted to talk to first, since he was concerned for the safety of his friend, Will Alexander. His second day in town, Dolf walked down to Hanratty's office. Mike looked up, and his face assumed a mock-sad look.

"Me old friend, Dolf Morgette," Mike said. "I suppose you blew in your stake and need a job as a beat cop, and I really owe you. But I don't have anything just now. However, I get one killed about once a week. First opening is yours."

Dolf shook the proffered hand as they both laughed. When Dolf was last in town, he'd held Mike's present position for a while and had given the newly pauperized Hanratty the job that got the Irishman's foot in the door of local law enforcement. Mike had shown up out of the blue and asked Dolf if he needed a cop, and Dolf had pretended that Mike, then pushing sixty, must have been asking on behalf of some tough *young* fellow that could handle the job. In fact, Dolf would have bet Hanratty could ramrod a suburb of hell and shake down the devil.

Their friendship was an unusual one, since they'd started out as enemies. Dolf had been roving troubleshooter for Will Alexander's score of wide-open pleasure palaces in Hanratty's precinct on the Barbary Coast, and the police captain was front man for Will's business enemies. The latter were trying to ruin Will by breaking up the lucrative vice enterprises that formed the cornerstone of his legitimate fortune. Hanratty had even tried to have Dolf shanghaied for a long cruise on a ship in the Oriental trade. Eventually they'd ended up with their eggs in the same basket and with a mutual respect of each other's courage and resourcefulness. Now, all was forgiven, and their case proved that there's no stauncher friend than a forgiven enemy.

"Pull up a chair," Hanratty said, and didn't miss the fact that Dolf placed it to face the door and, also, where he could see both him and his typist, Ed Kirby. Dolf eyed Kirby and wasn't deceived by the eyeglasses and short stature, suspecting that beneath the mousy exterior there was iron—it showed in the set of his jaw beneath a generous mustache.

Hanratty noted Dolf's appraisal and said: "This is Ed Kirby. I'd have to work if I didn't have him. You can talk around Ed."

"Howdy," Dolf acknowledged, but didn't cross the room to shake hands, and Kirby only looked up briefly, said—"Howdy."—and returned to his work.

Hanratty said: "I'd have met your train with a brass band, but I figured you'd have a big enough reception committee."

Dolf nodded. "I understand. At least, you weren't there to run me out of town as a vagrant, like Mulveen would've done."

Mike laughed. "If I had good sense, I probably would

have. Tobe's sheriff again, y'know. He told me you wouldn't be in town over a week before the lid blew off."

"Good old Tobe. How's he doing?"

"Fine. He may drop in."

"He'll probably slip the cuffs on me from force of habit."

"I don't think so. You ain't got a better friend in the world."

"It took old Tobe a long while."

"He ain't too swift upstairs, but he's a good man."

Hanratty knew why Dolf was there, other than for a social call, and got to the subject.

"I don't have a single lead on the blast up at Will's. Everybody figures the union pulled off the other two, but we can't prove anything there. In the first place, there's a whole raft of little unions all about as mad at each other as they are at the big companies. I'm not sure I want to catch the guys that blew up the company property. We got some of the oiliest dudes running the mines for Eastern big bugs that I've ever seen. They deserve whatever they get."

*That's really saying something*, Dolf thought. He wondered how long it would be before he met some of them. If he never did, it would be too soon to suit him. Will Alexander had already filled him in on what to expect.

Dolf got to what was on his mind about the bombing. "I hear Hank H. may have seen the guy that planted the bomb at the Wheat mansion."

"He saw somebody. It was still pretty dark, but he

thought whoever it was dodged down along the side fence and out beyond the stable. He didn't think much about it till the bomb blew. We got a lot of out-of-work guys wandering around looking for anything they can pilfer . . . some of 'em are pulling break-ins. A mouse like Hank wouldn't want to follow one of those, and best not."

"I don't suppose he could give you a description?"

Mike laughed. "Yeah, he did. A *big* guy." He laughed again. "A *bogey* man. You know how that goes."

"Yeah," Dolf said. "Maybe five foot two when you finally run 'em down. But, Hank H. isn't the fool everybody takes him for."

"I figured that out. I got a-hold of your brother-in-law, Buck Henry, and had him look for tracks. Pulled a blank. He said it ain't the kind of ground a man would leave clear tracks on except maybe tramped-down grass and weeds, and there was plenty of that. Something went through there, but he lost the trail down in the gulch out back of the house. Or rather he ran into a lot of trails . . . a pair of clodhopper brogans like most miners wear, most likely made by our man, kids tracks, coyotes, cats and dogs, and a bunch of deer."

"If Buck can't turn up something, no one can," Dolf said.

Hanratty took out a stogy and offered Dolf one, which he declined after seeing it was a villainous two-fer. Hanratty carefully lit up like he had a high-priced Havana.

"What else?" Dolf asked, knowing an experienced lawman like Hanratty had started a lot of inquiries.

"Our best bet may be the reward. Will probably told you he offered one thousand dollars, and Hal Green got the state to match that. That's a fortune to a starving miner . . . or any other kind for that matter. I've got my network on it . . . lots of guys out there owe me."

*And girls, too*, Dolf thought. He'd have bet a thousand dollars that Hanratty had recruited the best-looking one of them to replace his absconding tart, and would have won his bet. He speculated on the chances that the current one could roll the old boy for his new pot of gold, and would have bet another thousand it would never happen again.

"As soon as I know anything, you'll hear about it," Hanratty said. "This gives us all a black eye. I've got me rep to think about. Gonna try to nip this union bullshit in the bud, too."

"That'll be a tough one."

"I've thought a lot about it. Some of these union birds go 'way back to the Mollies in Pennsylvania. They should have been hung back then, along with the others." He referred to the infamous Molly Maguires who were responsible for a number of assassinations of mine operators over union organization in the Pennsylvania anthracite fields. Mike continued: "By the way, speaking of that, McParland was up here, and we had a talk about the local situation."

Dolf knew that McParland was a Pinkerton detective famous for his undercover rôle as Jimmy McKenna, who'd conned his way into becoming a leading light in the Ancient Order of Hibernians, the umbilical of the terrorist Molly Maguires. Through his work as a mole, ten Mollies had stretched rope, sixteen went over the road, and the organization died. Dolf merely nodded, waiting for Hanratty to continue.

"You know who McParland is, I reckon?"

Dolf nodded again.

"He's in charge of the Pinks' Denver office now. Anyhow, he gave me an idea. Mac said . . . 'Y' know, Mike, if we'd hung those ten devils first, it would have nipped the trouble in the bud!' I've mulled over what he said a lot."

He grinned, appreciating whatever he was thinking, and fixed Dolf with a stare from his pale blue eyes. These were eyes that had looked over the sights of a revolver and watched at least a dozen men—on the record—turn up their toes.

Hanratty went on: "Another real pro gave me a good idea. Do you suppose Chief Henry would hire out them deputy marshals he let you use?"

Dolf grinned, knowing he was the "pro" referred to. "How you talk, Mike," he said. He stalled for time to think that one over, meantime feeling he could get out a good cigar by now, without offending his thrifty friend. He offered Mike one, which was readily accepted and lit, the two-fer left to languish in the Arbuckle's coffee can full of sand that served Hanratty as an ashtray.

Dolf's erstwhile deputy marshals to whom Mike referred had been a bunch of Chief Henry's braves who'd helped him round up and hang a whole confederation of horse thieves that had operated between Canada and as far south as Utah. He'd been a U.S.

deputy marshal at the time.

Dolf looked at the ceiling as he blew out his first big puff of cigar smoke, and said: "I think I've heard of the outfit you mentioned, Mike. They might work again for the right party if the situation calls for it."

He didn't openly admit a thing, even to Mike, because public knowledge of the Indians' rôle in the matter would fuel the campaigns of the greedy land grabbers who wanted to steal even the small reservation given to Chief Henry's people after the Army drove them off their large, fertile one in Oregon.

"Let me know," Hanratty said. "And, come to think of it, I might have a job open right now."

"I'll bet," Dolf said. "A job as what, just as a matter of curiosity, old pard?"

"Chief investigator. I'd pay a hundred fifty a month and whatever he could steal."

"That's about what I thought. Tell you what I'll do, Mike. I'll keep my ear to the ground, and it won't cost you or anybody else a cent."

"I'll settle for that," Hanratty said. "Where will you be?"

"Fishing up around timberline, if I know Chief Henry. He goes up there to get away from it all in the summer."

"Christ! He doesn't exactly live in the city out where his camp is."

They were interrupted by the arrival of Will Alexander with a companion. Will ducked his head in, saw Dolf, and said—"I'm glad you're here."—and to Mike: "Mind if we come in?"

"Come ahead. Hello, Bradley." He greeted Will's

companion, without warmth.

His tone of voice placed Dolf on guard, so that he looked over Bradley more carefully than he would have. The man had dude written all over him, from the highly polished, russet, knob-toed shoes and pegged trousers to a derby hat. He was shaped like a turnip, as sedentary types who'd never sat a horse or followed one behind a plow were apt to be. A sack coat fell from his narrow shoulders, and he wore a fresh paper collar and red cravat, the only lively thing about his appearance. On top, looking like an absent-minded afterthought, was his high, narrow head, perched on a thin neck with a protruding Adam's apple. The healthiest-looking part of him was a luxuriant brown mustache beneath a pug nose that was entirely out of place between skeletal cheek bones. His black, shoe-button eyes seemed unable to remain on anything or anybody. When they settled on Dolf, however, they paused, and Bradley looked surprised for just a moment.

*He did a quick make on the face he's seen on* Leslie's *or the* Police Gazette *in some barber shop*, Dolf thought. *Probably read all about me, too, and peed down his leg.* Humorously he decided to play the Wild Bill rôle with this one if the opportunity ever arose.

Will said: "Dolf, this is Nick Bradley. Nick, meet my old friend, Dolf Morgette."

If Will had used the man's full name—Nicodemus, for which Nick was short—Dolf would have had a hard time stifling a guffaw. He didn't offer to get up, so Bradley had to step across the room to shake hands. Bradley offered his hand like a kid petting a lion he'd been told wouldn't bite him under the circumstances, an assurance he wasn't really sure about. His hand was white and his grip limp, like a frail old lady. Dolf noticed that his hands were even freckled like an old lady's. He was careful not to squeeze at all, having learned in the past how fragile some of these types were.

"Pleased to meet you, Mister Morgette," Bradley said.

"Howdy," Dolf greeted, poker-faced. He figured this one would probably go back East and tell it scary about shaking hands with the notorious killer. He wondered if the little pipsqueak knew Mike's record.

"Sit," Mike invited them. "What's on your mind, Will?"

"Not too much."

Will, as Dolf knew from experience, probably had more on his mind at any moment than ten average people. When he made a noncommittal remark such as that, there actually were dozens of ideas teaming behind a bland face. He said: "There *was* one little thing I wanted Bradley to tell you about."

Hanratty assumed a look of mild interest, waiting. Bradley looked like he was going to talk only because Will had twisted his arm.

When Bradley hesitated, Will said: "Bradley is going to bring in Pinkerton strikebreakers."

Hanratty fixed Bradley with a cold stare. "That's a god damn' dumb move," he said.

"That's what I told him," Will said. "By the way, Nick, you weren't planning to head back East on business before they get here, were you? Or maybe take a vacation in Europe? Carnegie was in Scotland when Frick pulled the trigger for him at Homestead, as I recall."

Bradley's expression answered the question. He protested: "I can't miss the board meeting in New York."

"Yes, it will probably be real exciting," Will dryly said. "But not as exciting as what will be going on here. We'll have a little war on our hands, if I'm any judge. Probably won't kill over fifty or sixty innocent people."

"Oh, really, now, Will. I don't see it that way at all. Besides, we're perfectly within our rights."

"That's the way Carnegie and Frick figured with the law looking the other way. Since then President Harrison woke up and worries it'll cost him reëlection. I hope to hell it does. But, of course, you're not running for public office . . . and you've got to protect your stockholders, just like the government has to protect free enterprise, right?"

Bradley said: "That's really true, and we can't sidestep it. And if these anarchists start trouble here, the militia will put a stop to that. Such barbarians should be run out of the community anyhow, if they don't want to work for a decent wage."

"A decent wage is the problem!" Will snapped. "The old-time owners paid a decent wage. Before you're through, you'll wish you hadn't cut wages. And I'll bet old Benjamin Harrison would side-step the hell out of Homestead, if he had it to do over again. His kind really love being President."

Bradley looked trapped. His eyes shifted to Hanratty, then Dolf, and then his shoes where he got more consolation than from either. He said: "All the same, we have to maximize profits. I have a board to answer to, Will, you don't. In the long run we'll come out ahead."

"In the long run you'll kill about a hundred or so men whose only crime will be trying to feed their families."

"Really, Will! You don't know that!"

"The hell I don't! I've seen it all before. I don't know a rattlesnake will nip me if I step on it, either, but I've got better sense than to give it a chance if I can help it."

"I don't have to listen to this," Bradley protested.

Will shrugged. "Well, I just thought I'd let Mike here know ahead of time what you're letting him in for. You'll be reading about it in the papers back in New York. Or were you maybe planning a trip to the continent, like Carnegie?"

Bradley ignored him and said: "I've got to get over to the office."

Will didn't offer to join him. Instead, he said: "Go ahead. And be careful when you open that gate in front of the building."

"What do you mean?" Bradley asked, looking nervous.

Will laughed. "There's something scary about gates in this burg. And maybe word got out what you're planning. If I was you, Nick, I'd get on that train East as soon as I could. Somebody might've read about Carnegie's vacation and will decide to get you before you get away."

Bradley looked at him, his face a mixture of disbelief

and fear. "You're joking, of course."

"Was the bastard joking that plowed up my front yard with dynamite?" Will asked. "I'm not joking. And it's not too late for you to settle the strike by jacking the wages back up."

"I'll talk it over with the board when I get to New York," Bradley said, and headed out the door, then paused, looking back.

"You do that," Will said. "And you'd better be damn quick about it. By the way, if you really *are* planning a trip to Europe, don't stop in Paris . . . these unions have connections there . . . I read somewhere that Paris is where most of their ideas about workmen's rights came from in the first place."

Bradley practically ran down the hall. When he was definitely out of hearing, Will said: "That ought to give the little bastard something to think about. I'll bet he'll be on the next train."

"It gives me something to think about, too," Hanratty said. "Like where I'm gonna get the money to pay for an extra hundred cops or so."

"They won't be a hell of a lot of help," Will said. "Don't forget the Haymarket riot in Chicago. The cops got their asses blown off."

Hanratty sighed. "I wish I was in Chicago."

Loud voices drifted up the hall from the front of the building, then heavy footsteps approached. A tall, broad man filled the door. He said: "Jeezus, Mike. Was that little bastard Bradley back here? You sure ain't particular who you associate with." He looked over the others and said—"Hi, Will."—but merely nodded to Kirby.

His eyes lingered speculatively on Dolf.

"If I was particular who I associate with, I'd see you to the door," Hanratty said.

"You and whose army?"

"One of the things I like about your kind is I never met one yet that was bulletproof," Hanratty replied. "But, now that you mention an army, Bill, I'd like you to meet an old friend, Dolf Morgette. This is Big Bill Cloverwood."

Big Bill didn't appear to Dolf like the type that he'd have to be careful shaking hands with for fear of breaking something. When he did, he felt the grip of a man who'd been a hard rock-miner before he got into union organizing. Cloverwood had come under the spell of Terrence V. Powderly and got the workman's rights message, but eschewed the former's gentlemanly philosophical approach and decided the only thing big business understood was naked force. He was trying to organize all the local unions into one to present Bradley and his kind with overwhelming force.

Bill accepted one of Hanratty's two-fers and lit it, then said: "I met that skunk, Bradley at the front door, and he had the poor sense to raise his hat. I grabbed it and stepped on it, then sailed it out into the street. I should have sailed him with it."

"I'd have had to run you in for assault," Hanratty said, but he was grinning from ear to ear when he said it.

"Sure, Mike. It was the only reason I didn't do it . . . in a rat's ass. I don't pick on girls." He threw back his head, laughing.

"What brings you here, other than airing your highfalootin' principles?" Mike asked.

"I just thought I'd let you know that about a hundred Pinks are on the way in here as strikebreakers, and probably another five hundred are ready to follow them."

"That's what I told him," Will said. "How'd you hear about it?"

"A little bird told me," Cloverwood said, and laughed.

"What're you aimin' to do about it?" Hanratty asked him.

"Me?" Cloverwood said, looking innocent and pointing a finger at his massive chest. "Why would I do anything about it. It's a free country."

## Chapter Three

All five men in Hanratty's office jumped when the building shook, followed by a heavy boom like a nearby clap of thunder. Glass shattered from the windows in the rooms across the hall and clinked to the floor.

"I hope that wasn't Bradley's front gate," Will Alexander said, as they jumped up and headed for the street.

On the front steps Hanratty ordered: "You stay here, Kirby, and keep an eye on things. I'll be over there."

He pointed to where people were running toward the site of the rising smoke and drifting dust that issued from behind Bradley's office building on the other side of the street and about a half block up. A horse, startled by the blast, was dragging a delivery wagon up the street at a run and almost ran over a man trying to hold his own rearing buggy horse.

Nick Bradley came toward them at a shuffling run, stopped once, and looked back as though he thought something was chasing him, and, when he reached Hanratty, he grasped his sleeve, face white and lips trembling. He gasped: "I might have been inside. I was just checking the front gate, since Will warned me, but I figured he was kidding."

"I was," Will said.

"Let's go get a closer look," Hanratty said.

They went around behind the three-story brick building, and arrived in a dead heat with the hook and ladder company whose station was only a block up the street. The rear wall had been blown off nearly half the building. Débris was scattered in all directions, and a large piece of the roof had been thrown across the alley into the empty lot that extended to the rear of Dawson's livery a half block away. Exposed floors sagged out into empty space and were smoldering, ready to leap into flames.

One of Hanratty's policemen ran up out of breath, followed shortly by a second. The chief said: "Keep the crowd away, Gorman. There may be another bomb set to go off, or some lunatic may throw one."

"All, right, keep back!" Gorman yelled, as he and the second cop tried to herd the crowd away, waving their arms. The crowd ignored him till he yelled: "The chief says there might be another bomb planted back here." That started a stampede back to the street, Bradley starting off to lead the pack. Hanratty grabbed him and prevented him from leaving. He struggled to get away, mouth open, still pallid and shaking. He managed to gasp: "Let me go, god dammit!"

Hanratty gave him a shove and turned him loose and watched with disgust as the mine manager ran off. Then the chief turned to look over the scene like a hound coursing for a scent. He stooped and picked up two pieces of copper wire and waved them in the air. "Same thing I found over at Will's. Let's circle out here across the alley and see if we can find the end of it."

Dolf joined him, Will trailing behind. Dolf noticed that Bradley, safely across the street, watched them but didn't come back. *His kind isn't cut out for much*, he thought, *except starving women and kids*.

They found no more wire and no tracks. Hanratty said: "About what I expected. But I'd bet a few bucks that blast was set off by a battery. The guy that did it reeled in his wire, but this piece blew off. We'll have to start questioning people to see if they saw anyone." He was talking half to himself. "The guy that set it off could have been across the street or up the alley. Could easy have buried a wire this fine under the dirt . . . it wouldn't take much to cover it." He walked up the alley toward the street, but the crowd had stirred up the ground. Hanratty looked at Dolf. "What do you think? If the bomber buried a wire, it was at night or someone would have spotted him. Maybe did. The odds favor it."

Dolf knew that was true. Criminals always thought they were undetected under cover of darkness, only to discover that someone just happened to look out a window, or put out their cat, or were sitting on a porch because they couldn't sleep; even drunks, sleeping it off in an alley, had been bleary-eyed witnesses who spoiled an otherwise perfect crime.

"Most likely he ran the wire across the empty lot," Dolf speculated. "It'd be easy to hide over in one of Dawson's barns, set it off, and walk away. Nothing but hay in those back barns . . . he'd have plenty of time to reel it in, especially with everyone's attention on the excitement over here."

Hanratty said: "Why don't you go over to Dawson's and ask a few questions? I want to hang around here till the crowd breaks up a little."

Before Dolf could comply, Sheriff Tobe Mulveen arrived on the scene, driving his buggy. He saw Hanratty and pulled over toward him. He carefully extracted his three hundred pounds from the buggy and attached his hitch weight to the bridle, then walked over to Hanratty's group. He stuck out his hand to Dolf and said: "I heard you was in town. It's good to see you back."

Dolf almost laughed. This was a different tune coming from that source. Tobe hadn't changed all that much, however. He turned his attention to the building and asked: "What the hell happened here?"

Hanratty looked at Dolf briefly, winked, and said: "I don't know, Tobe. That's what we were trying to figure out. Maybe some kid decided to celebrate the Fourth a little early." A sly dig that went completely over the sheriff's head.

Ignoring Hanratty, Tobe said: "Looks to me like the bomber got in another lick."

Bradley had rejoined the group and said: "Another minute and I'd have been in there."

"Where were you?" Tobe asked, not that he gave a damn. His opinion of Bradley was about like Hanratty's.

"Out front, just coming in the gate," Bradley said, laughing nervously. "Will, here, told me just a couple of minutes before I ought to look over the gate pretty close, just in case. If I hadn't spent a minute doing that, I'd have been inside."

*Pity Will didn't keep his mouth shut*, Dolf thought.

They watched the firemen playing a stream on the smoldering wood.

"I guess I'll walk over to Dawson's," Dolf said.

"What for?" Mulveen asked.

Hanratty showed him the pieces of wire. "Same kind I found over at Will's. Someone ran them over here from somewhere. Dolf figures the most likely place would have been from the barns over there. Easier to bury them and not be seen if he came from over there last night."

"You wouldn't even have to bury them except under the alley," Dolf said.

Mulveen shook his head. "Why run even that much risk? It'd be easier to touch off a fuse. Nobody would pay attention to someone walking up the alley here . . .

a slow fuse would take a long while so he could get away."

"Because whoever it is wants to pick the exact time the blast goes off," Hanratty said.

Mulveen scratched his head. "Yeah," he said. "That figures. I never thought of that. But why does he want to pick the exact time?"

"If I knew, I'd tell you," Hanratty said. "If we figure that out, we may be a lot closer to fingering our man."

Dolf was about to leave again when they were interrupted by one of Mulveen's deputies. "Hey, Sheriff!" he yelled. "Wait'll you hear this."

"Not so loud, Bill," Mulveen cautioned, noticing a few nearby spectators turning their heads. "Git down and spill it over here."

The deputy dismounted and looked over the men with his boss, then looked at Mulveen for the nod to go ahead, since he didn't know Dolf. The sheriff said: "These guys are all OK. I guess you don't know Dolf Morgette."

The deputy looked Dolf over carefully and extended his hand. "Glad to meet you, Mister Morgette." He might have added—"I've heard a hell of a lot about you."—but his look said it for him.

"OK," Tobe said, "spill it."

"The train up from the junction got blown up!"

"How'd you get word?"

"The train down almost ran into them and backed up here, bringin' back a bunch that was hurt. Somebody blew out a trestle. And there was a whole slew of Pinkertons on board."

Bradley incautiously let out what was crossing his mind and exploded: "Jesus Christ! The god-damn' unions!"

Big Bill Cloverwood, who'd been wandering around on his own, had just come over and joined the group. Overhearing Bradley's remark, he said: "I'd watch my mouth if I was you, Bradley. You don't know who blew up a damn' thing. I wouldn't put it past you to set off bombs yourself to make the unions look bad. Why would we try to kill Will, here, for instance? He's the only owner that's treated us decent. You bastards had more reason to blow him up than any union."

It was exactly what Hanratty had said to Will earlier.

Bradley, with two lawmen present, stood up to Cloverwood. "There's a big difference between that train full of detectives and Will. Are you accusing me of trying to kill Will?"

"If the shoe fits, wear the son-of-a-bitch," Cloverwood replied.

"All right," Hanratty interrupted. "This ain't getting us anything. Let's go down to the railroad station, or maybe the hospital." He turned to the deputy and asked: "Anybody killed?"

"I didn't wait to find out. I know for sure a hell of a lot was hurt, including a couple of women."

Dolf quickly swiveled his eyes to Big Bill and glimpsed what he took to be a momentary expression of discomfort on his face. Dolf exchanged a knowing look with Hanratty, who had observed the same fleeting expression.

The union organizer covered his embarrassment by

blustering at Bradley: "I suppose now you'll accuse me of getting women hurt?"

Bradley astonished everyone, perhaps himself most, by saying: "If the shoe fits, wear the son-of-a-bitch!"

Cloverwood undoubtedly would have knocked him down if the lawmen hadn't been present.

*Maybe there's more to Bradley than we figured*, Dolf thought. *If he isn't planning to leave town, he'd better go heeled from now on and learn how to use whatever hardware he packs, just in case he runs into Cloverwood all alone.*

## Chapter Four

The first person Dolf saw at the depot was his ex-wife, Theodora, stumbling along beside a stretcher borne by two men. Her hair was disheveled, and her face dead white, as though she were about to faint. Beside her, awkwardly trying to support her, was a strangely dressed man, whom he judged to be a foreigner.

He hardly dared look at the stretcher, being certain it was carrying his daughter, Amy. Closer, he could see the ashen-faced girl, unconscious, a bruise on her forehead, her mouth slack, and traces of dried blood flecking her lips. Cool as ice in a gunfight, he was shaken deeply by the sight of someone he loved threatened by death.

He called—"Theodora!"—and she saw him for the first time.

She rushed into his arms. "It's Amy," she said in a

quavering voice. "I think she's dying. Is Doc with you? Oh, this is just terrible!" She broke down and sobbed, shuddering against his shoulder.

Despite his own distress, a fleeting thought reminded him that this was vintage Theodora, a selfish woman who'd caused a lot of tragedy, unfazed personally until the evil results confronted her and caused her to go to pieces.

He was relieved to observe Amy take a big breath, sigh, then breathe strongly. Despite her pallor, she hardly looked like the people he'd seen dying. Regardless, he was deeply concerned and wished he could have taken her blow for her. He recalled the guilty look on Big Bill Cloverwood's face a short while before and resolved to have a little heart-to-heart talk with him.

He was relieved to see Doc Hennessey, coat off and sleeves rolled up, walking down the line of stretchers, making quick appraisals of those who might need immediate help. "Hey, Doc!" he yelled. Hennessey looked around for the source of the familiar voice, then trotted over.

Theodora moaned: "Oh, thank God!"

Doc took in the situation at a glance and bent over Amy, feeling her pulse, then placing his stethoscope to her breast. He listened a while, after which he put his hand on her forehead. Her eyes fluttered open briefly, then closed.

"She's dying, isn't she?" Theodora said.

Doc gave her a disgusted look, half inclined to leave her in suspense, then relented and said: "I don't think so. She may have a concussion, but, if she does, I'd guess it's pretty minor. She'll come around in a while."

"Thank God!" Theodora mouthed the words in almost a whisper. She bent over her daughter, placed her hand on her face gently, and said: "You poor baby."

Dolf was as relieved as his ex-wife. Amy had been the apple of his eye from the moment he'd taken her up and burped her after watching her nursing for the first time. He could almost feel the little mite again, soft, warm, and helpless, and thought how, later, when she was a toddler, she would come to him after her bath, put her little arms around his neck before going to bed, and say: "I love you, Pa." He'd carry her to bed, tuck her in, deliver her good night kiss, then turn the lamp low, because she was afraid of the dark until she was six or seven. Theo had welcomed his help with the kids, not being especially maternal with either of them, although he knew she loved them both in her own twisted way. This was obvious now; he was sure she had been genuinely terrified over the possibility that Amy might be dying.

For the first time the man with Theodora spoke up, saying: "See, I told you she would be all right."

Theodora seemed to awake from a trance and become more like her old, imperious self, recovering some of her compelling desire to hurt Dolf. His offense had been not returning to her at a snap of her fingers after she'd "found out" the man for whom she'd deserted him. That had been Sheriff Ed Pardeau, who Dolf had finally had to kill in self-defense. Theo didn't hate Dolf for killing Ed, in fact, had secretly approved; she'd threatened to kill Ed herself, aiming a Winchester at his head when he tried to beat her. Dolf's only offense had been his justifiably cool treatment of her, after she had killed his once blind love for her. He'd gently rebuffed her frantic efforts to rekindle it, which had only aggravated her angry frustration.

This was reflected in her tone and manner as she introduced her companion. "This is the Count Henri Leclerc Mandel-Pritolet," she said, and added with a malicious look, "we're becoming ever such good friends."

Dolf shook hands courteously as he looked over this latest specimen of his ex's taste. Dolf was a little surprised that this one didn't remind him of all the rest. He didn't look like a handsome, oily fortune hunter, and Dolf caught a surprised look on his face when Theodora mentioned what good friends they were becoming.

Those who knew both Dolf and Theo well had wondered how she'd had the good taste to pick Dolf the first time, and how he'd had the bad taste to pick her. No one was more conscious of her disastrous mistake in deserting Dolf than Theo. Dolf's subsequent marriage to an Indian woman only made it worse, particularly since Margaret Henry was both lovely and better educated than most white women, including Theo, who'd never even tried to read a book in all the years since she'd left school.

Dolf wondered what Junior would have to say about this latest friend of his mother's. Usually she showed outrageous indifference to the prosperity of the ranch, which was jointly owned by him, his mother, and his Uncle Matt. He could imagine how the count would make out if he tried to stick his nose into the ranch business in Theo's name. *Somehow this one doesn't look like a gold prospector*, Dolf thought, *but, if he turns out to be another one, Junior and Matt will probably drown him in the horse trough.*

Doc interrupted, saying: "The hospital will likely be full. I think we ought to put Amy in bed up at Mum's house."

"I won't have it!" Theo said. "We'll take her home to the ranch."

"Not if you expect me to examine her every day," Doc said.

Theo gave him a poisonous look that he ignored. He'd never got any other kind from her, even before she and Dolf were estranged. She'd resented any threat to the exclusive affection of her husband. She'd tried to put a wedge between them, even making up what she thought were disgusting stories about Doc.

Her face mirrored her thoughts, ranging from anger, through frustration, and then realization that she was not going to get her way, following which she forced a smile. She said: "All right. It's probably best. I wish I'd kept our place in town so I could be with her."

Dolf needled: "I'm sure there's room at Mum's, *if you want to stay there.* She'll be glad to see you." He could imagine Mum raking Theo over the coals every time she tried one of her transparent hypocrisies. If Mum welcomed her, he knew it would be because it would be a chance to poison her.

Obviously Theo got that picture, too. "I'll come in every day," she finally said. "If Amy's in no danger, like Doc says, you won't need me."

Dolf knew his ex so well he could practically hear her thinking that Doc's suggested arrangement would relieve her of the bother and work of taking care of a helpless person, and also permit her to be alone to court her newfound count as much as possible.

Tongue-in-cheek, Dolf said: "You should come up for a while till we get her settled where Doc can give her a thorough check-up. Besides, Mum has never met a count, and I'll bet they'll hit it off like old friends."

"Who is this Mum?" the count asked.

"My grandmother," Dolf said. "I thought maybe Theo had told you about her. Everyone loves her." He could have added truthfully: "With the single exception of Theodora."

Theo gave him a poisonous look, and Doc strangled a guffaw.

Amy's voice interrupted this exchange. "Pa!" she called. "Pa! I'm so glad you're here."

Dolf knelt beside her, leaned over, and kissed her dirty, bruised face. "Doc says you're gonna be just fine," he assured, taking her hand in his.

"I hurt," she said. "What happened?"

"You were in a train wreck," he said.

She looked at him steadily, and said: "I remember now." Her eyes closed again, and she muttered—"I never thought real people were in train wrecks."—then she seemed to lapse into unconsciousness.

Doc checked her pulse. He said: "I didn't want to dope her before I examined her, but I guess I'll give her a shot. Then we'd better scout up something to move her."

Dolf looked around for Theo and found her several steps away, holding the count's arm. She appeared totally unconscious of the need to be further involved in helping Amy—after all, Dolf and Doc were there, and hadn't men always fended for her? She took a mirror from her purse and passed it to the count to hold while she tried to straighten her hair and clean her face.

Doc said to Dolf: "I'll stay here with Amy while you scout up some kind of rig to get her out to Mum's. There's enough sawbones here without me. Besides, most of the rest who were hurt are Pinks, and they should have been strangled in the cradle."

Everyone in town with a conveyance that could serve as an ambulance was converging on the depot. Dolf spotted Mop Finn with Mum's wagon and yelled—"Hey, Mop!"—and motioned him over.

Mop and Dolf took over the stretcher and carefully put Amy in the bed of the wagon. "I'll ride back here with her," Doc said.

Dolf didn't think Theo would ride in the rude wagon, but looked around for her in case she might want to. She was nowhere in sight. As they drove down the street, he saw her on the count's arm, looking into a millinery window. He looked away and pretended not to notice her as they passed. None of this escaped Doc, who thought: *About what's to be expected there. I wonder how long it will take her to find out the phony count with her?*

At Mum's, Dolf went in first and told her what happened. She flew out to see Amy, certain she could help by touching her and willing some of her strength and determination into her even before she made up a special bedroom. She reached over the side of the light wagon with a lumberjack arm and put her hand gently on Amy's forehead. "You poor thing," she said. "Old Mum'll fix you up as good as new." Then, forgetting her crusty act for a minute, she looked at Doc and said: "And I ain't forgettin' Skookum Doc fer a minute. Druther have you here than any three sawbones in creation."

They got Amy into bed, and Doc said: "Me and Mum will take it from here. I'm gonna have to peel her down and give her a complete look see."

"Let me know as soon as you know," Dolf said. "I'll be downstairs or on the porch."

"Where's the girl's mother?" Mum asked Doc. "She oughta be here helpin' if she's able. Did she get hurt too?"

"Not much. A scrape or two. Last I saw of her she was on some fancy French count's arm, lookin' into a window at some hats."

"I'll break her neck if she shows up here," Mum said.

Doc nodded as he worked. "Seems like the good Lord never takes her kind."

"It ain't the good Lord that's gonna work on her case when the time comes, if I'm any judge."

A half hour passed that seemed like a day to Dolf, who paced up and down the porch, then went inside to thumb a couple of magazines and a newspaper, only to put them down, return to the porch, then walk in the yard, where Doc found him.

"The girl is OK," Doc assured, "except for a busted wing that I set and that bump on the head and some bruised ribs. Mum is with her, and she couldn't have a better nurse."

"Her mother should be with her when she wakes up," Dolf said.

On very infrequent occasions, Dolf's innate goodness pushed Doc's tolerance to the limit—this was one of them. He held his tongue with an effort. After thinking it over, he said mildly: "Maybe we should send someone looking for her."

The irony of Doc's remark completely escaped Dolf. "I might just do that," he said.

*I wouldn't miss what Mum says if Theo shows up for a whole bunch*, Doc thought. He hesitated, then said: "Come to think of it, I don't really think you should. The girl is going on eighteen. I'd guess she understands her ma by now and is used to her ways." He almost said "*selfish* ways".

"I reckon you're right," Dolf agreed. "At least, I'm going up and sit with her till she comes around, if you don't mind."

"Mind? I was about to suggest it."

Dolf went upstairs and pulled a chair up beside the bed, and held one of Amy's small hands in his big ones. He thought she looked a lot better than she had and figured the painkiller Doc had given her had helped.

Mum said: "I'm goin' down and fix some chicken broth for when she wakes up. I'll be back in a while, in case she needs to use that bedpan. Call me if you need me."

Alone with Amy, Dolf studied her face. It favored the Morgettes now that she was maturing. He'd seen her mother in her when she was a baby and had been happy about that. Now, he could see his own mother's features in her, and his mother's hair, brown with red tints in it. Amy was a beauty, no doubt about it. He hoped she'd have better luck with men than he'd had with women. He grinned, and thought: *I guess I'm gonna have to keep a loaded shotgun behind the door to drive away the kind like that count.*

He wondered what sort of a chaperone her mother had been. They'd been traveling in Europe for the sake of "broadening Amy's education". He'd rather have had Amy up on the reservation with Chief Henry's people, but knew that Victoria Wheat had become Amy's mentor. Amy wanted to be remembered as something besides a hard-working rancher's wife whose only monument, after she was gone, would be a stone buried in the weeds in a ranch burying ground. By contrast, Diana Alexander had happily traded all the privileges and opportunities his daughter was seeking to marry his brother Matt and be a ranch wife. And Diana had surprised everyone by not dragging Matt around the world every year in an effort to pump culture into him. As Mum had commented, after observing Diana's style when the chips were down: "The gal is aces with a shotgun."

Dolf was sure no one would ever have occasion to say that about Amy, but whatever Amy wanted to make of herself suited him. He'd financed her trip to Europe and intended to see that she got whatever formal schooling she wanted. After that, only time would tell if she'd become educated.

As he watched her, she stirred and opened her eyes, looked around the room, and then focused on him. "Pa," she said, "I'm glad you're here." He was relieved that she didn't ask where her mother was. Then she said: "It was awful. I thought I was going to be killed, and the only thing that went through my mind was I'd never see you again."

He didn't try to hold back or conceal the tears that came to his eyes.

## Chapter Five

After he was satisfied that Amy would be all right, Dolf headed back uptown. He wanted to learn what Tobe Mulveen and Hanratty had found out about the train wreck and the dynamiting that had caused it. He found Mike in his office with a visitor who, at the sight of Dolf, looked as if he'd like to jump out the window. Hanratty was looking at Dolf and didn't notice. He said: "This is Obie Pookay, who's in charge of the Pinks that came in on the train."

"We've met," Dolf said curtly. He might have added: *Two or three times too often for my taste.*

When he'd first met Obadiah, the detective had spelled his name Puecke, but changed it after getting into the Western hinterlands where he found that "crude" frontiersmen pronounced it Puke, either from ignorance or a desire to irritate him, in which they succeeded. His first acquaintance with Dolf had been when that "notorious killer's" six-shooter was pointed at him, an experience he'd never forgotten. At that time Dolf had just been released from prison, and the Pinks were shadowing him. They harbored the mistaken suspicion that he'd lead them to the hidden loot from a train robbery they thought he'd pulled off before he went to the pen. Puecke and another operative, Leverette Peeples, had been assigned his case.

Obie had run afoul of Dolf again in San Francisco a year later after he and Leverette Peeples had gone into business as private investigators. Obie was sincerely praying now that Dolf hadn't found out that it had been he whose avarice and stupidity had managed to get Diana Alexander kidnapped by a Chinese Tong at that time.

"Did you two meet in Frisco?" Hanratty asked. As a police captain there, he'd kept a suspicious eye on all the private dicks such as Pookay, knowing the types that were usually attracted to the business—principally blackmailers, natural born snoops, and troublemakers. (His virtuous nature had blinded him to the fact that the description fit most of the San Francisco cops, and cops in general, particularly him.)

Pookay said nothing, so Dolf put in: "Yeah, and up here before then."

Hanratty raised an eyebrow over that, but said nothing.

Dolf asked: "What have you found out so far about the blown bridge?"

"Not much. It's in Mulveen's department."

"It's a union job," Pookay said.

Normally Hanratty would have told Pookay's type to shut up, but in this case he agreed. Reading the chief's mind, Dolf asked: "Have you talked with Cloverwood?"

"He's been mighty scarce. I put out the word I want to see him, but wouldn't bet he's going to come in like a nice little boy."

Dolf chuckled. "No bet here." Then his voice hardened as he said: "My daughter was almost killed on that train."

Hanratty read in Dolf's eyes what that implied. He knew Dolf well enough to figure what he saw on his face was the foremost reason why Cloverwood might be keeping out of sight, if he had heard what had happened to Amy.

"How is she?" Hanratty asked.

"Shook up pretty bad, got a broken arm, some bruised ribs, and maybe a concussion. She'll live, but whoever blew that bridge didn't care about that sort of thing. Is that job you offered me still open?"

"You're hired," Hanratty said. "The pay ain't much."

"I'm not interested in that."

"It's got certain privileges, not as good as Frisco, but tol'able." He grinned, knowing Dolf wouldn't take a bribe or shake down anyone even if he didn't own a good paying gold mine and would rather starve first.

Pookay looked interested, but held his tongue. Hanratty explained what the Pinkerton obviously wanted to know. "You and Dolf will be working together, Obie.

He's just hired on as my special investigator for these bombings."

Pookay thought he'd better try to make his peace with Dolf, here, on neutral ground if he could. He said to Hanratty, praying his ploy would work: "Dolf might not want to work with me, and he's got plenty of reason not to. I got in a lot of trouble with Little Pete in San Francisco, and he forced me to try to kidnap Will Alexander's daughter, Diana." He tried to look Dolf in the eyes, but had a hard time of it, and looked at the floor, then at Hanratty. "Like a fool, I let him get me mixed up in it, but he threatened to kill my wife if I didn't play ball." *Hell, they don't even know if I have a wife*, he thought, *but I know Morgette is a soft touch about family.*

He turned his eyes to Dolf's face for reaction and noted it softening, and prayed harder that he'd made his case. "Anyway, I left town and never came back . . . went back home to Kentucky with the little woman and tried to make a go of it on a little farm and went broke. So I applied for another job with Pinkerton and got it, and I can say I sure as hell learned a lesson from the whole thing." He turned to Dolf. "I hope you can see the bind I was in and let me off. I really need this job. My wife is sick now, and I've got big doctor bills for that and have to keep another home in Chicago for her." He was a consummate actor when he had to be, and his eyes pleaded for understanding.

*The little rat is probably lying,* Dolf thought, *but how can I be sure? If he isn't, I can understand doing almost anything to protect the woman you love. And Diana really didn't get hurt. I guess even Obie's type can love someone. We've got to give him the benefit of the doubt. Besides, if he's running true to form and leaves here, he'll still be working for Pinkerton and might be a lot more trouble underground. Best keep him where we can watch him. I'll have to get to Will Alexander, though, and call him off, because he might kill the little son-of-a-bitch, and I can't say as I'd blame him.*

Dolf looked at Hanratty and got no signal there, so he said: "I'm going to buy your story, Obie, but you'd better stay out of Will Alexander's way until I see how he feels. He's apt to sieve you on general principles."

No one said anything for a moment, the only noise being Kirby pecking away at his typewriter. Pookay wished he'd stop—the sound grated on his nerves. He was thinking rapidly and asked himself: *How come the company didn't tell me this was practically Will Alexander's town? If I'd known that, I could have got out of this assignment just by telling them the problem. Maybe it ain't too late yet. I can make a run for it and get in touch with them from somewhere else.*

Cloverwood was closeted with his closest confidante, George Elm, in a miner's cabin at the edge of town. Elm wore grimy old miner's overalls and a dirty shirt, and had been living there for a couple of months with Clem McCoy, another in Cloverwood's inner circle, both under cover as shift miners. They were posing now as miners laid off by the strike.

Big Bill said: "I'm gonna hole up here for a few days until the heat dies down. Why the hell didn't those god-damn' Pinks come in on a special like Harry wired us they would? They'd be strikin' off medals for us right now if we'd just derailed a bunch of those bastards. I never counted on any women on the train, and worse yet two of 'em were Morgette's ex and his daughter. It looked to me like the girl was hurt bad. You know what that could mean if he suspects us, and he sure as hell will."

Elm stopped him there. "You want we should do up Morgette. From what I heard, it's been tried plenty before and got the other party killed every time, but he ain't bulletproof. Sooner or later his kind gets it. Maybe we can blow him sky-high. I sure as hell don't want to get in six-shooter range of him."

"No need to go after him yet. They can't prove anything on us. Besides, we might get someone else and be in even deeper than we are now. That's the trouble with bombing." Big Bill snorted. "Bradley is sure I was behind the try on him, and I'm halfway sure Alexander thinks Bradley might have had his place blasted to shake him up, since he didn't go along with the rest of the mine owners on cutting wages."

Elm laughed along with Big Bill, then shrugged his shoulders. "Could be any of the other unions that set off the shot at Bradley's. I can't imagine who would have done it to Alexander. It don't make sense."

"No, it don't. And the whole thing points up why we've got to get all the unions to merge into one. This ain't no way to fight. There's an old saying . . . 'divide and conquer'. Hell, they don't have to divide us, we're already divided, squabbling with each other. And on top of that maybe we've got a *shadow bomber* on the loose."

"What do you mean by that?"

"Some nut out on his own."

Pookay had arranged in advance to establish a Pinkerton headquarters at the Grand Hotel. He was busy writing telegrams to William Pinkerton in Chicago and dispatching them to the telegraph office by messenger. His latest, in code, deciphered as:

BEST HOLD OFF PLANNED REINFORCEMENTS UNTIL WE FIND OUT MORE ABOUT THE LOCAL SITUATION STOP BRADLEY IS RUNNING SCARED AND ISN'T SURE THE COMPANY MIGHT NOT MEET THE MINERS' DEMANDS STOP HE HAD THE BACK OF HIS OFFICE BUILDING BLOWN OFF THIS MORNING BY PARTIES UNKNOWN STOP NATURALLY THE UNIONS DID IT STOP STANDING BY FOR ADDITIONAL INSTRUCTIONS END

Pookay's chief assistant, Ev Bowman, sat in the room, reading a newspaper and chewing on a dead cigar. He was a man of many years' experience in situations such as this, although he was new to the Pinkertons. He'd been a lawman in several boomtowns, and had flirted with the other side of the law as a bounty hunter a time or two. Unlike most gunmen, he had no reputation as such, having played down his exploits, rather than blown off his mouth to the press to have his record enlarged far out of proportion to the facts, as some like Bat Masterson and Doc Holliday did. He didn't drink or squander his money on dance-hall girls, and, as a result, avoided the trouble such practices invited. In fact, he had his wife with him, a circumstance Pookay had taken with reservations. Hardcases usually didn't take their wives into situations like this. In any event, Pookay was glad to have him. He was sure Bowman could handle himself, might even be the man finally to take Dolf Morgette's measure if the need arose. Pookay reflected that he'd be just as happy if Morgette were somewhere else, including boot hill. *Why the hell couldn't Morgette have stayed in Alaska? For that matter, why the hell did the company send me back to this god-forsaken country again?*

He knew why he'd accepted the job. He'd tried to retire to his native Kentucky and live out his days on a small farm, the way he'd started out as a boy, and found out he didn't like to sweat or get calluses on his hands. Besides, he and his nagging wife had both been bored out of their minds living among the dogwood and magnolia. So he'd written William Pinkerton a letter, and was promptly rehired. The company cherished operatives as unscrupulous as they'd found him, and it was all in his record. It was what had got him this assignment; he was cut out for supervising a bunch of roughnecks running roughshod over ignorant laboring men, many of whom had families and hard-working ethics that belied the rough reputations of miners in general. Notwithstanding, Pookay wasn't the sort to shed tears over making widows and orphans.

As Bowman was going out, he passed Ed Kirby on his way in. Pookay looked up in mild surprise, wondering if Hanratty had sent him. Kirby shut the door behind him. He looked like he'd like to check the closet before he talked, which aroused Pookay's curiosity.

"Hanratty send you?" Pookay asked. "You look like you've got a real bee in your bonnet."

"Hanratty doesn't know I'm here. Best he doesn't find out." Kirby paused, weighing his next words carefully, taking reassurance from Pookay's apparent interest. He plunged in and asked: "How'd you like to stop worrying about Morgette . . . and Alexander for that matter?"

Pookay's answer to that was obvious on his face. "I'm all ears," he said. "Spit it out."

"What would it be worth to you if they both had a fatal accident?"

"I don't have the kind of money to handle that."

"Maybe money isn't too important. At least in the case of Morgette."

"You got something against him?"

"Maybe."

Dolf looked up Will Alexander as soon as he departed Hanratty's office and put Pookay's proposition up to him squarely. He practically had to restrain Will from leaping for the door. "Keep your shirt on a minute, Will . . . at least till you hear what I've got to say. If you're bound to get him, let's have him sent back to Frisco on a kidnapping charge and have him spend a few years in

Folsom. No sense in your buying a lot of trouble with a trial and maybe doing some time yourself."

"It'd be worth it," Will said, still hot as a firecracker.

"No it wouldn't. I've been there. You can't imagine what it's like. At your age you'd come out with a foot in the grave, if you even lived through it. You have to rub elbows with the scum of the earth and get along with them or get a knife in the ribs. It's hell. I didn't get too much of that, but I had a reputation as a killer. You don't. Besides, they'll know you're rich and that'll weigh against you. Don't even think of it, Will. Even if you beat the rap, the wasted time with a trial will make an old man of you."

Will listened and was obviously weighing Dolf's words carefully. Dolf was glad to read that on his face, and the fact that he seemed to relax a little. Finally Will asked: "What do you think we should do? Just let him get away with it?"

"Maybe not, in the long run. Let's give him some rope and, at least, pretend to go along with him for now. We know him and can figure him . . . if Pinkerton sent in someone else, we'd have no hold over him and maybe never figure him right. We can probably get Pookay to do what we want him to, up to a point. You want to settle this strike business without killings . . . our hold on him can be a key to that."

Will sighed deeply. He took out a cigar, offered Dolf one, and, after they both got their smokes going satisfactorily, Will silently looked out the window for a long while, thinking. He finally turned to Dolf. "You're right. We can use the little bastard, and, if he doesn't play our game, we can have him put away for a long while. There ain't no statute of limitations on kidnapping, and, if there is, he don't look bulletproof to me, and I won't have to pull the trigger myself." He grinned wickedly at the thought.

*With his connections on the Barbary Coast and his dough*, Dolf thought, *he could probably have almost anybody put out of the way.*

"Well, let's go down and look him up and arrange a truce," Will said, ". . . might as well get that over with."

Kirby had left Pookay's office well before Will and Dolf got there, and had left the Pinkerton chief deep in thought. *Why not play along with Kirby and take his proposition or leave it, depending on what happened?*

The meeting in Obie's office started as a frigid affair until Will, tickled at the sight of the cringing detective, began to enjoy it. They ended with a working arrangement that pleased Will, based on Dolf's earlier analysis of the situation. He even shook hands with Pookay on the deal, which Dolf observed with mild amazement. At the door, Will looked back and said: "The deal goes for me. I'd keep out of my daughter's way, though, if I were you."

At this remove, Pookay could bring himself to laugh at his last encounter with her in which she'd kicked him where it did her the most good, and him the least. "Amen," he said to Will. "And, Dolf, thanks for squaring things for me." He looked as if he'd like to kiss Dolf's hand.

As they walked away, Dolf thought: *Maybe the little such and so was telling me the truth. I know how I'd feel if Margaret was sick, and the chances I'd take to keep her alive. The little guy is really sort of likeable, aside from his tricky ways. Everybody has some good in them.*

After Dolf left Will, he looked up Hanratty and told him what deal they'd cut with Pookay. Hanratty said: "That gives us a handle on him, but I wouldn't trust that little bastard any further than I can see around a corner. We'll have to watch him."

"I know that. I'm sure Will does, too."

"Just remember, don't let your guard down for a second."

Kirby, back at his typewriter, smiled inwardly at that, thinking: *You can keep your guard up best when you know who to watch.*

## Chapter Six

Doe Darling's by-line was well known to readers of the sensational press. She'd been discovered by Ambrose Bierce and been hired as a writer on his recommendation by Willy Hearst for his San Francisco *Examiner.* Hearst had never found reason to regret it—in fact, was certain she'd increased circulation with her sob sister articles. She was adept at wringing the last tear from the plight of poor widows and abandoned orphans, and even frozen, starving mongrels and kitties trying to keep their pathetic litters alive (which always found them all a home) and getting the last ounce of drama from mine disasters, train wrecks, love triangles, suicides over unrequited love, and lost fortunes, as well as taking her readers into the hearts and minds of the frightened, homeless people victimized by natural disasters such as floods and earthquakes.

Hanratty, who'd known her well, *and not always happily*, in San Francisco, was not surprised when she appeared in the door of his office. She smiled innocently and said: "Long time no see, Michael."

He was actually glad to see her and showed it, getting up and crossing the room, taking her by both hands and saying: "Come in dahr-rling. I thought you'd never get here."

She misread his ploy and asked, surprised: "You knew I was coming?"

He laughed. "Not really. But the situation is cut out for your peculiar talents, my dear."

"And I wouldn't have been surprised if your long nose found out I was coming. Ah, Michael, we know each other like books."

He laughed, looking her over approvingly. She was a high-breasted eyeful, and her figure complemented a pretty, round face with winsome cupid's-bow lips, shining almond eyes, and radiant brown hair that showed glints of auburn, a genuine crowning glory, now pulled into a bun to fit under a wide-brimmed, bright red straw hat. He had reason to know that, when she let it down, it reached to her waist. She realized he was taking her all in and pirouetted for his benefit.

Kirby was out, so he asked: "Private showing later?"

She laughed, a bell-like, breathless sound, not

averting her eyes. "Michael," she said with a stagy sigh, "you are my guiding star. You never change."

"Not about some things. That ain't one of 'em. I'm a full-fledged rube cop, though, and like it. The Barbary Coast was never like this."

"I noticed. There's a church. It looked like about the same number of saloons though. Does Will Alexander own them?"

"Nary a one."

"I'm surprised."

"Have you seen him lately? You just missed him. He may be back in."

"I haven't seen any of the old crowd for a long while. I've been on the road, taking in strikes and interviewing moguls. I caught Andrew Carnegie in Scotland."

"What's he like?"

"Like what Mark Twain says you can't toss a rock in a crowd without hitting."

Hanratty cocked his head, inviting her to elaborate. He wasn't a reader. She didn't realize that, and he finally asked: "And how is that?"

"A hypocrite."

"Were you surprised?"

"Uhn-uh."

She eyed his office, which was really rather spare and plain compared to what he'd had in San Francisco. She noted the Arbuckle's coffee can ashtray and took a pack of cigarettes from her purse. "Want one?" She offered the pack.

He shook his head. "I'm strictly a cigar man. How about dinner with the old man tonight. Believe it or not, the Grand has a good restaurant. The chef cooked for the White House."

"That's no guarantee. I got the worst meal I ever ate there."

He laughed. "Then this guy wasn't the cook."

"OK. I'm staying at the Grand. I'll pump you mercilessly about the bombings."

"If you find out all I know, you won't know much."

Dolf, who had been over at Pookay's headquarters, stepped in, saw the woman, and turned to leave.

"Come back here!" Hanratty called. "I want you to meet an old friend."

The old friend had got a glimpse of Dolf, did an instant make on him from pictures she'd seen, and had time to put on exactly the cool, disinterested look she wanted to project. She'd heard about him from Diana Alexander, and regretted that he'd been in San Francisco for only the few months during which she'd been globe-trotting.

"Dolf, this is Doe Darling from Frisco . . . she writes for Willy Hearst."

Dolf looked her over with interest and nodded. "Pleased to meet you. I reckon you're the Doe Darling that all the boys in Alaska read whenever they can get hold of an *Examiner*."

She smiled blindingly. "Oh, surely, a bunch of rough men can't be interested in what I write."

He wondered if she were putting him on, then it occurred to him that she really might not know what a bunch of sentimental men peopled the far places, often with wives and children at home—most lived for the time they could return to them. He said: "A lot of 'em cry over your articles."

This took her off guard. It was the last thing she expected to hear from a noted gunman. She didn't know what to say.

"Honest," he assured her. "You write some real . . ." —he skirted what he'd intended to say, which was "tear-jerkers" and said—"stories that get them right where they live."

"Even you?" she asked.

He smiled. "Even me. But especially my wife, Maggie. She reads everything you write that comes her way. And my grandmother, Mum."

This meeting had taken a turn that Doe had little expected, but she liked it. She also liked this man she'd been led to believe would be a hard-as-nails killer.

"I don't know what to say," was the best she could do.

"When I get in a corner like that," Dolf said, "I don't say anything. But it's the truth. You carry a lot of the boys back home with what you write."

If someone had asked her, she'd have said she wrote for money or reputation, but Dolf's innocent remarks made her realize that deep down the reaction he said her work evoked in people was what she was really striving for. It gave her a warm feeling, and she found herself genuinely liking this big man she'd expected she would have to handle somehow—a man who her ambitious nature normally would have taken as a conquest, especially from what Diana had told her. She'd thought of him as another potential male hide to tack on the wall until he'd spoken in his friendly down-to-earth manner.

Now she was overcome by an emotion she normally reserved only for her family. Nonetheless, she wanted this man as more than a friend. And Doe generally got what she wanted.

"Michael and I were just going to supper over at the Grand," she said. "Why don't you come with us?" She didn't look at Hanratty as she said this. If she had, she'd have been surprised to detect no chagrin. He knew Dolf well enough to realize that she'd have tough sledding in case she was planning to throw him over her shoulder and carry him off. In fact, he was rather anxious to see how she made out with her familiar tactics on a man as impervious as Dolf to the wiles of women like her. He'd seen Dolf fend off Mornét Dumond, the all-time *femme fatale*, who had managed Will Alexander's Latin Quarter on the Barbary Coast, a move that had almost cost Dolf his life due to her resentment. He didn't think Doe Darling's wrath was apt to be so poisonous, but he was certain she was headed for a strike out if she attempted to add his friend to her long list of conquests. And he read the signs rightly. She had already made up her mind she was going to try.

At dinner she carried most of the small talk. Dolf was preoccupied with how he was going to tell Maggie that he would be in town a great deal of the time, working on the bombings. She wouldn't say much, but he knew what she'd be thinking. In this case she could hardly object to his desire to find the criminals who had almost killed his daughter.

Doe was saying: "I understand that Will Alexander was the target of the bombers. Why him? If I got it right, he's the only mine owner who met the union demands, the only one whose mine is still operating."

Hanratty said: "He thinks the other mine owners may have planted a bomb because they don't like him being *soft* on the miners."

"What do you think?"

"I gave him the notion in the first place. A fellow named Bradley, who you'll want to meet, is the front man for the other mine owners. I wouldn't put much past him. If he did it, it was to scare Will, not kill him."

"What do you think, Mister Morgette?" Doe asked.

Dolf shrugged. He didn't think Bradley had the guts for that sort of thing.

"Any clues?" Doe pressed, recognizing that Dolf wasn't going to commit himself.

Dolf looked at Hanratty to answer the question. Mike said: "We found electric wires at the scene of all the bombings, so we know they were set off by someone who was probably watching from a distance."

"Why would they want to do that?"

"In Will's case, to make sure they didn't get the wrong party . . . which would be him if they just wanted to make him mad at the unions, too."

Doe thought about that. "That makes sense in Will's case even if they just wanted to scare him. They don't know him very well, do they?"

Hanratty nodded. He'd known Will since the days of '49 in San Francisco. He was certain in his own mind that the other mine owners had been behind the bombing at Will's, but identical tactics used on Bradley didn't make sense. On the other hand, the unions had the record to prove they could be absolutely ruthless in going after Bradley's kind.

"I want to see Will's daughter, Diana," Doe said, "for sure while I'm here. I understand she married a rancher and is perfectly happy, which is a matter of wonder to all her old friends."

"My brother Matt," Dolf said.

"Really?" *If Matt is cut off the same piece of cloth as his brother*, she thought, *I can understand why she's perfectly happy.* She wondered what it would be like to be Dolf's wife. *The man I marry, if there ever is one, will have to be like him, big, fearless, a fighter, and handsome.* Something warned her not to try to flatter him with a remark such as: *If he's like his brother, I can understand why she'd be happy.* Instead, she said: "Where is their ranch?"

"Not far from town," Dolf said. "I aim to go out there in the morning. If you want to see Diana, you can come along."

"I'd love to. How is she?"

"About to have a baby."

"Diana? Somehow I never thought of her having babies."

Dolf laughed. It fit the picture he'd got of Diana when he'd first met her. Life was full of surprises. Now, if he were any judge, she loved the idea. He had a notion she'd make a wonderful mother.

"You laughed," Doe said. "I understand you knew her well a few years ago. Were you thinking what I was?"

"I don't know. What were you thinking?"

"That she was the last woman on earth who would

want to settle down and raise a family."

"Something like that," Dolf said. He wondered how much this woman suspected of his previous relations with Diana. She had undoubtedly read the newspaper surmises that he and Diana were headed for wedding bells. *Well*, he thought, *it might have happened . . . I thought Margaret was dead . . . if I hadn't gone back to Alaska for a final search and found her, I guess I'd have married Diana . . . and been happy, too, after I got over losing Maggie and the kid. I'm glad it turned out the way it did, though.*

Doe was watching him, but couldn't read his thoughts. She asked: "Where will I meet you in the morning?"

"Here at the hotel will be OK. I'll drive by about nine and drop in here for a cup of coffee, if that suits you."

"Fine." Later that evening would have suited her better, or even in the middle of the night. The thought of being alone with him thrilled her. She couldn't honestly imagine that leading anywhere on brief acquaintance with a man like this, but she made up her mind to stay around for a while longer than she'd originally planned.

Dolf excused himself, saying: "I've got to mosey up to my grandmother's place. She worries if I stay out after dark." He smiled at his own little joke. "I phoned and told her I wouldn't be home for supper and got a lecture on taking care of myself."

"It beats not having anyone that *really* gives a hoot," Hanratty said.

Dolf thought he sounded a little wistful.

Doe said: "Well, Michael, you have me to mother you now."

Hanratty looked happier, and Dolf left them chatting. He nodded to Pookay and Ev Bowman on the way out. He'd seen them come in to dinner earlier, and wondered who the woman with them was. Oddly he was only vaguely familiar with Bowman's background, which was exactly the way Bowman would have wanted it.

Bowman gave Dolf an appraising examination, without being obvious, and wondered where he carried a pistol, since none showed. He doubted that a man with as many enemies as Dolf, particularly in this community, could be so rash as to go unarmed. He knew of others like Dolf, trying to put a reputation behind them, who had gone unarmed to their sorrow, such as Milton B. Duffield in Arizona who had been done up by a scared kid who couldn't believe him when he swore he was unarmed.

## Chapter Seven

Dolf drove Mum's steady old nag, Lucretia. He'd selected her since he wasn't sure whether Doe Darling would be comfortable behind a snortier horse, although she hadn't impressed him as the type to be scared by much. He found a place to leave the horse and buggy up the street from the Grand and left Lucretia tied to her hitching weight, even though he was sure she'd have stood all day hitched to nothing, patiently waiting for him to return. When he turned to walk away, he was confronted by a ragged boy who said: "Can I watch your horse, mister?"

Dolf was about to say she didn't need it when he caught the desperately hopeful look in the boy's eye. "How much? I'll be inside the Grand a while."

"Ten cents," the boy said, but looked like he didn't expect to get that much. He was barefoot, not too well fed, but clean.

Dolf couldn't suppress a smile, and the boy turned red and started away. "Hold on, sport," Dolf said. He fished out a quarter and flipped it at the kid who made a dive for it and managed to catch it.

He looked at it, then at Dolf, and said: "Jeez, mister. I ain't got any change."

"Keep it," Dolf said. "You look like the kind that really will watch Lucretia. She gets pretty tough to hold sometimes, so don't let her get away."

In fact, she was already half asleep.

"Jeez," the boy said again. "I'll sure watch her good, mister." He was looking at the quarter as though he still couldn't believe his luck.

Dolf fished in his jacket pocket and took out an apple he'd brought along for the mare. "Give her this," he said, tossing it.

The boy caught it with one hand, holding tight to his quarter with the other. Dolf guessed he seldom had that much money to call his own. He smiled and walked away, then turned after several paces and caught the kid taking a big bite out of the apple. The boy saw him and again blushed beet red.

"I didn't mean to eat her apple," he said. "But I ain't

had anything to eat today, and it looked so good."

Dolf came back and produced another apple. "You eat that one, and give her this one later."

The kid took it, not meeting his eyes and still blushing. Dolf could remember when he was a bashful farm boy in town, always doing the wrong thing or thinking he had and feeling embarrassed. He could see himself again in this boy and wondered who he was. From his looks he sure didn't belong to a family that had much, but he was polite and willing. Probably the kid of some miner out of work trying to help out the family.

"What's your name, son?" he asked.

"Persimmon."

"Persimmon who?"

"Just Persimmon. That's what everybody calls me."

"How about your ma and pa?"

"I ain't got a ma or pa," he said, and looked embarrassed, but didn't blush, or look like he was going to cry, either, so he must have been on his own for quite a while.

"Where do you live?"

"Nowhere." Then he quickly amended that to: "Around."

"You don't have a home?"

"No, sir."

"Do you go to school?"

"No, sir."

He got red again, remembering how he'd stopped going there because everyone made fun of his poor clothes, and once he'd been so hungry he passed out and fell out of his seat and the teacher thought he had some disease the rest might catch. She'd called the principal who sent him "home", and he never had the nerve to come back. Nobody at the school ever bothered to inquire what had happened to him, he guessed.

"Where did you sleep last night?" Dolf asked.

"At the livery stable. Mister Dawson lets me sleep in the loft and sometimes gives me some work, but I heard him tell someone I wasn't strong enough to earn my keep." Here Dolf could see tears rising close to the surface. "It ain't so," Persimmon said. "I can whip any boy my size in town." He didn't realize he'd been eating the apple while they talked, and started on the other.

"How old are you?" Dolf asked.

"Twelve, I guess."

He was mighty small for his age, if he was twelve, maybe because he never was fed up right. Dolf thought of taking him up to Mum and having a square meal thrown into him; he looked at his watch and realized he didn't have time if he was meeting Doe Darling at nine.

"How'd you like to come up to the Grand with me and have breakfast?" Dolf asked.

Persimmon looked like he thought his ears were deceiving him. The closest he'd come to a meal at the Grand was to look through their garbage for something edible if the kitchen crew didn't catch him and run him off.

"C'mon," Dolf urged. "You can have anything you want."

Persimmon fell in beside him, and he shortened his stride so the kid could keep up. He'd have liked to take his hand but knew it would embarrass the boy, perhaps frighten him into thinking he was taking him somewhere else.

Since the Grand made out to be a high-toned place, a head waiter met them at the entry. He looked from Dolf to Persimmon.

"Two," Dolf said. "Maybe three, depending."

"I'm sorry, sir," the man said, "but I can't let anyone in dressed like the boy."

Dolf looked at the man impassively. "He's hungry," he said.

"House rules," the man insisted politely, but ready to become firm if he had to.

"You could hide us at a back table," Dolf said. "I'm supposed to meet someone here at nine."

The man shook his head. "All the same, like I said, it's against the rules."

"Who's the house? . . . maybe I can talk them into making an exception for a hungry kid," Dolf suggested.

"Me. I'm the restaurant manager."

Dolf shrugged. He wasn't the kind to push around little people or use his name to scare them, and the man had his job to think of.

"OK," he said. "How about giving a message to a Miss Darling who's expecting to meet me here, and tell her I'll be across the street at the hash house."

The man nodded. "Who should I say left the message?"

"She'll know," Dolf said, and turned, saying: "C'mon, Persimmon. We've got to get some grub in you."

Persimmon had been listening and looked like he'd like to hide because he knew he'd embarrassed his new friend.

As Dolf turned he almost bumped into Alby and Victoria Gould. "Dolf!" Alby exclaimed. "We heard you were in town." He wrung Dolf's hand vigorously.

Victoria hugged him and presented her cheek for a kiss. He could smell her familiar perfume, which brought back pleasant memories.

"Join us for breakfast," Alby said, "or are you finished? At least have a cup of coffee with us."

Dolf laughed. "Can I come over in ten or fifteen minutes? I'm taking my sidekick here across the street to get him something to eat."

Alby asked: "What's the matter with here? It's the best place in town."

"I like it fine," Dolf said. "I suspect the kid would, too, but they don't like his fancy get up. I hardly blame 'em, but he doesn't look any worse than I did at his age."

The head waiter was taking all this in, his mouth open, suspecting he might have performed a maneuver commonly known as "doing it in your own boot". He wondered who Dolf was but knew who Alby was. He owned both the hotel and restaurant.

Alby got the picture completely. "I guess we can bend the rules this time," he said, and signaled for the head waiter to seat them.

Dolf said—"C'mon, kid."—and turned to find him almost to the door. He trotted after him and grabbed his shirt tail.

"Where are you headed in such an all-fired hurry?" he asked Persimmon.

"I don't want to cause anybody trouble. I'll go watch your horse and earn that quarter and get something to eat afterward. I'm used to being hungry."

Dolf suspected his real reason was his embarrassment over his shabby appearance in front of such obviously prosperous people as Alby and Victoria.

Dolf took his hand and held it firmly. "C'mon," he said, "nobody's going to have any trouble on your account."

He'd seen enough of Persimmon to be sure he deserved help and didn't intend to let him slip away before he could arrange something. He hoped that Doe Darling would be as taken with Persimmon as he was, and knew Alby and Victoria both judged people on what was inside of them, not on appearances.

Dolf helped Persimmon get his chair close to the table and, since it had arms, was sure he wouldn't bolt for the door. Persimmon's stomach felt queasy, and he wasn't even hungry any more, praying he wouldn't let go in his pants and embarrass himself. He thought again of running.

The Goulds sized up the situation at once, and Victoria said: "I'm Victoria, and this is my husband, Alby."

Alby shook the boy's hand. Persimmon sat, mouth open, too impressed to blush. Everyone in Pinebluff knew who Alby Gould was. He'd seen him from a distance before, and he seemed to be a giant close up. He wasn't able to say a word.

"His name is Persimmon," Dolf said.

"Pleased to meet you, Persimmon," Alby said. He figured the boy would be more comfortable if the men ignored him and talked business; he nodded slightly to Victoria to guide the kid over the unfamiliar course.

"I'll help with the menu if you're not sure what you want, Persimmon," she suggested tactfully, since she wasn't sure he could read.

Persimmon cautiously eyed this lovely, well-dressed lady, and finally got up the courage to say: "I never ate in a restaurant before."

"I remember my first time," she told him soberly, "and I was a little scared even with my father along."

Persimmon was beginning to relax and feel better. He asked: "Where was your mother?" Persimmon asked.

"I never knew her. She died before I was very old."

"Aw, that's too bad," Persimmon said. "My ma is dead, too, but I can remember what she looked like. She was like them angels on calendars."

Dolf and Alby both had an ear cocked to the proceedings, even though they were talking. Alby winked at Dolf. Victoria was masterfully putting the scared boy at ease.

"I have a picture of mine. She was pretty, too, but not exactly like an angel."

Persimmon didn't know what to say, so he looked at the menu, but didn't really see it. He would have said he'd like to see the picture of Victoria's mother, but was afraid that would be impolite.

"You can have anything on the menu," Victoria said.

"I only got a quarter, and I ain't earned that yet," he said. "I'm supposed to be out watching his horse." He pointed at Dolf. Dolf realized that the kid hadn't really believed anyone would buy the likes of *him* a meal, or anything else.

"You won't have to pay anything," Victoria said. "My husband owns this place. We want to buy it for you. Do you want breakfast or dinner or supper?" She used the terms, as she knew local people did, meaning dinner at noon and supper in the evening.

Persimmon said: "I'd like a steak, then. I never had one, except maybe buffalo when I was little. I ain't sure about that, but, before he got blown up, Pa told me we did back in Montana."

Victoria would have liked to question him about that, but knew better than to do it and perhaps spoil the boy's pleasure, so she ignored that leading remark. But she intended to find out more about it later, if she could.

"Steak it is, then," she said. "What do you want with it?"

It hadn't occurred to him that he'd get anything with it, but he thought about that. "How about ice cream?"

All three adults managed to keep from laughing.

Victoria said: "Ice cream it will be. But you can have mashed potatoes and gravy and bread and butter with your steak first, and a glass of milk, if you'd like one, and have ice cream, afterward, for dessert."

Persimmon's eyes were shining at the thought and his mouth watered so it hurt. "I'd like that," he said.

Dolf got a kick out of watching Persimmon tie into what was probably more food than he'd ever had at one time. Dolf had eaten earlier at Mum's and was having only coffee.

Alby took out his cigar case, and offered Dolf a Havana. "Hard to get these out here," he said.

Dolf laughed. "Where I've been, it's hard to get so much as a two-fer most of the year." He turned to Victoria for permission to light up.

"Go ahead, I love the smell of them. Father always smoked them."

Alby said: "It's the smoke of kings. Prince Albert smokes a dozen a day, they tell me. Duchesses kill to stand next to him and tell him what Victoria just said, whether they mean it or not."

"I mean it," Victoria said. "They smell rich. I don't especially like cigarette smoke, but I don't see how anyone can object to cigars."

Alby laughed. "In New York they're putting special dining rooms in the best restaurants for sour-faced old ladies who pretend they object to smoke. It mostly drives more business away than it attracts, though."

"I don't smoke yet," Persimmon said.

"That's good," Victoria said. "Don't start till you're older."

"I chew when I can get it," he mentioned calmly. "Huck Finn wasn't any older'n me and he smoked a pipe and chewed, too."

That got a laugh from everyone, and Persimmon was beginning to feel so comfortable he joined in, instead of blushing.

Dolf thought it was a good time to change the subject. "How'd you like to come out to my brother's ranch with me and Lucretia, Persimmon, if you're not going to be too busy today?"

He said absolutely seriously: "I don't think Mister Dawson will want me for anything. I'd like to go with you first rate, Mister . . . ?" He realized for the first time that he didn't even know the name of the big man who'd befriended him.

"Call me Dolf."

"What's your last name?"

"That'll do for now. I'm kinda like you, Persimmon. One name is enough."

The Goulds knew why he was being evasive. There was no doubt that a boy would know Dolf's name, just as everyone still remembered Wild Bill Hickok, who'd been famous for the same reasons Dolf was. Dolf wanted the boy to find out he was just like other people before hero worship set in.

Persimmon's ice cream arrived just as Doe Darling entered the dining room. Victoria saw her and called: "Doe! What are you doing here?"

Doe came over rapidly. "I might ask you the same thing." She took both of Victoria's hands in hers.

"I live here. That is, we live here part of the year."

"How come a nosy reporter like me didn't know that?"

Victoria turned to Dolf. "This is Doe Darling, Mister Hearst's famous globe-trotting news lady."

"We've met," Doe said. "He's taking me out to see Diana."

Victoria realized she had no logical reason to feel a pang in her breast when she realized that what had been between her and Dolf years before had to be all over. She was married and that was that. But she knew Doe

Darling all too well, and was glad Persimmon would be with them. That gave rise to an inward smile since she'd have bet that little Doe wasn't going to relish the chaperonage.

Alby and Dolf were listening politely. Alby invited—"Join us, Doe."—and arose to bring over another chair. The head waiter almost broke both his legs trying to beat him to it. He hadn't been over six feet away since he had served Persimmon his ice cream personally, saying: "There you are, sir."

Doe seated herself and looked closely at Persimmon for the first time.

Victoria said: "Doe, this is Persimmon. He'll be going out to the ranch with you and Dolf."

If Doe was distressed at the news, Victoria could detect no evidence of it, and she'd been watching closely.

Doe extended her hand to Persimmon, who accepted it with remarkable aplomb, considering the fact that until a half hour before he was terrified of women like her. Victoria had achieved a remarkable transformation with her natural, warm manner. In fact, the thought had crossed her mind that Persimmon had the stuff that would make him easy to civilize—and she and Alby had no children. *Alby would probably swoon if he guessed what I'm thinking*, she thought to herself.

She'd have swooned if she knew the same thought had crossed Alby's mind.

Doe pumped Persimmon's hand as a man would, and said: "Hi, sport. Did anybody ever tell you that you look like Wild Bill Hickok?"

Persimmon managed a grin. "Yer ribbin' me," he said, but loved it anyhow. His grin broadened.

"No, I'm not. Don't you people think he looks like the younger pictures of Wild Bill?"

With his sandy hair and freckles Dolf thought he looked more like his pal when he was in prison, Knucks Geohagen, who was a professional boxer and wrestler.

"Now that you mention it," Alby agreed, going along with her ploy, "I think I can see what you mean." Actually he thought the main resemblance was that Wild Bill had also had blue eyes.

"I watched you finish that ice cream," Doe said. "Why don't you have another dish of it while I eat something? I'm starved."

Persimmon was absolutely positive he was going to like this pretty woman with the friendly brown eyes and big smile. He was also looking forward eagerly to riding out to a real ranch with her and Mr. Dolf, his new friend. He wondered if maybe he'd died and gone to heaven, and thought: *Jeez, I woke up hungry this morning and lonely enough to drown myself and fell into all this.* He pinched himself and hoped no one noticed. He was out of luck there, since Dolf did and quickly shifted his eyes away.

## Chapter Eight

Obadiah Pookay was a good man for his job. He'd had operatives combing the town to discover where Big Bill Cloverwood might be holed up until things cooled down, assuming he wouldn't try to skip out one jump ahead of Morgette's six-shooter. Obie was convinced that Cloverwood had pulled the trigger on the bombing of the trestle that aimed to get a bunch of Pinkerton hirelings maimed or killed. His offer of a reward for information on Cloverwood's whereabouts, in a town full of half-starved miners, got predictable results.

Pookay wired in code to Pinkerton headquarters:

HAVE LOCATED CLOVERWOOD STOP SUGGEST WE HANDLE OURSELVES SINCE WE DON'T HAVE THE GOODS ON HIM YET STOP THE LAW WOULD PROBABLY HAVE TO TURN HIM LOOSE AFTER A PRELIMINARY HEARING STOP ADVISE END

He didn't have a long wait for a reply.

PROCEED AT YOUR DISCRETION STOP IT WOULD BE BEST IF CLOVERWOOD WAS CAREFULLY TAKEN OUT OF THE PICTURE STOP OBTAIN AGENTS OUTSIDE THE COMPANY TO PERSUADE HIM TO MOVE ON END

Pookay read this reply with satisfaction. He interpreted the message correctly as: *We don't care how you get rid of Cloverwood, but do it soon.*

The urgency suggested to him that more might be at stake for the company than he'd been told. Maybe Bill Pinkerton thought his reputation was on the line with this particular job. But, more likely, they'd been offered a big bonus to bring this one to a conclusion in a hurry. He had mixed feelings about that.

Pookay didn't like this backwater, but the pay was a lot higher than for routine assignments, and he needed to accumulate a new nest egg after going broke on the farm. He'd lied about his wife being sick, but the longer he spun out the local assignment, the better for him. The bigwigs in Chicago didn't know it, but he realized that the trouble wouldn't go away if Cloverwood were disposed of. Even Big Bill's own union wouldn't fold without him. Someone else would step into his shoes. Pookay reasoned that his company figured only a man of Big Bill's persuasive talents had the ability to organize all the little unions into one large amalgamation and force Bradley's company—indirectly Pookay's source of income—into coming to terms. Obie turned all this over in his mind and saw no reason not to follow company instructions; otherwise, he would have dragged his feet.

Obie considered who to get for the job that needed to be done. Dolf Morgette might be his man, since Pookay was aware Dolf thought, as he himself did, that Cloverwood was behind the bombing that might have killed Amy Morgette. He turned the idea over and recalled that in San Francisco Morgette had brought his man, Forrest Twead, in for the courts to deal with, much as he'd have liked to avenge the death of his friend, Harvey Parrent, who Twead had undoubtedly drygulched. After further consideration he decided it wouldn't be worth his time to bring it up with Dolf. Who else was there? He had a roster of about a hundred men that he'd brought in, and most were not directly connected with the company except as day employees. A few of the more seriously injured were in the hospital, but the others were now out. He had set them up in a tent encampment at the edge of town. The majority of them, he was well aware, were from the lowest criminal classes of the Coast cities, and a few even from Chicago and New York, both places noted for a violent underworld. He wondered if Hanratty's assistant, Ed Kirby, might be his man, since he was willing to dispose of Morgette, or Will Alexander, for a price as yet unspecified. He'd put him on the payroll and instructed him to wait until he got the word, shelling out a few of the company's double eagles to make sure of his man. Even if he didn't use him, Kirby was a pipeline into Hanratty's office.

When Ev Bowman showed up at their office, Pookay handed him the deciphered telegram from headquarters. "You've been dealing with our boys . . . does someone fit the bill for doing up Cloverwood?"

Bowman laughed humorlessly, a dry rasp in his throat more than a laugh. "Hell, if there's enough money in it, any of them will do." He wondered if Pookay was denser than he thought, and was possibly unaware of the conscienceless types that had to be recruited for a job like strike-breaking, especially in an out-of-the-way place like Pinebluff.

"OK. You pick our man. It's good for a few hundred bucks . . . give him one up front and the rest on delivery. I've already arranged for a cabin with a good clear shot at the front door where Cloverwood's hid out. Get somebody with a Winchester in there as quick as you can before our bird flies."

"Suppose he has guards spotted around the neighborhood?"

"A chance we'll have to take."

*A chance some dumb bastard has to take*, Bowman thought, *but not this low life I work for . . . or me, come to think of it.* Dry-gulching wasn't the kind of job he'd ever taken, and he didn't have much stomach for even working as Pookay's go-between, but the money was good and he had to retire someday and was working on a nest egg to do it. *When I was a raggedy-ass kid grubbing out stumps on a farm in Wisconsin,* he thought, *I never imagined I'd end up like this.* He sighed and headed for the door. On the way out, he said: "I'll send you your man."

"Don't send him here! I don't want him to so much as suspect the company is involved."

Bowman looked at him disgustedly. "Who the hell do you suppose he'll think is putting up the money? The local diocese?" He waited for that to sink in, wondering if Pookay knew what a diocese was. Then he added: "Hand over the dough if you want *me* to handle it."

Pookay went to the office safe, carefully shielded his moves from Bowman as he worked the combination, and opened the door, blocking a view of the contents. Finally he closed the door, turned, and handed Bowman five double eagles.

Bowman looked them over and asked: "A lousy hundred bucks? How much for the whole job?"

"Maybe five hundred."

"What do you mean, *maybe?* I don't want the kind of bastard willing to drill Cloverwood with a Winchester, looking for me because you welsh on him. Hand over the whole thing or you can do the job yourself, or find someone else as go-between."

Pookay assumed a pained expression. "Don't you trust me?" he asked, not recognizing how stupid the question was.

Bowman looked at him silently. Pookay didn't like the look, especially since he was one of the few who knew Bowman's background. After a moment, he turned back to the safe and counted out the rest of the five hundred. He was so unnerved that he didn't shut the door but turned to Bowman and carefully counted out the gold pieces, one at a time.

"You want a receipt?" Bowman asked, almost grinning.

"Just get the job done," Pookay said, not recognizing the implied humor and totally unable to conceive that Bowman was capable of being funny.

Pookay had just completed that transaction and come down for breakfast, when he ran into Dolf leaving the dining room with Doe and Persimmon. He was the last person Pookay wanted to see at that moment. The whole deal upstairs had left his nerves raw. He nodded and tried to brush past, getting shouldered out of the path of Doe and the boy by Dolf.

" 'Mornin', Obie," Dolf said cheerfully.

Obie recognized Doe, who he'd seen on occasion in San Francisco and hoped she didn't get a make on him.

He was satisfied to observe no sign that she had. All Pinkerton needed was a sob sister bleeding for the miners in the nation's dailies, and they did have a habit of picking up her stuff and re-running it. She was known even on the Continent. He didn't need the kind of roasting from headquarters in Chicago that he was sure he'd get if she cut loose on a bunch of cold-hearted, mercenary strikebreakers. It hadn't penetrated his dense skull that she would probably do that anyhow, that it was why she was here, and no matter what he did or didn't do, it would happen as sure as death and taxes.

He mumbled—"Good morning."—to Dolf, and quickly sidled by as soon as the path was clear. He was out of luck in thinking that Doe hadn't recalled his face, although she couldn't immediately place where she'd seen it. Obie wondered what she was doing with Dolf and wasn't consoled over any of the reasons that occurred to him. He made a note to find out.

"Who is that bug-eyed little man you called Obie as we were coming out?" Doe asked Dolf after Obie was out of hearing.

"Does he look like someone you know?" Dolf asked, suspecting where she'd known Obie.

"I've seen him some place, but I can't remember where."

Dolf grinned. "Probably San Francisco. His name is Pookay. He's the big cheese for the Pinks that just came in."

That brought back to her mind a courtroom where she was covering a murder case in San Francisco with this man, Pookay, testifying on the stand. There had been a few other scandalous cases in which he'd been prominent, but she couldn't remember the details. "Yes," she said, "he was a private detective then. I wonder where the Pinks found him?"

Dolf shrugged. "He used to work for them."

"How come you know all of this?"

They were outside by then, Persimmon following and listening to every word. Dolf debated telling her his entire connection with Pookay, but decided not to, at least not until he knew her better. Instead, he said: "I think Hanratty must have told me the other day when Pookay showed up here."

Dolf found Mop Finn waiting for him at his buggy.

"Mum sent me," Mop said as soon as Dolf was in hearing. "Your brother's wife is due to throw her kid, and Matt brought her to town. Mum figured you oughta know so it would save you a trip out to the ranch for nothing. They're over at Matt's house with her mother."

That changed Dolf's plans. He wondered what Mum thought about Diana's going over to their own place, where Clemmy would likely fuss over her like Mum would have. He knew his grandmother like a book; even though Clemmy was Diana's mother, Mum would be sure she could nurse her better. It caused him an inward chuckle. He bet it wouldn't be long before Mum showed up for an inspection.

"OK, Mop. Thanks. Tell Mum I'll go over there."

He knew Persimmon would likely be bitterly disappointed over missing a trip out to a real ranch, and he reassured him: "We'll still go out to the ranch one of these days." He saw Persimmon's face fall, and read his mind. The kid thought he was just trying to make him feel good, that his idyll was actually coming to an end and he was being let down easy. Dolf said: "I want you to go with Mop and stay over with my grandma. I'll be over in an hour, or so, and we'll go out to the ranch, maybe even this afternoon. If we don't, we'll go for sure in the morning. You can stay overnight with Mum if we have to wait till tomorrow. She's just about the world's best cook."

Persimmon brightened right up.

"Take him along, Mop. I hear he's aces with hosses. Works for Dawson. He can help you around Mum's place while he's over there."

Mop grinned. "Me and Persimmon are old pals," he said. "I'll see he gets taken care of."

The fact was that Mop had slipped Persimmon a dime or quarter from his own meager wages from time to time when the boy looked especially hungry. Mop knew all too well what it was to be down and out. When Pinebluff had practically turned into a ghost town for a few years, before the new mineral discoveries, Mop had survived on what little he could make as swamper in the one thinly patronized saloon that stayed open. It hadn't been much. When Dolf got out of prison, Mop had been one of the few who greeted him as an old friend, rather than crossing streets to avoid meeting him. Dolf had put him in charge of his newfound pup, named Jim Too after his former favorite dog, Jim, then got Mop a job with Mum. She'd just come to Pinebluff to stay and bought a big old house with a stable. Mop had been in charge of that house and Mum's horses while she lived in Alaska with Dolf.

Steady work had got Mop off the bottle, and he looked better than Dolf had ever seen him. Where he had formerly seemed like an old man, he now appeared to be a pretty well preserved sixty, which probably was close to his real age.

Dolf turned to Doe, and asked: "How will it suit you to go over and see Diana at their place, since that's one reason why you were going out to the ranch?"

"I'm game. But with her expecting pretty soon, maybe I'm the last person she'll want to see."

"How well do you know her?"

"Well," Doe said, "she was probably my closest friend in Frisco."

"Come along, then. You'll probably meet my best friend over there."

"Who?"

"Doc Hennessey. Best midwife on the globe. He saved my wife's life in Alaska."

She assumed he meant in childbirth, although he didn't elaborate.

They had a slow trip over to the Matt Morgette house behind plodding Lucretia, who reluctantly woke up for the job. Dolf led the way to the door, and his brother Matt answered his rap almost at once. He shoved a cigar at Dolf. "Too dang' late to help," Matt said. "We got here just in time and it popped out easy as pie."

*I'll bet!* Doe thought. *He ought to have one, not that I ever have, either, but at least I can imagine it's no picnic. Most men act like they think it's a hangnail.* Nonetheless, she was glad to hear that her friend hadn't had a bad time of it.

The sound of a baby's squall could be heard from upstairs.

"Boy or girl?" Dolf asked.

Matt looked nonplussed. "I forgot to ask, and nobody said. They were all pretty busy. Clemmy yelled downstairs a few minutes ago and said . . . 'You're a father and stay down there a while till we get things cleaned up.' I wasn't about to ignore that lady."

"I wouldn't, either," Dolf said.

"Must be something to drink around," Matt said, then seemed to see Doe for the first time. "Pardon me," he said. "I'm a little disorganized."

Doe grinned and put out her hand, which he took. "I'm Doe Darling," she said, thinking: *He didn't really have to tell us he was disorganized. I'll bet he isn't nearly as disorganized as Diana, but she's probably relieved that it's over.*

"Doe Darling," Matt said. "Diana wanted me to meet you on our honeymoon, but you were in China, or some place, I can't remember exactly."

"China," she confirmed. "You have a good memory."

"She talks about you all the time," Matt said.

"Then I'm glad I came just now. I thought it might be a bad time."

"I don't think so. Uh, how about joining us in a toast? Maybe some wine."

She made a face. She wasn't the wine type, even if it was some Diana had imported. "How about some sour mash?"

He did a retake on her and laughed, joined by Dolf,

and finally by Doe herself. "I'm a hard-bitten, globe-trotting news hound," she said. "I join the boys in whatever they've got. Sometimes I even carry a six-shooter like Ambrose Bierce."

"He carries two," Dolf said.

"You know him?"

"A little. I'm surprised *he* isn't up here in Idaho with you."

"He's probably on his way. He was set to come with me, but there was a train wreck, and Hearst has him make any bad luck the S.P. has look like the end of the world."

Dolf rather sympathized with that, being familiar with the tactics of the Southern Pacific with Huntington calling the shots. He recalled that they'd been responsible for killing Clemmy Alexander's brother down in the San Joaquin Valley over their land-grabbing schemes.

They were just pouring drinks when Doc came down the stairs, sleeves rolled up, wiping his hands on a towel. "Ah," he said, eyes lighting up, "how did you know the presiding genius was in need of a small libation?"

Dolf held up his glass to Doc. "We'll wait. And if I know the presiding genius, it won't be a small libation."

"*Comparatively* small," Doc said. He looked over Doe with an approving eye, and she read the look quite precisely from long practice. "And who is *this*?" Doc asked.

"Doe Darling," Dolf said. "Doe, this is Doc Hennessey."

She gave him her hand and smiled. "I believe I've heard of you."

"I believe I've heard of you," Doc said. "If you're the Doe Darling that makes all the boys up North think of Home Sweet Home."

She smiled even more broadly. "That's what Dolf told me, but I didn't quite believe him."

*So it's Dolf already, is it?* Doc thought. *My boy isn't losing his touch. And this one is a rare chicken if I'm any judge.* He poured himself a big hooker and raised the glass, then tossed it down in a couple of swigs. "Ah," he sighed. "The nectar of the gods." Then, seeming to recall his business, he said: "Oh, by the way, Matt, it's twins. Girls, at that. Big healthy ones, too."

Matt took that as well as could be expected in a country where there weren't enough men to go around for all the manual labor that kept the country running. "I'll make hands out of them, anyhow. If they're half as good with cows as their ma turned out to be, they'll beat boys."

Doc poured himself another half tumbler of whisky, but only held it in his hand, looking at the new father. He said to Matt: "I hate to disappoint you, if you'd *really* rather have girls, but I was kidding. It's a big healthy boy, and the ugly critter looks like his pa, sad to say."

Matt smiled broadly. "I ought to wring your neck," he said.

"Been tried by better men than you, kid."

Clemmy came down and announced—"You lummox men can come up now."—then saw Doe Darling, and exclaimed: "Doe, where the hell did you pop in from?"

She rushed over, and the two women embraced. "Will Diana ever be surprised to see you. And glad, too. And wait'll Will gets home . . . you're his favorite *other* daughter. I sent for the new mother's daddy, but Lord knows where he's got to. Probably down some damned dark, dripping mine with a bunch of roughnecks."

A cavalcade headed for the stairs, Matt leading and Doc remaining behind, sipping his second whisky and eyeing Doe's wiggling rear as she mounted the stairs. "I've been," he said to no one in particular.

Diana lay under a fresh coverlet, nursing the baby and looking at it with that special gaze that only captures a woman's eyes at such times. Dolf thought she looked especially angelic, but he couldn't say much for the baby since he was one of those that thought all boy babies should be kept out of view until they were at least ten days old.

Diana glanced up, saw Doe, forgot the father in her surprise, and exclaimed: "Doe! You're the last person I expected to see!"

Doe laughed and went to her, touching the top of her head gently, then stooping to kiss her cheek. "That's what everyone says nowadays," Doe said.

They both laughed, joined by the others. "Ouch," Diana said. "It hurts when I laugh."

Clemmy took over then. "All right. You've had your look. The lummox that caused this affair can stay and get acquainted with his new wrangler. Everybody else out."

"Who, me?" Matt asked. Up till then he'd been standing with his mouth open, looking at his son.

"Yeah, you. I'll teach you how to hold your son without dropping him as soon as he's done nursing. Also, how to change diapers."

Matt was in a daze, his eyes shifting from Diana to the new boy. Finally he got up his nerve and kissed them both. It was the last thing Dolf saw as he left the room, and he smiled, thinking of his clumsiness with his own newborn kids, and at the same time recalling his choking sense of love for the mother and baby, and overwhelming sense of protectiveness. He was sure he knew exactly how Matt felt.

At the bottom of the stairs they ran into Will. "Clemmy might not let you up there," Dolf said, grinning.

"The hell with Clemmy," Will said, "I'm a grandpop. And it's a boy."

*What's the matter with girls?* Doe thought. Then she noticed the way Doc was eyeing her and decided maybe girls were all right, after all. She'd heard a lot about Doc, and, although he wasn't a big, strapping fellow, there was the appearance of steel in the way he carried his body and moved and, especially, in his piercing blue eyes. She understood he'd killed a dozen men or so in his day and, to compensate, delivered a few hundred babies into the world.

He noticed her looking his way and said: "Doe. I always wondered how you got that name. Maybe you'd like to join me for dinner tonight and let me in on that."

She grinned, locking her eyes with his. "If I tell you

now, will you still take me to dinner tonight, anyhow?"

"Why not?"

"You might not after you hear," she said but didn't pause. "My name is Sarah Rabinowitz, and Doe Darling is the name Ambrose Bierce hung on me to write under."

Dolf recognized a good time to make himself scarce. "Doc, how about running Doe back uptown when you go, unless she wants to leave right now."

Doe said: "I think I'll stay around and gab with Clemmy. I can walk uptown if need be."

"Not on your tintype," Doc said. "I'm not letting you stroll up the street alone with the crew that's wandering around town these days."

*He doesn't know about my six-shooter*, Doe thought, *but then I wouldn't want to bother with a coroner's hearing. Besides, Doc looks like good company. Maybe my stay here is going to be a lot more interesting than I thought.* She hadn't forgotten that she wanted to know Dolf a lot better, as well. And his brother Matt looked like a younger carbon copy of him.

## Chapter Nine

Big Bill Cloverwood had dealt with the Pinkertons before and was at least as shrewd as they were about the cat and mouse game. Consequently he knew Pookay had engaged a nearby cabin almost as soon as the deal was cooked. However, he wasn't sure the Pinks might not simply want to spy on him. Naturally he had to take care of all the other more likely possibilities as well.

He and his right-hand men, Elm and McCoy, talked that over at length. Elm finally suggested: "Why don't we just get you out of here? We'll take care of whoever they hide over there."

"Tonight, maybe, I'll pull out. Let's give 'em a little rope. If they wanted me arrested, they'd have had Hanratty up here before now. Knowing that rotten crew, my guess is they'll smuggle a couple of birds in there tonight with Winchesters, ready to give me a Pinkerton welcome the first time I step outside. I wonder how they located me."

"Money talks," Elm said. "I'm sure some of the boys must at least suspect you're up here."

"All the more reason to pull out quick," McCoy put in. "Some of our boys have places you can hide back in the hills where they'll never find you, and they ain't the kind to talk. Even if someone spots you leaving, we can ditch them. You're right next to the timber here. I can get you a good, fast horse."

"Nobody's gonna chase me out before I have a little fun out of it," Cloverwood said. He laughed. "I've got an idea how to do just that. We'll have to wait till after dark to pull it off, though."

When Mop and Persimmon were in sight of Mum's, they could see a lot of activity going on in her small pasture behind the stable. They were not yet close enough to be sure what was happening.

Mop pointed. "Now what the devil is all that about?

Your eyes are likely a lot better'n mine . . . can you make it out?"

Persimmon squinted. "A bunch of people and horses, but I can't tell what they're doing."

Then they both saw the first teepee being raised.

Mop said: "I know what that is. Some of Chief Henry's crowd is down in town for something. We always let 'em stay there. Most people are scared of 'em, or at least don't like 'em."

"Indians?" Persimmon asked, although he could see for himself.

"You bet. Dolf's family. His wife Maggie is a full-blood Injun princess . . . Chief Henry's daughter."

Persimmon knew all about Chief Henry and how he and his braves had whipped the U.S. Army to a frazzle years before. "You suppose the chief is there?" His heart beat faster, and he was a little bit afraid, recalling the stories he'd heard all his life about wild Indians.

"I wouldn't be a durned bit surprised. He and Dolf are good friends."

"Who is Mister Dolf, anyhow?" Persimmon asked.

It dawned on Mop that Dolf hadn't let on who he was to the boy.

"Didn't he tell you?"

"Just that his name was Dolf and one name was good enough, just like Persimmon."

Mop grinned. "I reckon maybe I shouldn't tell on him, but you'll find out soon enough, anyhow, so best you get it straight. He's Dolf Morgette. I s'pect you've heard of him."

Persimmon's chest tightened at the realization that

he'd been rubbing elbows with a notorious killer, and he felt his pulse quicken again. Who hadn't heard of Dolf Morgette, especially in Pinebluff? He wondered why it hadn't come to him in the first place. But the big man had been so kind and friendly and soft-spoken. He smiled a lot, a real friendly smile, too, and knew how to make a kid comfortable, just like he was a big kid himself, knowing how a boy felt, especially a hungry orphan.

"I can guess what you're probably thinking," Mop said. "But let me tell you, all those stories are bosh about him bein' a real mean man. There ain't a finer or more considerate fellow drawin' breath anywhere. When I was a drunken bum, down on my luck, he always treated me like a king . . . kept me in grub, tried to get me off the bottle, and saw I had firewood up at the shack where I lived . . . that is, when he was in town, which was mostly before they made a killer out of him. Then they railroaded him up the river, and I didn't see him for five years, but the first thing, after he was back, he treated me the same." Mop laughed, remembering that day. "I seen him a-comin' up the street with a big stray half-growed pup he'd just picked up. Bought some bones for him from the butcher and was stoopin' down and givin' the poor, starvin' critter another one as fast as he finished one. Then he spotted me and said . . . 'Is that you, Mop?' Just like he left the day before, and he got that big grin on his face and come over and pumped my hand. Then he gave me two bits for a drink, which he knew I probably needed pretty bad, and asked me to hang onto the pup for him till he found a place of his own to stay. That's the kind of man he is, kid, and don't let anybody tell you any different."

Persimmon was taking it all in, trying to square it with the stories about bodies found all over the district with the Morgette earmark on their taking-off. Persimmon believed Mop because the man he described was the one he'd met. He couldn't see Dolf as that other mean fellow people talked about, the fellow about whom mamas told their kids—"If you ain't good, Morgette will get you."—to scare them into minding. He said: "I don't care what they say about Mister Dolf. I know he's just like you said. I felt like my pa was back when I was around him."

"Jest so," Mop said. "And don't ever let anybody make you feel any other way about him. Whatever else he did, he was drove to it by a bunch of skunks."

By then they were close enough to make out Mum standing out back, supervising the Indians who were putting up teepees. A smaller woman was with her.

"That's Dolf's wife, Margaret, up there," Mop said, "and his grandma, Mum. You'll like 'em both. Cut off the same bolt of cloth as Dolf."

"Can his wife speak English?" Persimmon asked.

Mop guffawed. "Better'n you er me. They sent her away to school back East after the Army caught her pa and sent the tribe away for years to Injun Territory."

Mum saw the buggy coming and went to meet Mop and Persimmon. The boy was surprised to see the size of this woman, having expected a granny to be a wizened and stooped little thing, instead of this six foot, broad-shouldered lady with a young face and piercing blue eyes that fixed him with a stare as soon as they came close.

"What have you got here, Mop?" she asked.

"Friend of Dolf's. This is Persimmon. Meet Mum."

Mum's face immediately lost its severe look. She sized up the boy in a glance. "C'mon in. I aim to leave these heathens out here on their own."

Margaret had followed and was close enough to hear her remark: "How about this heathen? She hasn't had a morsel since before sunup."

"You best come in, too, I reckon. I made a bunch of fritters from your recipe, and we can start on them and coffee while I fix some real grub."

It sounded good to Persimmon, even though he'd finished his steak less than an hour before. He remembered that Dolf had told him that his grandmother was about the world's best cook, not that he cared how something was cooked as long as it filled him.

Mum said: "This is Maggie, Persimmon." And to Margaret: "I reckon this is another one of my grandson's charity projects . . . I guess you're used to them by now."

"I was his first one," Margaret said with a little laugh. She examined Persimmon with an experienced eye for judging character, liking the direct look he gave her.

"Howdy, ma'am," he said and, taking his cue from having watched the Goulds, offered his hand. Margaret noted that it was surprisingly clean, considering his shabby looks. His hair was even slicked back as well as he could do, using fingers in place of a comb and water from a public horse trough. Overall, she liked what she saw and remembered that Mum had a trunk with some of her grandsons' cast-off clothes in it. They could probably tog Persimmon out a lot better than he was.

Dolf got back before they were finished with breakfast, put Lucretia up, and fed her a little hay, then headed over to the Indian campground. Chief Henry came forward and greeted him heartily. "We got your message," he said, "and my daughter decided to come to town for a while." He made a face when he said "town". "Your horse Wowakan is with the other horses." He signified where with his thumb. Dolf looked and saw the big black and wondered if he would remember him after three years, and, if he did, if he'd forgive him for having left him.

Dolf approached the rope corral slowly and whistled the distinctive signal that he'd used to call the black before—a sound that summoned him from as far away as he could hear it. The fine head shot up, ears pricked, and he turned his eyes on Dolf, but stood like a statue, perhaps assessing whether he'd heard right, or trying to recall who this man was. Dolf whistled again, softly, and Wowakan lowered his head and came forward at a dancing trot, tail high, stopping a few feet away. He snorted, then extended his nose, nostrils flared. Finally he stuck his head over to the ropes and stood, showing no nervousness, waiting for Dolf to extend his hand and touch him, which he did, sliding his hand up and down his neck and on his forehead, then lowering it to tickle his upper lip and chin as he used to do. Wowakan emitted a great rumbling sound of satisfaction and danced a little, eyes bright as hot coals.

Dolf slipped under the rope and rubbed his back, then rubbed him all over, up and down his legs, picked up his feet, and examined his strong black hoofs and their undersides. They were clean and well cupped, but like all Indian horses he was unshod.

"Who's ridden him?" Dolf asked.

The chief pointed a finger to his chest. "Only me." It was almost true. He had put young Henry on him and discovered that the stallion turned into a docile buggy horse with a child, as though he knew he must care for this cargo because it wasn't yet mature enough to do that for itself. But the chief had been afraid to turn the boy loose with this big bundle of dynamite until he'd been seasoned on more docile animals. He had no intention of getting his only grandson killed.

Young Henry burst from a crowd of boys with whom he'd been running when he spotted his father, and came on the run, rushed up to Dolf, and cried: "Pa!"

Dolf swung him high in the air, then hugged him, only to have Henry push him away. Dolf had forgotten that this wasn't manly among Henry's new friends. He put his son down, and the boy walked over and scratched Wowakan's nose, which was all he could reach, then hugged one of his front legs.

"I rode your horse," he said, exposing his grandfather's white lie.

Dolf turned to Chief Henry in mock reproach and found him looking away, suddenly quite deaf and very interested in watching the little boys playing. Dolf knew he wouldn't have risked the boy any more than he himself would, and it was obvious that whatever had happened young Henry had survived, and apparently both he and the horse had loved it, loved each other.

"You old fraud," Dolf said to Wowakan. "And I thought you were a fire-eater."

Chief Henry laughed. "He is a different horse with your son."

"You bet," young Henry said. "And I aim to ride him a lot."

"If I say so," Dolf said. "And I'll teach you how, or your grandfather will, and no sneaking around on your own. You might get your neck broke."

The boy didn't seem to be listening, and Dolf spoke in a firmer voice: "You hear me, Son? I'm not kidding."

"Yeah, Pa."

"And you promise to mind me?"

"I promise."

Young Henry had lost interest in view of the direction of the conversation, and his eyes wandered back to his new friends. "I gotta go," he said, and yelled something to them in their language that got a return yell, then he rushed away, and they all headed for the nearby timber, in full cry, Henry gaining on them with his hard, little legs churning like pistons.

Dolf couldn't restrain a pleased laugh in which the chief joined him. It was obvious what he thought of his grandson. Dolf wondered where Little Maggie was and bet she was in the house snoozing. He knew she was good about her naps. In fact, her mother called her a slug-a-bed, always adding: "Like her pa." Actually, at that moment, Little Maggie was contentedly snoozing on his daughter Amy's bed, where she'd been temporarily deposited while Mum and Margaret went outside.

Dolf said to Chief Henry: "I shouldn't have to be here in town too long. Maybe we can go fishing again, soon." He had a picture of the isolated lake, near timberline, where he'd spent a restful vacation on his last visit to the district. Not many vacations had fitted into his life since he'd been a boy, and he recalled that one with great pleasure.

Chief Henry smiled at the memory. "I go there every year. I have waited this season till you could come along."

It was an oblique suggestion that Dolf forget about whites and their petty problems and learn to enjoy life while he was young enough. The chief was not yet sixty himself and spry for his age, as Dolf had reason to know from watching how he mounted a horse, as though shot from a catapult.

"Let's mosey over to the house," Dolf suggested, "and check on the supply of vittles. I reckon Mum has some fresh huckleberry pie."

That lit up Chief Henry's face. "Good."

Dolf led the way, knowing Mum would pretend she was pained to have to entertain her heathen Indian relative and secretly pleased to have him around to trade insults with. Dolf had a suspicion that she harbored more than respect for this true fighting man, Indian or not, knowing how grudging she was at showing real affection for fear of appearing weak and being taken advantage of. He would have bet a lot that the chief had never taken advantage of anyone in his life.

They found the two women with Mop and Persimmon, sitting around the big, round, oak kitchen table. Dolf read Persimmon's look at the sight of the chief in his Indian regalia, and almost grinned.

"Hi, kid," he said, clapping him on the shoulder. "I meant to get you something to eat earlier."

Persimmon said—"You did. Don't you remember?"—unaware that he was being ribbed.

"Alby Gould bought that," Dolf said, "so it doesn't count."

As he'd expected, Mum gave the chief a frosty look. He ignored her and looked over Persimmon with intense black eyes, probing as his daughter had for the boy's inner worth and, like her, approving of the direct gaze he got in return. He might have grinned at the obvious awe and avid interest that were plain on Persimmon's face, but stood on rigid formality.

"This is Persimmon," Dolf said. "I hired him this morning to help out Mop. He'll be livin' here." He looked at Mum to get confirmation of the arrangement. She looked pleased. He speculated that Persimmon was in for a lot of grandmothering and that the boy would love it.

Chief Henry, recognizing what was expected of him after the lecture he'd gotten from his grandson the other day, said—"*Hau*."—and looked stern. He wondered how his grandson would take to this older boy, who was obviously destined to be a new member of the family. Rather well, he suspected, from the way young Henry took to his Indian relatives and they to him.

A sudden vibration shook the house, followed by the *boom* of a distant explosion. Dolf suspected immediately that they had another bombing on their hands. He'd intended to go up and see Amy before he did anything else, but changed his mind. "Get my old saddle out," he said to Mop. "I'm goin' down and get my horse, then ride over and see what happened. Mike Hanratty will likely send for me, anyhow, if I don't."

Margaret restrained a desire to say—*Be careful.*—and an even stronger desire to say—*Why should you care what old Hanratty wants?* But she knew better, knew it would only get her a patient explanation of why he had to go after the men who could have killed one of his most precious possessions. She realized that they were not going back to their beloved home in Alaska until he had seen justice done, or died in the attempt. It was the latter possibility that she dreaded.

## Chapter Ten

Dolf mounted Wowakan for the first time in three years and felt the old eagerness in the big animal. It was wonderful to have a horse between his legs again. Running behind a dog team kept Dolf in shape, but a dog driver never got the feeling of oneness, the inimitable feeling only obtained from an animal you were in direct contact with and from which you sensed and subtly controlled every movement, knew what your horse was thinking—a good horseman and his animal became almost one. You could watch a man and horse and see the difference between a real horseman and someone who thought you just sat on a horse and tried to make it do what you wanted with a bit, quirt, and spurs. That kind always thought horses were dumb as fence posts, and often said so, not realizing how stupid they sounded to the ears of real horse people.

Dolf gave Wowakan his head for the quarter mile to the edge of town, then lightly reined him in, and said—"Trot."—to see if he still responded to his voice cues as he'd been trained to do. Wowakan gave signs of wanting to keep up his wild pace, but his early training had been ingrained, and he responded. Dolf grinned, feeling the thrill of knowing he'd trained this animal well, and that he was still his, giving willingly as he always had. Chief Henry, a born horseman, hadn't spoiled him as some cowboys would have with unnecessary gear, rough hands, and harsh reining and spurring. Dolf had never used spurs on him once, had never encountered any reason to, since body and voice cues and light reining were enough.

Dolf looked for smoke or evidence of a crowd as he passed several streets. He knew he wouldn't find Hanratty in his office, so he kept on, finally spotting a diminishing cloud of smoke still rising. He headed that direction and saw the crowd around the Pinkerton tent city. Many of the tents had been blown flat by the explosion, but few people had been hurt, since most of the men were downtown, carousing in the saloons.

Hanratty stood talking to someone whose back was to him. Several doctors had arrived, but only a couple stayed since the explosion had only hurt of couple of men badly and just shook up the rest. The big mess tent was flattened. Other tents had been blown down.

As he drew near, Dolf recognized Pookay as the man talking to Hanratty. He was waving his arms. Dolf dismounted, and left Wowakan standing on dropped reins. Hearing his approach, Pookay turned, red-faced and scowling.

"Some son-of-a-bitch is going to pay for this!" he growled. "The company is gonna put out a big reward this time. It was that bastard Cloverwood's work."

He wasn't about to tell Dolf or Hanratty that he already knew one way he was going to exact quick revenge. He'd have his assassin in place after dark; as soon as Cloverwood poked his head out after shooting light in the morning, he would be done for. It had occurred to Obie that his quarry might pull out before morning, but he hated to think of that possibility. He was also thinking of having someone sneak up in the dark and dynamite Cloverwood's cabin, which would be riskier.

Dolf thought *any* of the unions, not simply Cloverwood's, might have bombed Pookay's men, but he didn't see any reason to get all het up about a bunch of tents being blown over. *It'll be the day*, he said to himself, *when the Pinkertons pay a reward to find someone who blew up a few tents, as tight-fisted as they are.*

"This blast doesn't necessarily have the earmarks of our old friend," Hanratty said. "I didn't find any wire. There was a wagon of provisions parked in here this morning, and that's where the charge was set. Probably a timer inside. I haven't found any parts of a clock yet, but I'll bet we will. I've got some of the boys going over the ground."

Dolf noted a couple of uniformed policemen cruising around, and some men in plain clothes. "Where's Mulveen?" he asked.

"Out to the mines. Mexican cook brained some guy with a shovel for complaining about his cooking. Mulveen probably heard the blast from out there. I expect him to show up any minute and ask what happened." He grinned, took out one of his two-fers, bit off the end, spit out the tobacco, and struck a match on a pant leg, cupping it as he touched it to the cigar. Once it was lit up to his satisfaction, he said: "Let's mosey around and see if we can find anyone else that saw it happen. One of my boys was on the way over here when the charge went off. That's how we know it was in the wagon. He said the wagon was there one minute and gone the next. A piece of the seat damn' near got him."

Dolf spotted Hank H. among the crowd of watchers and remembered he'd wanted to talk to him after Bradley's office building had been blown but hadn't got around to it. "I'm going over and see if Hank H. saw anything," he said. "You asked me to talk to him the other day, but I haven't yet."

Hanratty nodded. "Good idea. He hears things that other people wouldn't, since a lot of folks think he's dense, and talk as though he isn't even around."

Pookay asked: "Who the hell is Hank H.?"

"The town halfwit," Hanratty answered, and didn't elaborate.

Pookay turned away, then walked off to join the men

118

poking around in the wreckage.

Hank H. saw Dolf coming and grinned. "Hi, Dolf. Some excitement, huh? I guess old Dawson is out a wagon."

"Hi, Hank. Good to see you." They shook hands. "How's that again about the wagon?"

"I drove it over this morning with a bunch of supplies. That's what the bomb was in. The wagon was what blew up, and I almost saw it happen myself. Somebody must 'a' put a bomb in it."

Dolf's ears pricked up. "Were you with the wagon when it was loaded?"

"Naw. I left it over at the platform behind Crowder's store for a couple of hours while they got the stuff in it, and then I came back and drove it over here."

"Did it blow right after you left it?"

"Gosh, no. I was lucky. Must 'a' been an hour after I dropped it off at least. I unhitched and took the team back to Dawson's, since those fellows didn't seem in a hurry to unload. I was just coming back down this way, wondering if they'd unloaded the wagon yet, so I could bring a team to get it, but I wouldn't have needed it till tomorrow. I wasn't looking right at it when it blew up, but I looked that way right after, and the wagon was gone, just disappeared . . . one minute it was there and the next nothing was there . . . and I saw the tents flying." He guffawed in the strange boisterous manner that had given him his reputation, his head and hands flying around seemingly not under his control. Then he recovered and looked embarrassed.

Dolf thought of asking Hank about Persimmon, since

the kid worked for Dawson when he could, but thought better of it. Persimmon didn't need a recommendation from Hank H. He was his own recommendation. Before he walked away, Dolf asked: "Do you have any idea how a bomb could have got attached to your wagon?"

"What do you mean . . . attached? Somebody put it in there."

Dolf shook his head. "They unloaded everything in the wagon. If it was in there, it would have blown up inside that big mess tent."

Hank thought about that, then shook his head. "Search me," he said. "Maybe you ought to ask down at Crowder's. Holy smokes, that thing could have gone off while I was driving the wagon." He laughed, this time fairly normally, and added: "Then Dawson would have been out a team, too."

"And you, too," Dolf put in. "He'd be looking for a new driver."

"Yeah," Hank said, "I'd be pushing up daisies if they found enough of me to bury." But he didn't seem particularly disturbed by the thought.

Dolf said: "I'm working on these bombings for Chief Hanratty. Did you see anybody suspicious-looking around Dawson's when Bradley's place got blown up?"

Hank thought about that. "Not anybody out back in the hay barns where I was. There's always strangers out front, nowadays. The kid was back there, sawin' wood in the hay, and naturally he woke up when the blast went off. I didn't see him, though. He mentioned it later to me and Dawson."

"What kid?"

"Persimmon. The kid that hangs out with us."

"Nobody else?"

"Nary a soul that I saw."

Dolf turned that over in his mind. He'd have bet someone had been back there somewhere to reel in the remains of the wires that set off the bomb. It was the only logical place. There were three big barns in a row, and the bomber could have been in either of the other two. He was convinced that whoever it was had to have been in one of them and made a note to ask Persimmon if he'd seen anyone.

"You described the fellow you saw over at Will's place to Hanratty, I guess. Have you thought of anything else about him? Do you think he saw you and got out of the way?"

"The feller I saw didn't seem to be in a hurry or trying to hide . . . he just walked down the fence like anybody would. I thought maybe it was someone goin' home from a night job downtown. After the bomb went off, I started thinking maybe he set it off."

"So you didn't pay any particular attention to him, is that right?"

"I see a lot of night owls when I walk to work in the morning. Even saw a bear once. And deer almost every morning. I don't know what they like about town, but I heard they ate up Miss Allenby's roses and she raised hell with Chief Hanratty about it. Hanratty asked her if she wanted him to arrest the deer if he ran across 'em. She didn't like that and said she wasn't goin' to vote for him at the next election. I guess she don't know the cops are hired, instead of elected." He laughed, and Dolf joined in.

Dolf decided he'd have to tease Hanratty about that, having himself had the memorable experience of a dressing down from the indomitable Artemisia. He wasn't surprised to learn that Hank knew police were hired rather than elected like sheriffs. He'd run across those characteristics in him before, which was why he always told people not to underestimate the man. Hank read a lot.

On the spur of the moment he asked Hank H: "Who do you think is setting off the bombs?"

Without hesitation Hank said: "I think Bradley had the one set off up at Will's."

"Who gave you that idea?"

"Nobody. It just figures. Bradley is a real bastard. He's mad at Will for not cutting wages along with the others."

It was the first time Dolf had ever heard Hank use strong language.

"Let me tell you something about Bradley," Hank said. "Persimmon's pa got killed in a blast in the mine, and Bradley made a big show of coming to the funeral. This was before the strikes. When they were throwing in the clods and the kid was standing there crying, Bradley came up and gave him a dollar. Imagine that, a whole god-damn' dollar!"

Dolf was learning a lot new about Hank H. the longer he talked to him. He'd just cussed again and stronger than the first time.

"Where do you live?" Dolf asked to keep him talking.

"Out on the edge of town in an old cabin. It belongs

to Hal Green, and he lets me have it for nothing."

"How long have you lived there?"

"Since before they sent you . . ."—he paused, realizing what he was about to say, then decided to plow ahead and finished with—"to the pen."

*That's over a dozen years*, Dolf thought. *I wonder what Hank has learned about the town in all those years, listening and overhearing God knows what?*

"And you worked for Dawson all that time?"

"Worked for old Mark Wheat when I first came to town."

Dolf hadn't known that. He'd worked for Victoria Wheat Gould's father himself, very briefly.

"What did you think of him?" Dolf asked on the spur of the moment.

"Another real bastard. I overslept one morning and didn't get the stove going in his office early enough to suit him, and he fired me. I was sick as a dog, and told him so, and that I was sorry, but he fired me anyhow. I can't imagine how he ever had such a nice daughter."

*And that isn't the half of it, in either case*, Dolf mused. *I might be married to Victoria today, and I probably should have killed her father for getting Pa and my brothers killed . . . I guess that wouldn't have set too well with her.* It reminded him what a hell of a life he'd had in Pinebluff. And here he was up to his ears in the community's troubles again, as usual. *If I have a lick of sense and get out of here with a whole skin this time, I should never come back.* It wouldn't be easy to manage with his wife's Indian family here on the reservation and his own out on the ranch. He was probably saddled with being in and out of the place as long as he lived.

"Well, Hank," Dolf said, "thanks a lot. If anything comes up that I ought to know about, I'd appreciate your getting word to me. I'm staying with my grandmother, or you can always leave a message with Hanratty."

He shook hands with Hank and headed back to where Hanratty was talking to Tobe Mulveen. The sheriff had finally shown up for the party, although town wasn't exactly in his jurisdiction.

"What did Hank H. have to say?" Hanratty asked.

"Probably nothing you don't already know. He said you're one of Artemisia Allenby's *fave-o-rite* public servants."

Hanratty chuckled. "How the hell would he know that?"

"How does he know anything? He keeps his ears open and, mostly, keeps his mouth shut."

Tobe said: "He's a good man, actually."

Dolf said: "Did you know he drove that wagon over here, Mike?"

"Hell, no! Did he have any idea how a bomb got in there?"

"It couldn't have been in the wagon with the supplies because they were already unloaded and in that mess tent before the explosion."

"Yeah, I know that . . . somebody must have hitched a bomb under the wagon somewhere. Did Hank have any notion how someone could have done that?"

"Nope. He left the wagon over at a store called Crowder's . . . must be new since my time . . . and they loaded it, then he picked it up and drove over here. It could have got planted over there, but that's a pretty far-fetched idea."

Hanratty interrupted, saying: "By the way, while you were jawin' with Hank, we found this." He held up a small, bent, smoke-smudged brass gear from a clock. "Bomb timers built from clocks ain't too damned certain, I hear, so you can bet whoever set that calling card in the wagon wasn't around, leastways not if they knew their business. They've been known to go off a leetle early." He paused, then said: "I reckon you're planning to go over to Crowder's and make a few inquiries."

"Unless you say different. Why don't you come along?"

"Nope. That's what I hired you for. Besides, I ain't one of old Eb Crowder's favorite people."

Dolf figured maybe Mike had tried to shake Crowder down for more than he was willing to pay for having someone rattle the back doorknob on his store a couple of times a night.

"I'll let you know what I find out. I aim to go over to the hospital after a while, too, and ask around for anyone that saw anything suspicious. Where's Crowder's place? It must be new since I was here last and I don't remember seeing it since I blew in this time."

"On Second Street right back of the Grand."

Dolf mounted Wowakan and set out at a trot, taking a short cut through the alley beside the Grand over to Second. He glanced up and was surprised to see Doc Hennessey looking out of a second-story window at him. He halted Wowakan.

Doc grinned. "Me and Hippocrates draw the line at Pinkertons. Besides, I had an emergency up here."

He was stark naked as far as Dolf could tell, and grinning like the end man in a minstrel show. Dolf could imagine the kind of emergency that took precedence over medicine with Doc, and knew Doc would be especially susceptible to distractions where natural born sons-of-bitches were the only neglected parties. He hadn't realized that Doc was staying at the Grand.

He urged Wowakan on without looking back, thinking: *I'm almost certain Doc is staying at the Cosmopolitan.* Then he remembered what lady journalist was staying at the Grand, and mused to himself: *Old Doc is working like lightning on this emergency . . . I wondered why I didn't see her nosing around down at the big excitement.*

At Crowder's, he asked for the boss and got a wary look from a clerk who said: "I'll have to tell Mister Crowder who you are and what you want. He don't see just anyone."

Under the circumstances, Dolf had a notion to say: *Tell him I'm Dolf Morgette, and I aim to shoot up the place if he doesn't trot right out.* He'd have bet that would get some action, especially in Pinebluff. Instead, he produced the badge Hanratty had given him. "I'm investigating the bombings. The wagon that was carrying the bomb that went off this afternoon was loaded over here a few hours before the explosion."

The clerk's mouth opened wide and stayed that way. His eyes were a picture of apprehension, which Dolf guessed was due to his mouse-like character rather than any guilty knowledge. Finally he said—"I'll tell Mister Crowder."—and trotted away, disappearing through a door that had PROPRIETOR, NO ADMITTANCE painted on it in large letters.

After a long while, the clerk reappeared and approached Dolf. He said: "Mister Crowder is busy right now and says to come back tomorrow."

Dolf smiled deceptively. "You don't say. I wonder if you'd go back and ask him if he'd like me to drag him down to headquarters and grill him as a suspect. And tell him we'll get a warrant if we have to."

Dolf was not surprised to receive an invitation to visit the inner sanctum. Inside, seated behind a desk, he found a tall, thin man, about fifty years old, with thinning gray hair, wearing granny glasses through which a watery pair of blue eyes were staring at him. His odd appearance wasn't improved by the green accountant's shade that topped his head. He gave Dolf an impatient look.

"I want to talk to whoever loaded a wagon here this morning that Hank H. from Dawson's Livery drove over to the Pinkerton camp," Dolf explained. "It blew up and injured a lot of people. We naturally want to try to figure out where a bomb got in the wagon." He shaded the truth a little to keep his investigation simple. He figured it unlikely that anyone would know enough to have a bomb ready and quickly attach it to a wagon here, or even know where the wagon was bound until it arrived. They certainly couldn't have planned on enough time to get the job done unseen. If the bomb had been planted in the wagon, it would have been a simple matter of slipping in an extra box. Nonetheless, he wanted to see if someone here had seen anything unusual about the appearance of the wagon. There weren't many places a person could hang much dynamite to a wagon without having it show.

Crowder eyed him without speaking. Finally he said: "I can assure you that no one here put a bomb in any wagon. We're a respectable business. I investigate all my employees before I hire them. They don't smoke or drink or gamble, go directly to dinner, and then their rooms after work and read their Bibles till lights out at ten p.m., and I require them to go to church on Sunday. I also save part of their salary for them and bank it."

*This guy is a small-time edition of Henry Huntington*, Dolf thought, *who, according to Will Alexander, is at least runner up for the biggest son-of-a-bitch that ever lived.*

"That's the kind of upstanding men I like to talk to," Dolf said. "They tell the truth. One of them might have seen something suspicious and *naturally* would want to tell me about it." He decided to put out some bait. "Maybe they saw the bomb sitting in the wagon before they loaded it and didn't know what it was. It could have been in a box or a bag." He, of course, knew that wasn't the case, but figured it would accomplish his purpose of talking to whoever loaded the wagon.

The success of his ploy lifted the frown from Crowder's face—it had dawned on him that this possibility would certainly divert suspicion, hence bad publicity, away from his establishment.

"I'd like to talk to whoever loaded the wagon," Dolf said, figuring that the sooner he did it the better, just in case Crowder added a codicil to his pious rules and slipped in one about "lying for the boss".

Crowder said: "Your man is Elton Dean Mulcahey. He's out back now, working in the warehouse."

Dolf couldn't believe his ears, in case this was the Elton Dean Mulcahey that he knew from the old days, the biggest rounder and tinhorn in the West, and there couldn't be two of them with a name like that.

"I'll send for him," Crowder said.

"Why don't I talk to him privately?" Dolf asked. "A man sometimes won't talk to an investigator with his boss listening. I'm sure neither of you have anything to conceal, and the sooner we establish that the better."

As he hoped, that made sense to Crowder, and, if the man he was to question was the Mulcahey he knew, Crowder had to be the world's most gullible goose under his crusty exterior.

Crowder went to the door, and called: "Oh, Felton, come here." This fetched the clerk who'd first talked to Dolf. Crowder instructed him: "Take this officer back to talk to Mulcahey, and tell Elton I said it was all right to tell him everything he knows."

Dolf followed the clerk into a large, high-ceilinged warehouse that smelled of all sorts of trade goods, particularly vinegar and spices. They found Mulcahey on the rear loading platform sneaking off a smoke, which he quickly tossed away. If Felton noticed, he didn't let on. He'd probably lied to get his job, too. And it was, indeed, the old Mulcahey that Dolf remembered. Dolf slipped him a broad wink that he hoped would forestall his blurting out something like: *Well, Dolf Morgette, what brings you here?* The Irishman's inborn caginess might have accomplished that anyhow, but Dolf wasn't willing to take the chance.

That was exactly what Mulcahey did say when they were alone.

Dolf replied: "I might ask you the same thing. How the hell did you get a job from that old hypocrite inside? And why?"

"I got the job by lying like hell. It beats gambling. This is a sure thing. I steal more from this old fart than I ever made at the tables."

"How come he hasn't found you out? He looks like a real snoop that doesn't miss much."

"In the first place, he's too snooty to talk to anyone that might give me away. And I'm his fair-haired boy. I even teach the Sunday school class and Bible school on Wednesday night. He's fired three guys I told him were stealing the stuff I've got away with."

"He'll catch you sooner or later."

"Who cares? I'm gettin' like Huck Finn's old man with the widow. It'll be a relief to get found out and go back to my comfortable old ways. Meanwhile, he's building up a bank account for me. I never saved a cent in my life before."

"What're you aimin' to do with it when you get it to keep?"

"Blow it."

Dolf didn't have to ask on what. Here was a man with a philosophy that Chief Henry could appreciate. If he knew he had an hour left, he'd say: *C'mon, guys, let's live! Don't shed any tears for me.* And if he had any money, he'd set up the drinks. Dolf got down to business. "I actually came over to question whoever loaded a wagon this morning for Hank H. Word has probably got over here by now about why I want to know."

"Happens it hasn't."

"It had a bomb planted in it, and it went off over at the Pinkerton camp."

Mulcahey's face expressed interest, but no more. "I heard it go off," he said. "They're getting common as Fourth of July around here. If I was facing the other way, I wouldn't turn around and look at the dust settling."

"Was there anything suspicious-looking about the wagon when Hank left it here, before you loaded it?"

"Maybe, now that you mention it. But there wasn't any bomb in the wagon. All I hustled into it was canned truck for the cook over there. I'll bet there's canned goods scattered in the brush for a mile around. Good thing. A lot of the miners and their families are almost starving. But I think I know where your bomb might have been. There was something attached to the evener, like a long bundle wrapped around it and tied on."

"Easy to see?"

"Nope. You could see it from a distance, but not close up. I first noticed it when I went over to get the wagon and pull it up to the loading platform."

That set Dolf to wondering why Hank H. hadn't noticed it. Then he remembered that Hank was nearsighted. Hank had asked him to teach him to shoot once, and Dolf discovered that Hank could see the sights all right, but not a small target any farther away than fifty feet. Hank had been surprised to learn that everyone didn't see like he did. But he'd never seen any reason to get glasses, since he could read without them and harness horses and do everything he really had to do.

Dolf asked: "How come you didn't investigate to see what was fastened down there?"

"Because it wasn't any of my business."

Dolf didn't even blink at that. "Could anybody have monkeyed with the wagon after you loaded it?"

"Sure. It must have sat out there an hour before Hank H. came back and drove it away."

"He left it here, with the horses hitched to it?"

"Nope. He tied the hosses over there in the shade under that tree. He's a good man with horses and don't let 'em stand out in the sun like a minister, or other Bible-thumping sons-of-bitches like old Crowder."

"And you didn't see anyone around the wagon?"

"Nope, I went back inside. Could have been half a dozen people around the wagon after I loaded it, but if that thing on the evener was the bomb, it was already there."

That made absolute sense to Dolf. Before he left, he asked: "How long do you think you'll last here?"

Mulcahey laughed. "Till I get caught. Maybe a long while, or until Crowder finds out I've been having women over at night . . . I got a room over here and act as night watchman."

Dolf joined him in another laugh. He shook Mulcahey's hand. "Good luck. I'll see you around."

## Chapter Eleven

Dolf decided his investigation of the hospital could wait till morning. He looked up Hanratty to report Mulcahey's revelations, and found him in his office, feet on his desk, two-fer in hand, entertaining an unexpected visitor—Ambrose Bierce, who Dolf knew well from his Barbary Coast days.

Bierce rose and came forward, hand extended. "Ah," he said, smiling, "my favorite cold-blooded killer."

Dolf grinned. Knowing Bierce, he could picture him telling St. Peter he needed an appellate court due to his record of bad decisions; not much he said shocked anyone who'd known him long. He said: "I wondered why Doe Darling called you Sweet-Lips. I thought maybe you two had something going between you."

"Don't I wish," Bierce said. "I'm a little old for her taste."

*That's what you think*, Hanratty thought. He'd seen her earlier in the day with Doc Hennessey, and entertained suspicions regarding why she hadn't been snooping around at the scene of the latest bombing. Doc wasn't exactly a spring chicken, either, but he could be a ladies' man with the best of them when he wanted to pour it on. Hanratty didn't have a jealous bone in his body, probably due to his sacred reverence for women, which was so minor as to be almost nonexistent. He was definitely not a romantic. *I may have to give Bierce some advice and counsel for his own good. The last man I ever thought might need it.* He was ill-equipped to suspect a broad moral streak in Bierce such as he knew Dolf possessed. He occasionally wondered how deep that might run in Dolf, too.

"You won't believe what I found out and who I got it out of," Dolf said.

Hanratty eyed him expectantly. "Try me."

As a preliminary Dolf said: "By the way, did you know Elton Dean Mulcahey is working for Crowder?"

Hanratty let out one of his wheezy laughs. "Everybody does. It's the joke of the town. But nobody is apt to tell Crowder, unless maybe Artemisia Allenby."

"He wouldn't believe her if she did," Dolf said. "Mulcahey's got Crowder thinking he's honey on a stick."

Bierce asked: "Who, may I ask, is Elton Dean Mulcahey?"

Hanratty felt he'd better lay in a little background, like the good storyteller he was. "Before I tell you, you oughta know who Crowder is. He runs a general store and won't hire anybody who isn't a Sunday school boy . . . no drinking, gambling, whoring, late hours, you gotta read your Bible, go to church, save your money. Mulcahey is actually teaching a Sunday school, I hear."

"That's what he said," Dolf contributed.

"So," Hanratty picked up, "the town's former leading sporting man conned Crowder into hiring him. He actually lives in back of the store as night watchman and has a different whore in almost every night. Naturally that isn't cheap, but he's likely stealing Crowder blind."

Dolf snorted. "He admitted it to me. Said that, so far, he's managed to get three guys fired by convincing Crowder they stole the stuff he's lifted."

Bierce grinned. "I'm beginning to like him. How long do you think he'll last?"

"That's the rich part of it," Dolf said. "He told me he's getting like Huck Finn's old man and would like to go back and sleep with the hogs. He'll probably arrange to get caught so he can relax. Anyhow, he was a mine of information. He said Hank H. left the wagon that had the dynamite charge in it at the store to be loaded, and went off somewhere for an hour or so. Mulcahey himself loaded the wagon."

"Did he say *he* put the bomb in it?" Hanratty asked, straight-faced.

"Nope. But he said he noticed something bulky wrapped around the evener and tied on."

"And he figures it was the bomb?"

"So do I."

"Why didn't he ask Hank H. what the hell he had tied under there?"

"Said he didn't figure it was any of his business."

That would have made sense to a majority in any Western community and certainly did to these three.

"How come Hank H. didn't see it?"

"Mulcahey said you could only see it from a distance, and I know for a fact Hank H. can't make out much except close up. I can vouch for that . . . can see big stuff well enough to drive a team, but he had me teaching him to shoot years ago . . . I wondered why he was pretty good close up and couldn't hit the broad side of a barn at fifty feet, even with a rifle. That was why."

"How do we know he didn't put that bomb under there himself?" Hanratty asked.

Dolf didn't consider that for long. He asked: "Are you serious?"

"Crazier things than that have happened."

"He ain't the type in my opinion," Dolf said.

"Mine, either," Hanratty agreed. "I've been a cop too long . . . suspect everybody. Besides, why would he? So I guess we have to backtrack from there. If it had a timer on it, someone put it on that wagon after they knew it was the one that would carry those supplies down to the Pinks' camp. Who knew that, and when?"

"Why don't you ring up Dawson and ask him? He'll know. Or we can bring in Hank H. and talk to him, but he's apt to think we suspect him and get scared. Lord knows what he might do."

"Probably get the whips and jingles and giggle like a maniac," Hanratty said.

Bierce had been shifting his sharp eyes between the two as they talked, and now couldn't help but ask: "Who the hell is Hank H.?"

Hanratty said: "He's either one of two things . . . the village simpleton or a hell of a lot shrewder than he looks and acts, and maybe a little of both, come to think of it."

"Never underrate an idiot," Bierce said. "Some make President. Sounds like I ought to do a feature story on this one."

"Maybe Doe Darling will beat you to it."

"We can share a by-line. Where the hell is she, by the way?"

Dolf maintained a poker face, although he thought he could answer that question. He said: "She's staying over at the Grand."

Hanratty got on the telephone as they talked. "Dawson there?" he asked. "Chief Hanratty," he said. As he waited, he said: "Jesus Christ, Dawson is getting persnickety . . . prosperity must be spoiling him. . . . Dawson. Hanratty. I got a question. When was the first anyone knew what wagon you was gonna send over to Crowder's to pick up groceries for the Pinks?" He listened, then looked disappointed. "OK," he said, "thanks . . . what the hell do you mean, why am I asking? The son-of-a-bitch could have killed some people. As it was, it hurt some pretty bad. I'm investigating. . . . Yeah, I know they were Pinkertons, but it's still against the law." He looked disgusted as he hung up.

Dolf and Bierce looked at him expectantly. He said: "Helluva big help that was. He said he always uses the same wagon, everybody knows that, and the order for it came in last night, so the whole world had all night to gimmick it if they were a mind to. No sense in asking him if they saw someone suspicious around it, but I'd better call him back, just in case."

He rang him up again, went through the same rigmarole on getting him to come to the phone, and then said: "Was anybody suspicious fooling around that wagon before Hank H. left with it?" He nodded, eyes on Dolf as he said into the phone: "I was afraid of that." He hung up. "Dawson said they don't keep any night watchmen. I oughta run the smart-mouthed bastard in on suspicion. That might get him thinking about putting on a night watchman from now on. The way this burg is running, it might not be a bad idea. I'm getting so I half expect to hear another blast any minute."

"I think I'm going to like it here," Bierce said.

"I did up till a couple of months ago," Hanratty said. "But I'm already sure I'm not gonna like it here much longer. I might get a small place somewhere that's warm in the winter and raise vegetables."

Somehow Dolf couldn't see Hanratty in bib overalls and brogans, but you could never tell. He grinned.

Hanratty asked: "What the hell's so funny about that? I got a gal that was raised on a farm in Iowa. She could show me how."

"How to what?" Bierce asked, and got a withering look.

"The only question there is *when?*" Hanratty said.

Riding back to Mum's, Dolf detoured to the edge of town so he could let Wowakan have a run. His first couple of hundred yards were his usual thundering, clod-throwing burst of motion, then Dolf eased him down to a long lope, feeling the pleasure of a rocking-chair gait that usually only came from a horse like this, with long, springy pasterns. After a mile or so, he pulled him in and turned back, setting him into a fast trot, then a walk. When they got to Mum's, the big animal was scarcely breathing hard and hadn't sweated up at all. Dolf gave Chief Henry high marks for keeping Wowakan in prime shape.

When he got to Mum's, he found her sitting on the porch with Little Maggie, looking like an impish doll, asleep on her lap, a slight smile curving her lips. Mum said: "I seen you runnin' that fool horse over there on the back road. Did anybody ever tell you a horse might stub its toe and go paddle wheel over pilot house?"

Dolf grinned. "I can't say as they put it exactly that way. Pa used to say I'd break my fool neck someday, though."

"Well, your pa had good sense. You ought to mind his advice."

Dolf laughed and turned away, riding to the barn, where Mop and Persimmon met him. "Seen you two throwin' up clods over yonder," Mop said. "That's a hell of a horse."

Persimmon's eyes were big, looking at Wowakan and at the same time trying to stay out of his way, since the horse was still *up* and didn't want to stand.

Dolf dismounted, and handed the reins to Persimmon. "Walk him around a little while," he said, "then let him have some water." He turned and took off the saddle himself, since it was a little too high for the boy to manage. He put it on the rack and sat on the bench by the stable door, watching to see that Persimmon wouldn't get himself in trouble. It was obvious that the boy wasn't the least bit afraid of this big, explosive animal, and Wowakan sensed it right away and followed him willingly. He ducked his head down and cropped a mouthful of grass, and Persimmon let him do it, but then pulled him away, taking a shorter lead on him. Dolf took out a cigar and got it going, feeling himself relax completely.

He asked Mop: "Where're Maggie and little Dynamite?" The latter referring to little Henry.

"The kid's with his grandpa over in camp, I reckon. Yer wife said she'd be over to yer brother's place. Your son brought in his wife who's about to pop. She said to tell you to come over there for supper."

Dolf nodded. "I guess I'll go up and see how Amy is first. Keep an eye on the kid and have him rub down Wowakan and show him what to feed him. I got a notion it'll be good for 'em both if I let him take special care of him."

Mop had been watching Persimmon and nodded. "That's a hell of a good kid," he said. "Good all the way around, but good with hosses, too. He must have picked up a lot over at Dawson's."

"Fine," Dolf said. "I figured him for a keeper. Now we'll have to decide how to make it legal. Shouldn't be too hard."

Mop watched Dolf's departing figure, thinking: *That's just about the goodest son-of-a-bitch I ever laid eyes on. They don't make many of 'em . . . his pa was another one. Runs in the family, come to think of it.*

Mum was still on the porch, and Little Maggie had awakened and was looking around. She spotted him. "Yer back, Pa." She extended her arms to be taken up. He picked her up, swung her high in the air, and dropped her quickly to give her the butterflies in her tummy that she loved.

"Careful," Mum cautioned. "She ain't been to the pot for a couple of hours."

Dolf said—"Then that'll be our next stop."—and hugged Little Maggie, placing her cheek next to his.

"I don't have to go yet," Little Maggie said seriously. "Tickle me with your mustache."

He obliged as he always did.

Mum said: "While you two are being mushy, I'll go up and see that Amy's presentable and pretty her up before you go up to see her. Yer fool dog has adopted her."

When Mum finally yelled down for him to come upstairs, Dolf carried Little Maggie up with him. He found his big hound, Jim Too, faithfully guarding Amy, just as he'd guarded Maggie in the final days of her pregnancy when the dog had sensed that she might not be able to care for herself.

Dolf kissed Amy and carefully hugged her like he was afraid she might break. "How you feelin', honey?" he asked.

She smiled. "Better. Good enough to be hugged a little harder than that. I really feel like I'm going to live. But not too pert yet."

"Takes a while," Dolf said. He remembered when he was shot, he'd wondered for a week or two if he was apt to die, and didn't much care if he did. This couldn't be as bad as that, but Amy might not be as tough as he was.

Jim Too got up and stretched, nosed Amy, then made it plain he'd like to go out now and tend to necessities. "OK," Dolf said. "I'll let you out."

Outside, he found Mop and Persimmon headed for

the house. Mop stayed in a room behind the kitchen, and Mum had set up a cot there for Persimmon till they decided where to put him. Jim Too went about his business, then returned and inspected Persimmon.

"This is Jim Too," Dolf said. "If he don't like you, you'll be the first kid he didn't take to."

Persimmon carefully extended the back of his hand and squatted down as he did. Jim Too sniffed it, and then accepted an ear scratching and patting, wagging his tail. Persimmon extended his face to be licked, but was disappointed.

Dolf, watching, said: "He ain't the lickin' type since he growed up. Must be beneath his dignity."

*I'll have to teach him*, Persimmon thought, *if we're together long enough.*

Mum showed up at the door, saying: "I'm aimin' to fix supper. I suppose you're gonna desert us and go over to your brother's place?"

Dolf thought about that. Finally he said: "They got enough folks over there without me. I suppose Doc is over there by now, too." *I hope the scoundrel has enough strength left for another delivery*, he thought, then told Mum: "I'll call over and tell 'em not to expect me. Where did Little Maggie get to . . . did she go in with you?"

"Upstairs on the job with Amy again."

"I guess Amy'll be eatin' off a tray for a few more days," Dolf said. "Fix me one and I'll eat with her. I want to talk to her. I've been gone too much. How about feeding Little Maggie down here?" Then he said: "Persimmon, I reckon you ain't met my daughter Amy yet. C'mon up for a minute."

When he knocked on the door frame, Amy said: "Is that you, Pa?"

The words were part of an old game they used to play when she was a kid. Recalling, he played his part and said: "No, it's a big wooly bear."

Little Maggie, with whom he also played that game, yelled from inside the bedroom for both her and Amy: "Ain't either. It's you, Pa?"

He peeked around the door frame, and Little Maggie rushed to him, squealing, and was picked up and hugged. "You always figure me out," he said.

Persimmon listened and watched, totally flabbergasted, thinking: *This ain't exactly the way I figured Dolf Morgette would be.*

After the game was over, Dolf led Persimmon over to the bed. "Amy, this is a new member of the family. We call him Persimmon."

She looked him over, and thought: *Isn't that just like Pa to take in a ragamuffin?* She approved of the bashful kid she saw, though, poorly dressed as he was, and obviously embarrassed. He had an honest pair of eyes that looked directly at her, even if he was blushing, and obviously feeling awkward, as though he'd like to run.

"Hi, Persimmon." She extended her good hand, and he took it, feeling its soft warmth, and blushing even more deeply.

"Howdy, Miss Amy," he managed to get out, thinking: *She's beautiful, even if she is sick. She's about the prettiest girl I ever saw.*

Later, after Dolf and Amy had finished eating, Dolf

pulled up a rocker and sat, holding Amy's hand. It was getting fully dark out, normally the loneliest time of day, but he felt far from alone, and hoped Amy felt the way he did. He said: "I'm sure sorry this had to happen to you, honey. I'd have done anything to keep you from it."

She smiled. "I know, Pa. You always did."

"I'm gonna get the skunks behind these bombings, too," he promised.

"Why don't you smoke your after-dinner cigar? I know you love them after a meal. I love the smell of them, always have from the first time I knew what that rich smell was, when I was hardly walking yet."

He got one going to his satisfaction. A cool night wind had picked up and billowed the curtains, bringing a mingled scent of evergreen and assorted mountain plants to mix with the cigar smell. He was relaxed and content, wishing life could stay this way forever, but experience had taught him that destiny probably never intended his path to be tranquil. He was reminded of that when the house shook, followed by the sound of the explosion that came on the heels of the shock wave. A flash outside was as bright as lightning.

Amy started, then looked at him for reassurance. "They're still at it," he said. "I'll have to go." He leaned down and hastily kissed her.

"Do you have to, Pa?" Her eyes pleaded, fear for him plainly expressed in them.

"The danger is over, now," he reassured her. "We've got to catch whoever is doing it."

Mum came through the door as he was leaving.

"I suppose you're goin' over there like an idiot," she said. "Go on, I'll stay with Amy and Little Maggie."

When he got downstairs, the phone was ringing, and he picked it up. It was his brother Matt.

"Wait a minute," Matt said, "Maggie wants to talk to you."

He grinned, even under the stress of the situation, knowing Maggie was still reluctant to try to call central and get a number for herself. She sounded breathless. "Are you going over to the bombing?" she asked, knowing the answer.

"Of course. It's my job just now."

"I wish it wasn't. I wish we'd stayed in Alaska."

"So do I," he said.

"Be careful." Then added: "This one is a girl."

He almost said—"This what?"—having momentarily forgotten about his son's wife Catherine. He suddenly realized what she meant and said: "Holy Cow! We're grandparents. How's the mother?"

"Just fine, and the father shows signs of surviving, too. Be careful," she repeated. "I'd die if I lost you. I'll be back over there in a little while."

He hung up, turned, and found Persimmon with Little Maggie on his knee, bouncing her. Persimmon was saying—"Bup, bup, bup."—at each bounce, but stopped long enough to say: "Mop is out saddling up for you. I wish I could go with you."

"We need you here."

He realized how true that was. This kid was going to be a true helper like Mop, who he found outside with a lantern, holding Wowakan.

## Chapter Twelve

Lanterns were bobbing where rescue workers were moving around all over the area of the latest blast. The fire department and Hanratty had beat Dolf to the scene. Hanratty didn't look too happy when Dolf reached him, hair uncombed and shirt carelessly tucked in, flapping out behind. Ambrose Bierce was with him, and, this time, Doe Darling, as well. Dolf asked: "Whose place was this?"

Hanratty drew him aside and said in a low voice: "The Pinks had a guy in here. I'm not sure anyone knows that but me and one of my boys, and now you." He added: "Pookay didn't tell me, naturally . . . we found it out on our own."

"Where's Obie?"

"A little bird told me he went up to the junction on the Bullet and hasn't got back yet. He'll be fit to be tied when he does."

"How'd you find out he had a man in here?" Dolf asked.

"I was watchin' the place sorta by accident. I had Clem Yoder and a couple of others out in the hills, glassing the camp to see if Cloverwood poked his head out of some hole. He did . . . in a cabin about a hundred yards over there." He pointed. "I reckon Pookay found out Cloverwood was up here and slipped somebody in the cabin that just blew up. You can imagine why Pookay had a man here."

Dolf thought that over briefly. "I reckon the coroner

might be working on Big Bill in the a.m. if he hadn't found out about it, right?"

"It figures. They blew the poor bastard Pookay had in here sky-high. I wonder who he was. We'll likely be pickin' pieces of him off the trees in the morning." He was interrupted by muffled cries of some kind that sounded like an injured animal.

Dolf said: "Sounds like somebody's cow got caught in the blast."

The whole crew heard it, and a hush fell over the group as they waited for the sound to be repeated. When it came again, it was recognizable as someone calling for help. A fireman yelled: "He's over here somewhere!" Several men with lanterns converged on the sound, the rest of the crowd following. Hanratty shoved people out of the way and trotted over, followed by Dolf, who realized that Doe Darling was beside him when she said: "Isn't this exciting?"

He had to agree, with the reservation: *Provided you don't have your guts blown out, or something.*

The frantic yelling for help was coming from under a pile of splintered boards and seemed to be under the ground. Realization of what the mess had once been caused Dolf to grin despite the plight of whoever was caught in it. Hanratty put words to it. "Some poor son-of-a-bitch must have been in the shithouse . . . or, come to think of it, maybe some lucky son-of-a-bitch."

Reluctant hands fished through the mess and finally helped a sorry sight to emerge. He cried: "Ooh! Ooh! I can't stand it! My pins are busted." Then he passed out.

Dolf realized that Doc Hennessey was there when

Doc pushed into the front of the group around the injured man. "Hold those lanterns up so I can see him. We might kill him if we don't get him out of here just right."

"It's a sawbones," someone said. "Let him through."

"Christ!" Doc said. "Phew! Somebody get a couple of buckets of water, and we'll slosh him off before I examine him."

Doc discovered that the fellow had compound fractures of both his lower legs, and temporarily splinted them to move him to the hospital. "Have to fix these so he doesn't move his legs on the way to the hospital and cut an artery. Bleed to death sure as hell if he does. I'll ride down with him. Give me a couple of lanterns so I can keep an eye on him."

Doe Darling said: "I'll come along and hold the lanterns." She hiked up her dress and agilely climbed over the wheel of the light wagon that served as an ambulance, to the edification of the male watchers, since there were enough lanterns on the job to light up a lot of leg.

Bierce watched her with admiration. *I guess I know how to pick 'em. On the other hand she can run down to the hospital if she wants to. I'd rather go back and order another dinner because the one I was working on when the blast went off is sure as hell cold by now.*

Hanratty turned to Dolf. "Not much we're gonna see here till morning. I'll have a couple of the boys keep the crowd out of here, and we can look it over then. By the way, I got a new guest down at the Hotel-du-Hanratty," he said, using the popular name that frontier newspapers applied to local jails—hotels named for the local marshal or police chief. Pinebluff's newspapers were no exception.

"And who might that new guest be?"

"Cloverwood. I had a couple of good men watching his place, and they picked him up just after dark when he headed out of that cabin. I suppose he was planning to get out of town . . . or, at least, he was getting to hell away from here . . . the blast went off about fifteen minutes after he cleared out. If I'd been using my head, I'd have figured what he might have his boys do to Pookay's man in this pile of kindling after he got clear. Want to come up to the jug while I talk to Cloverwood?"

"You bet," Dolf said. "I gotta get my horse."

"I'll meet you up at my office," Hanratty said.

When Dolf arrived, he found Hanratty, Bierce, and Tobe Mulveen there. "I'll bring up the guest of honor," Hanratty said.

Dolf wondered what he meant by "up", since the cells were all behind the office so far as he knew, but the jail was new since his time. Hanratty explained: "I got a special suite for him. He can't even hear the bow-wows bark from down there . . . and, more to the point . . . no one can hear anyone yelling from down there."

"Want me to come along?" Dolf asked.

Hanratty gave him a pained look, as though to say: *You must think I'm gettin' too old to handle the tough ones!*

On due reflection, Dolf knew that Hanratty would as

soon shoot a prisoner as look at him, if the fellow got too rough. He also knew he carried a heavy, shot-loaded sap in his back pocket, was an expert at using it, and still quick as a snake. More to the point, Cloverwood would also know that and, most likely, valued his life and an undented head as much as anyone, for all of his bluster.

Cloverwood looked decidedly unhappy when he joined the group. "Have a chair, Bill," Hanratty offered sociably. "How about a seegar and a little pop of something?" He handed him a two-fer and brought a bottle out of his lower desk drawer. Cloverwood gratefully accepted both, taking a big swig from the bottle, wiping his mouth and letting out a satisfied "Ahhh!" He got his two-fer going well, and looked at Hanratty.

"What the hell you got me in the clamp for?" he asked, trying to appear innocent and aggrieved. He avoided meeting Dolf's eyes after looking at him once and getting the notion he was being measured for a pine box.

Dolf was thinking: *This man thinks he's goin' to the Promised Land someday for tryin' to get workin' men a livin' wage, and is blind to anything else, just like John Brown was about freein' the slaves. Well, old Brown got to the Promised Land and somebody else freed the slaves, and, if I find out he had that train bombed, maybe I'll help him to the Promised Land, and we'll leave it to someone else to get his workmen a livin' wage.*

His conflicting thoughts expressed the split in his character that few but his closest friends understood and appreciated. Hanratty was one of that number and hadn't missed the look he'd directed at Cloverwood or its significance.

Big Bill noticed the look as well. *Maybe I should take up Elm on sending Morgette over to the majority . . . if I ever get out of here.*

To Cloverwood's question, Hanratty replied: "I guess you can figure out why you're here. One of those guys that was on that derailed train croaked this afternoon. And somebody just blew a cabin sky-high over next to the one you were holed up in and killed the guy inside."

Neither statement was true, but Cloverwood didn't know that. "You'll play hell hangin' those on me. Especially with a jury in this camp."

"That's what we're here for. Playin' hell. And who do you suppose a jury would think had the motive in both cases if the D.A. got a change of venue to get an honest trial?"

Cloverwood didn't like the sound of that. "I got a right to a lawyer."

"Not in my town. I read somewhere that Abe Lincoln suspended the writ of *habeas corpus* in an emergency. I figure this damn' community is havin' an emergency." He turned to Tobe. "How about you?"

Tobe rose to the occasion. "Whenever Dolf, here, is in town, it's an emergency."

Everyone laughed, even Cloverwood.

"That ain't exactly what I meant," Hanratty said, "but it's a fact, come to think of it."

"Thanks," Dolf said, looking bland. "It's a knack I have. It's really nice to be appreciated by your friends."

"How about another pull on that bottle?" Cloverwood asked. Hanratty passed it to him.

"How about the rest of you guys?" Hanratty offered after Big Bill handed the bottle back.

"No thanks," Bierce said, having noted the label and deciding he'd rather have varnish remover. Dolf waved his hand, but Tobe took a pull, followed by the chief.

"You didn't bring me up here to have a party," Cloverwood said.

"I brought you up here to cut a deal," Hanratty told him.

Cloverwood looked interested. "Start cuttin'," he said.

"I don't especially give a damn about a couple of dead Pinks. But I figure if you was out of town, we'd have one less problem. Why don't you sashay back to Colorado or somewhere and start some trouble there?"

Cloverwood laughed. "In so many words, you want to run me out of town."

"I didn't say that . . . exactly. I just think you could use a vacation."

"But it boils down to that . . . *exactly*. No son-of-a-bitch ever run me out of any town."

"Bullshit!" Hanratty said. "If you went back to a couple of them, they'd fine you for having violated curfew slippin' out of town after dark. I'm givin' you a fair chance to slope, or I aim to send you up the river, or get a rope around your neck. Take it or leave it."

"Suppose I take it, and don't leave?"

"Suppose I find you're still around and shoot you on

sight? I don't trust you, Cloverwood, but I figure you got good sense."

"Go to hell," Cloverwood said, and was escorted back to his dog house in the basement. After Hanratty locked Big Bill back in his cell and was a few steps away, Cloverwood yelled after him: "I get to see a lawyer, don't forget."

Hanratty laughed. "I know just the man. It happens Dolf Morgette was licensed in the territory. I suppose he can practice in the state, too." He knew the last man Cloverwood cared to be alone with was the well-known gunman whose daughter had almost been killed on the bombed train. "Want I should send Dolf down here?"

"Go to hell. I'll catch up on my sleep. You'll have to get me a lawyer sooner or later. If the boys find out I'm down here, they'll tear your jail down."

"Don't be too damn' sure about that," Hanratty said. One of Cloverwood's boys had put the finger on him just before Hanratty's men picked him up with field glasses, and it had been the one Big Bill would have suspected least—George Elm. George had had the misfortune of having Hanratty see him around town and make him as a former San Francisco thug who'd gone "over the road". The chief reasoned that he was out of Folsom way too early, unless he'd been pardoned, and checked up, discovering that Elm was an escapee. Some pious lawmen would have picked him up for return to California, but Hanratty simply recruited him as a member of his grapevine intelligence service. Elm had debated not ratting on Cloverwood for a couple of days, then considered the consequences if he got caught holding out after Hanratty put out the word on Big Bill. He decided to sing about the same time that his boss was spotted, anyhow. However, Elm saw no reason to tell Hanratty about the dynamiting he had arranged after Big Bill was clear. He felt sure he could claim ignorance of that and get away with it.

When Hanratty rejoined the others in his office, he said: "I guess you all realize that nobody needs to know I got Cloverwood here . . . not for a while, anyhow."

They all nodded in agreement.

He arranged that just in the nick of time. Pookay's rapid footsteps echoed down the hall, followed by those of a couple of others. He entered the office and started babbling. "They bombed one of my boys." He spotted the bottle and added: "And what do I find the law doing?"

Hanratty said: "Something it would do you some good to do. We're *thinking* before we go off half-cocked. What's your idea about what we should do?"

Behind Pookay was Nick Bradley, with Will Alexander and Hal Green closely following. The other two grinned at Hanratty's acid remark.

Pookay was undeterred. "I had that guy that was blown up tonight up there on the look-out for Cloverwood."

"What did you aim to do if you saw him?"

"Get you to pull him in, so we could put the heat on him. He's behind all these bombings, and we all know it."

Hanratty snorted. "Sure you were, and maybe send him over a hamper of sandwiches just in case he got hungry before I got there. Why didn't you get a couple of my boys to come up there to sit on look-out with your man?"

Pookay's face took on an evasive expression as he realized he couldn't answer truthfully and that everyone in the room knew it. He spotted Bierce. "Don't I know you?"

Bierce shrugged. "Maybe. I know you." He didn't elaborate, which left Pookay damned little further to say on that subject.

Pookay turned to Hanratty: "I came here to get down to business. Does this man have any right to listen in?"

Hanratty said: "I just hired him as a private investigator to help out Dolf here. He's one of the best snoops I know." He grinned at Bierce, whose face remained impassive. "You probably heard of him. His name is Bierce. Ambrose Bierce. He's got a great nose for digging out the truth."

Pookay looked like he was going to have apoplexy. Bierce had done a series of scathing articles on strike-breaking tactics in the U.S. After the Homestead massacre of workers by militia and Pinkertons, he'd skinned everyone in print as only he could, including the President, who'd stupidly sanctioned the use of troops.

"I ain't talkin' with him here!" Pookay exploded.

"Good," Hanratty said. "That's the first good news I've had all day. Stay right where you are, Bierce."

Will Alexander broke in. "I've got no objection to talking while Ambrose is here." He turned to Pookay. "If Bierce says he'll keep something confidential, he will. It's common sense in the case of a man in his position, and, if it wasn't, I'd vouch for him as a man of honor."

Bradley broke in. "I don't care who the hell is listening. These latest two bombings are the straw that broke the camel's back. There's going to be hell to pay."

Hanratty regarded him coolly, obviously not impressed. "So? There's already hell to pay. Cut loose your wolf. What's brewing?"

Bradley wisely ignored the question, but Pookay said: "For one thing, after today about half of my boys want their time and a ticket out of here."

*If that's the case*, Dolf thought, *it's damn' dumb of him to mention it here.*

Bradley lost his temper and plunged in heedlessly, sputtering: "That won't stop us. We're going to bring in as many more men as we need to repossess our property and hire men willing to work."

Hal Green spoke for the first time: "I think you're making a big mistake. You guys all remind me of a couple of dogs that start out playing, till one bites a little too hard and a real fight starts."

Bradley looked at him resentfully. "You, of all people, should be standing up for the law," he protested. "Property rights are sacred under the Constitution in this country, thank God."

Hal said mildly: "Funny the same guys that framed the Constitution didn't think of that earlier when they mentioned 'life, liberty, and the pursuit of happiness'. I suppose you think that should have been pursuit of money."

"It boils down to the same thing," Bradley snapped.

"*In your case*, you might add."

"In everybody's case. If these miners weren't all lawless, they'd have money to feed their families."

"The argument is over how much, as I recall," Hal said. "They tried it and weren't making out too good. You ought to try supporting a family in one of these shacks on three dollars a day with the price of groceries what they are way out here, to say nothing of medicine and doctors' bills if they have someone in the family sick, and most do. And your friends, the railroads, aren't helping either, with rates jacked up sky-high."

"So now it's the railroads."

"Not entirely. Just the rate fixing they like so well when it comes to giving big business a break and small labor and farmers a compound fracture."

Bradley practically had steam coming out his ears. "I own railroad stock," he said.

"I'd have bet on it. Probably a lot of it, too."

"Look, god dammit! I'm bringing in as many men as we need to uphold the law if no one else will."

Will Alexander said: "And if I'm any judge, based on past experience, all you'll get is a big expense and a lot of corpses. The Army will come in then, and your Pinks will get run out of camp. You may get your mines back in your control, but you might wish you hadn't in the shape they'll be in after the miners figure out they'll never work there again."

"What the hell does that mean?"

"I guess you've read the papers over the years. It means they'll know you're bringing in a bunch of scabs to replace them, and they'll dynamite in every shaft you ever cut."

"By God, Will, I believe you want these criminals to put us out of business so we won't compete with you. I wouldn't put it past you to be bank-rolling them."

For his age Will had a nice punch. He dropped Bradley like a pro. Hal Green caught Bradley's slumping body and let him down to the floor, easy.

Pookay's eyes stuck out far enough to hang a hat on. "You'll go to jail for assault and battery for that," he said.

"Not in my town," Hanratty said. "I never saw a thing. How about the rest of you?"

"I saw something," Pookay blurted out, and quickly realized he shouldn't have.

"You'll likely see stars if you don't shut up," Hanratty said. "Will, there, packs a good punch, and he still looks mad as a wet hen to me."

Pookay backed away quickly, recalling the shifty ground he was already on with Will. He had no desire to do a stretch in Folsom for kidnapping.

Bradley was coming around slowly. He shook his head, obviously still dizzy and not seeing straight. "What happened?" he asked. He really didn't know. He'd never been in a fist fight in his life.

Pookay, the only one willing to tell him, was by then afraid to open his mouth. Will Alexander relieved him of the responsibility. He said: "I poked you in the snoot for shooting off your big mouth. Not only that, but I have a notion you had my front gate blown off to try to scare me into playing your dirty game."

Bradley's eyes were by then focused. He said: "Somebody help me up."

Pookay rushed over and gave his bread and butter a hand. Bradley half rose, then, still dizzy, fell over again. He struggled around on his hands and knees, shaking his head. Finally he made another try and was able to stand. He regained some of his nasty disposition. "You'll pay for that, Will Alexander."

"Not likely," Will said. "And if you don't shut up, I'll slap your face a few times to remind you to have respect for your betters."

Bradley looked at Hanratty, who hadn't even risen from behind his desk. "You're the law here! I demand protection!"

Hanratty grinned. "I've seen a lot of guys like you protected a lot better than I ever could by just learning to button their lips."

Bradley then turned to Hal Green. "You're the lieutenant governor. Why don't you do something?"

"What?"

Bradley realized he was beaten and turned to Pookay. "Let's get out of here," he proposed.

It made a lot of sense to Pookay, who, like most of his type, was only brave when backed by a bunch of plug uglies in his employ. He had no desire to be punched in the snoot, and like Bradley had never been in a fist fight in his life.

As they left, Will Alexander yelled after Bradley: "You'd better think about my proposition!"

Down the hall, Bradley muttered under his breath: "Go to hell."

In Hanratty's office, Hal Green asked Will: "What proposition?"

"Alby Gould and I are ready to buy them out."

Dolf smiled. It was the first ray of hope he'd seen in the miserable local situation. Gould was an old-timer who sympathized with his neighbors of many years, and Will was fast becoming one. Dolf wondered why there weren't more like them in business. It occurred to him that there were very few like them anywhere, and in business they were as scarce as cowards in boxing rings. *In business you only get punched in the snoot by accident and derned seldom at that.* He grinned inwardly, savoring what Will had just done to Bradley.

As the group broke up, Hanratty said to Dolf: "Drop by in the morning . . . not early . . . and we'll mosey down to the hospital and over to the latest mess together."

"OK," Dolf said. "I'd better get home now . . . Maggie will be waiting up for me."

Bierce said: "Anybody want to join me for a late dinner? I still haven't managed to get one finished."

"I'll have a cognac while you eat," Will said. "Join us, Hal? Chief?"

"Nope. I've got to get out the paper."

He was mulling over a headline and liked a possibility he knew he couldn't publish:

ANOTHER PINK MISSES PERDITION!
TOO BAD!

## Chapter Thirteen

Doe Darling had seen a lot worse hospitals, or what went by that name, in a good many places in the world. Pinebluff's was clean enough and didn't smell too bad, but was suffering from overcrowding due to the recent bombings. It had two large wards and a half dozen private rooms in a separate wing that had been included for the well-to-do. All had been pressed into full use, with four persons in each of the private rooms. A fourth wing contained the operating room and offices. Doc took Doe there, put her in a white attendant's gown, and said: "Come on, they'll have him ready by now."

Doc Priddy, who'd taken over Doc's practice when he'd pulled out for Alaska for good, and a male nurse were there to help. Doe noted the bruised flesh of the victim's legs, the broken bones protruding, but she was not the kind to get sick at such sights, never had, even when she was a child. Since then, of course, she'd seen a lot of victims of violence all over the world, felled by accidents, natural disasters, crime, and wars.

Pookay's assistant, Ev Bowman, had been at the scene of this latest bombing and had come to the hospital to get Doc's professional opinion regarding the man's chances. Unlike Pookay, Bowman considered their force of private police as something more than pieces in a chess game, and knew that this fellow, Charley Molton, had a wife and a couple of kids in Seattle. As a good manager, Bowman had made it a point to meet, and recognize by name, the men they had brought in, and he'd learned something about those like Molton, who were willing to talk to him. Bowman had a retentive memory for names and faces, one of the reasons he'd been a good lawman, but, if he hadn't, he'd have worked at it until he knew them anyhow. It was good business, he'd found. In talking to these men, he'd discovered a number who simply needed work and would take long chances to make money, usually to support a family, others to start a business or farm after acquiring a nest egg. Molton had been one of these and had been unaware that Blackie Wilson, who had been assigned to the dynamited cabin with him, was a professional killer whose mission was to dry-gulch Cloverwood. Blackie had figured he wouldn't be needed till daylight and hadn't shown up yet by the time of the explosion. Bowman would have shed no tears if the blast had caught him. The majority of the men Pookay had employed were Blackie's type, professional rowdies at best, and thugs and murderers at worst. Bowman didn't buy Pookay's callousness or his tactics, but he needed a job, too. He'd thought of going over and hitting up Hanratty for a far less lucrative job as a beat cop to get out of the nasty business, and hadn't given up the idea entirely.

Bowman had been waiting outside the operating room when Pookay burst in. This was before he'd gone down to Hanratty's office with Bradley, and, of course, was the reason he'd gone.

"What the hell happened?" Pookay blurted.

He already had a general idea. Talk of a new blast had been the first thing he'd heard on all sides when the night train got in. He'd asked the first man he could buttonhole for details, and was told: "Some poor sap had his legs just about blown off up in a cabin. Nobody knows why it was blown up." Pookay concluded correctly what had happened, and swore under his breath: "That bastard, Cloverwood, has spies all over this town! He read us." It instantly occurred to him that Big Bill might have a mole among the Pinks, of the sort Hanratty had in Cloverwood's outfit, not that Pookay was aware of Hanratty's informant.

Bowman told him all he knew, which was simply the externals.

Pookay growled: "This is the union's dirty work. They knew somehow we had that cabin staked out, damn them. I'm going to look up Hanratty. You stay here. If that guy croaks, I want to know about it right away and get out a murder warrant for Cloverwood. And remind me to take the boob off the payroll in the morning." He missed or ignored Bowman's look when he said that and left for Hanratty's office, looking for an outlet for his frustration.

Pookay's order to stay there prompted Bowman to wonder where Pookay had thought he was going to be. He resented the pompous little man's excessive orders. *If that bastard takes Molton off the payroll, I'm quitting flat right then and there.*

Doc came out of the operating room, wiping his hands on a towel, followed by Doe Darling.

Bowman stepped up. "How is he?"

"You a friend of his?" Doc asked.

"He works for me."

"He's doped up to high heaven," Doc explained, "but he'll live. He was lucky and didn't lose much blood, but in any case he won't be running any races very soon."

Bowman nodded. "Thanks. I've got to write to his family."

Both Doc and Doe looked surprised.

"I'm Doe Darling. You may have heard of me. I'd like to talk to you about doing a story on the trouble here from your side."

"I guess just about everyone's heard of you," Bowman said. "But the story depends on what you want to know."

"The human angle. Nothing confidential. These men are doing a job, and you seem to me a lot more concerned over their welfare than most I've ever met in jobs like yours."

Bowman smiled thinly. "It's good business."

"Is that all?"

"Some of 'em have families. Lots of 'em show me pictures of their wives and kids somewhere, waiting for them to come home, and likely praying that they will. Of course, others are pretty hard and, if they have a family, keep it to themselves. But there's something about that kind . . . they stick together in places like this even if they'd be at each other's throats back in a city somewhere."

"Honor among thieves?" Doe ventured, and made sure she smiled when she said it.

"Some are a lot worse than that." Bowman held up his hand. "Don't put that in there. I've got to keep my job. I've got a family, too. I brought my wife with me."

"Any kids?"

"Three. Two boys and a girl. She's married and lives on a farm in Iowa. One boy's a lieutenant in the Army."

"How about the other one?"

Bowman again gave his thin smile, but this time without humor. "Killed at Wounded Knee with the Army. He was a private . . . just got in a few months before."

"Oh," Doe said softly. "How terrible for you and his mother." She put her hand involuntarily on his shoulder. "I'm so sorry." This was the big-hearted Doe to whom people wanted to talk because they recognized that she genuinely cared about them and their affairs.

"The wife's still takin' it pretty hard. She tried to keep him out of the Army. In fact, I'd just as soon have had him do almost anything else."

"How about the lieutenant?"

"She's proud of him. So am I. But we'd both rather see him walking behind a plow back home."

"Where is back home?"

"Wisconsin. Dodgeville. I was born there on a farm."

*So many of these men out here are from farms*, Doe thought. *I guess almost anything beats getting up with the chickens and sweating and grunting all day till you fall back in bed so tired you're asleep before your head hits the pillow.* She remembered Ambrose Bierce telling her that most of the recruits in the Civil War weren't there because of patriotism, but to escape boredom back on farms and in hick villages. He was probably right.

"Have you been in this business long?" she asked.

"Not with Pinkerton. I've been in law work most of my life."

"Where?"

"Here and there. All over."

She recognized his evasiveness and wondered why, but got off that tack. Nonetheless, he didn't look like the kind that would be ashamed of anything he'd done, except perhaps what he was engaged in now. He'd popped out with—"Not with Pinkerton."—quickly, defensively.

"What does your wife think about you being in this business?"

"That I'm going to be killed someday and leave her alone when she's too old to take care of herself." He looked her directly in the eyes.

"What do you think?"

"I hope she's wrong. I'm salting away a nest egg to go somewhere and raise chickens." He smiled, this time openly. "Maybe Arizona. It's warm in winter and there's plenty of good farm prospects there . . . it's not all desert."

His talk hadn't been what she'd expected. She planned to do some interviews with the miners and their wives to write a balanced article, showing both sides of this question. She suspected that the man in charge of the mines who had cut wages would be a reluctant interviewee, a professional mining man by the name of Bradley who she intended to look up in the morning—not early. She was tired, and thought: *Doc looks fresh as a daisy, considering what we've been through together today.*

"Thank you very much, Mister . . . ," she began, and realized she'd almost forgotten the first thing you asked in an interview.

"Bowman. Ev Bowman. You're welcome. Don't have me saying too much that I didn't, or you'll get me fired." He smiled again, his narrow smile, but this time with real humor.

She laughed and assured him: "I won't, and thank you again. Somehow I feel you wouldn't be too unhappy if you *were* fired."

He only grinned.

Doe turned to Doc. "I don't know about you, but I'm going to hit the hay."

Doc dropped her off at the Grand, and headed for the Cosmopolitan, thinking: *I guess I'll move over here as soon as I can get a room. Save shoe leather.*

When Doe came down to breakfast, the first people she saw were the Goulds and Will Alexander at a table. Victoria saw her and motioned her over. "Please join us. The men are talking business as usual, so we can have a good gab fest."

Alby and Will both rose until Doe was seated, then resumed their earnest conversation, which Doe listened to with one ear.

Will was saying: "We should be able to raise enough capital to buy out Bradley's outfit."

"No problem at all," Alby responded. "It's one of the best-paying gold propositions in the country . . . or was until these fools overreached and made it one of the worst. If we can get our hands on it before they force the miners to blow it to smithereens, we can have it putting out a million a month again in short order."

On Doe's other side, Victoria was saying: "You've got to come over and see the babies. We've got two of them up at the house now. Dolf's son's wife, Catherine, had hers, too, and both women are over there, with Clemmy fussing over them, to say nothing of a couple of awkward husbands, unless they went back out to the ranch. You'll find out that in this country *calving* runs neck and neck with *birthing*."

"I don't want any part of either one," Doe said.

Victoria's face was sad for a fleeting moment, and Doe read what she was probably thinking. Victoria was the kind who would have liked a house full of kids, and it looked as though she and Alby couldn't have children. She wondered which one of them had the disability. *Probably him*, she guessed. *Overbred, old money.* Then as an afterthought: *Not that I have anything against money, new or old.*

Alby and Will were deep in their business talk while Doe finished breakfast, then Alby said: "I heard somebody say something about seeing babies. Will and I have a business call to make, so why don't you ladies take the carriage over to dote on the newborns?"

*I'll bet they're going over to see Bradley*, Doe thought. *I'd like to horn in but don't see any way to do it just now.*

Neither Diana nor Catherine looked like *birthing* had unduly undermined their constitutions, in Doe's opinion. And all babies were dear, in her opinion, so long as someone else had carried and given birth to them.

There were voices and bustling noises downstairs at the front door, after Doe had been visiting for a few minutes, followed by heavy footsteps on the stairs. She wondered what man would be coming up here, and hoped it was Dolf. Clemmy entered just ahead of a large, older woman.

Mum barged in, noted Doe but ignored her, and went to her girls and the babies, berthed in separate beds in the huge master bedroom, which had become the maternity ward. "You both look like a million bucks," she pronounced in a booming voice. "I'd have been here sooner, but, as you know, I got a nursing job over to the house."

"How is Amy?" both of the new mothers asked almost in unison.

"Fine as wine, now," Mum answered. She turned to Doe, and asked no one in particular: "Who is this?"

Doe put out her hand and took Mum's, saying: "I'm Doe Darling."

Mum looked surprised for an instant and repeated what the men had all said: "You're the Doe Darling that makes the boys up in the camps get all teary thinkin' of home fires, I reckon? I heard you was in town. Pleased to meet you."

She offered her hand, and Doe took it innocently and was thankful to get her hand back, not realizing that Mum had thought she was being very careful not to crush it.

"I've heard of you, too. Doc Hennessey mentioned you."

Mum sniffed. "What did that reprobate have to say?"

Doe grinned. "Nothing but the best. And that I ought to meet you,"—and then the mind that made her a great newswoman prompted her to add something Doc hadn't said—"and that I ought to do an interview with you . . . that you're walking history, and, besides that, the boys in Alaska would love it."

Mum grinned. "We could give 'em something to think about, couldn't we? Make up a big bunch of lies, like I'm fixin' to get married to a young preacher who's after my gold mine."

Everyone laughed at that. "We'll do it, then," Doe agreed. "When can we get together?"

"Why don't you come over to the house with me after I'm done oohing and aahing and kitchee-cooin' over these little darlings and their mamas. I'll feed you lunch. Take you over and see that heathen Pa-in-law of Dolf's, too. Chief Henry. You probably heard of the old murderer. You'll meet Dolf's wife, Margaret, too. I don't see how a hardcase like the old chief had such a nice daughter . . . must 'a' come from her ma's side."

If Doe read her face right, Mum didn't hate the chief all that badly.

Mum continued: "You'll meet Dolf's daughter, Amy. She almost got killed when the train derailed. She's a sweetheart."

This was getting to be more than Doe had hoped for. Here was a bonanza of exactly the type of stories that her readers ate up, the rare human profiles that had made her famous because she did them better than anyone in the business.

"You won't need me," Victoria interjected. "I think I'll stay here and be nurse maid till Alby and Will show up."

## Chapter Fourteen

Mum's house was a mansion by small town standards and was more impressive than Doe had expected. She didn't know that Mum had come to Pinebluff when the town was on the skids before the new discoveries and places like hers went for a song, or for delinquent taxes. Doe took in the trim hedges and flower beds, all kept that way in Mum's absence by Mop. As they drew up in Mum's preferred transportation, a farm wagon pulled by two draft horses with a plank across the front for a seat, Mop was the first member of the establishment that Doe saw. He came to take the horses, followed by Persimmon.

After climbing down over the wheel before anyone could help her, Doe turned and said—"Hi, Persimmon!"—then stooped and took his face in her hands and kissed his cheek. He smelled her perfume and wondered at how soft her hands were, blushing deeply. Nonetheless, he was tickled, not really embarrassed, and measured up by saying: "Howdy, Miss Darling. I'm glad to see you again."

Mum interrupted, saying: "Doe, this is my right-hand man, Mop. I couldn't get along without him."

Doe went to him, and shook hands. "Hi, Mop. Pleased to meet you."

He stunned both her and Mum by recalling a dim past that prompted him to say: "My pleasure, ma'am." He even bowed slightly from the hips, which Mum didn't miss, prompting her to remember to inquire regarding the origin of that habit. She thought: *I really don't know a thing about Mop's past . . . only that it made a solid gold man of him before he went on the skids . . . well, he ain't on the skids any more and never will be again if I can help it.* She kept an eye on him for signs of having a bottle stashed around the place, but had never seen the slightest indication of it.

Mop and Persimmon went off with the horses. Mum pointed after them. "You can see Chief Henry's village stickin' out there behind the barn. But he's probably in the kitchen with his daughter about now, eating me out of house and home."

She proved a prophet. He was at the table with a piece of his favorite huckleberry pie and a cup of coffee that Mum knew would be about half sugar. She'd once acidly commented—"You like a little coffee in your sugar, don't you?"—and discovered that Doc Hennessey had been coaching the chief for about a month so he could say, without twisting his tongue: " ' 'Tis a consummation devoutly to be wished.' " She suspected Doc's hand in the matter, but didn't get him to confess till later. At the time, her jaw had dropped, and the chief had grinned broadly.

Later she'd asked Doc: "You think he had any idea what he was saying?"

"Sure," Doc said. "I've been reading him Shakespeare. He likes it, aside from thinking Falstaff is too mouthy."

Whatever the truth was, she never learned it to her satisfaction and gave up trying to find out.

Margaret and her father looked as though they'd been caught with their hands in the cookie jar, which disturbed Mum. She had tried for years to make Dolf's wife realize she was fully accepted as a Morgette, whether she had Indian blood or not, but her indoctrination at the Indian school—whose principal impact was the exact opposite of its stated aim—had too strongly conditioned her to feel inferior.

Chief Henry, a man with an eye for the ladies, looked Doe over from head to foot. Mum ignored him and introduced Doe to Margaret first. "Maggie, this is Doe Darling. This is Dolf's wife, my favorite grandkid."

Margaret got up, smiling and extending her hand. "You're Doe Darling. I love your articles . . . and cry over a lot of them and laugh at others. I never thought I'd meet you. The men up in Alaska love you, too."

Doe was immeasurably pleased at confirmation of what Doc and Dolf had told her, especially coming from this source. She smiled broadly. "I've really been looking forward to meeting you. I've heard a lot about you, and every word of it good, so you needn't worry."

Nonetheless, Margaret couldn't help thinking: *She really wanted to meet me only because I'm an Indian. And Chief Henry's daughter, at that.*

Doe wouldn't have denied it, if confronted with the charge, but she also thought: *How pretty and poised she is, and her English is perfect. No wonder Dolf loves her.*

"And," Mum said, not knowing or caring how much the chief understood of what she said, "this is Maggie's Pa, the old scoundrel."

Margaret said something to him, and he rose and accepted Doe's hand. Still conscious of his grandson's reproof regarding too much lack of ceremony, he said: "*Hau.*"

Mum didn't want to embarrass them further in case Maggie really did feel she didn't have a perfect right to feed her father there. "We're gonna leave you two for a while and go up to see Amy." She led the way upstairs.

"Are you decent for company?" Mum called while still out in the hall.

"Wait," came a little anguished cry. "Who's the company?"

"It ain't no male come courtin', so relax." She peeked in, and said: "You look in apple pie order, as usual. I see you got your sidekick there." She referred to Little Maggie who spent a lot of time dozing next to Amy and imagining she was being her nurse the rest of the time. Jim Too got up, but wasn't hostile since Doe had come with Mum.

"Come on in, Doe," Mum invited.

Amy looked at the sophisticated strange woman and wondered: *Who in the world is Mum bringing to see me?*

"This is Doe Darling. I reckon you've heard of her."

Amy's astonishment registered on her face. This was close to the last person she'd expected to visit her, or even to see in her whole life for that matter. She'd hoped her mother would visit, but she hadn't yet. Amy knew why—because Theodora detested Mum and, moreover, feared her acid tongue that stripped her of pretense and emphasized her numerous failings, especially as a mother.

Doe crossed to the bed, and took Amy's hand. "I hope I'm not intruding. Your father spoke so highly of you, I just had to meet you."

Amy smiled, very pleased. "I'm so glad you came. I've always wanted to meet you. I've thought of trying to write myself. It must be wonderful to be so good at it and get the recognition you do, and travel like you do."

Doe said: "To be perfectly honest about it, sometimes it's a chore. Especially when you're trying to find a hotel in Calcutta or some place that doesn't have cobras in the bed."

Amy laughed. "Not really, I hope."

"I'm exaggerating, of course, but it can get to be a real job . . . other times, when I manage to do something really useful, I wouldn't trade it for anything."

"I think that's what I'd like to do," Amy said.

Little Maggie, next to her, squirmed into a more comfortable position but didn't awaken. Amy said: "This is my half-sister, Little Maggie. She's got to be my pal. I never saw her until a couple of days ago, since she's been living in Alaska."

"She's a cutie," Doe said, and genuinely meant it.

Jim Too had decided he'd better put his formal stamp of approval on Doe, and nosed her gently. She patted his head and scratched his ears, which satisfied him so that he lay down again and sighed, keeping one eye on her, just in case.

Doe said: "If you really want to be a writer, I'll bring a famous one over to see you. He knows your pa and is in town to cover the news just like me."

"Who?"

"Ambrose Bierce."

"I'd be afraid of *him*," Amy gasped. "I always thought his name ought to be Ambrose Fierce."

Doe laughed. "I'll have to tell him that."

"Please don't."

"He's not at all like people think. You'll love him, and he won't get mad at something like that . . . he'll think it's funny, and, besides, it's true sometimes."

Amy didn't appear convinced.

"I'll wait'll you're able to get around, if I do bring him. No woman wants a strange man around for the first time when she's in a sickbed, unless he's a doctor, and even then I'd want an old, gray doctor."

"Doc Hennessey has been taking care of me. Have you met him?"

"I believe I have," Doe said. "A most charming man, as I recall."

Listening, Mum humphed and put in: "He's almost as bad as Chief Henry. They're both old reprobates."

"They are not," Amy said. "You just like to make out they are."

Mum said: "Somebody with common sense has to protect the public from their type."

Doe was glad that Amy asked the question for her: "What type is that, Mum?"

"Tricky."

They were interrupted by the sound of new arrivals downstairs. Mum said: "Let me go down and see who that is."

She was not pleased to see the newcomers. She recognized Theodora, and was not surprised to see her on the arm of one of her typical *gigolos*. She'd heard a little about this one. Margaret had let them in, and there was a frosty silence surrounding them, since Theodora had never forgiven Dolf for remarrying so far beneath him, especially after she'd made it clear he could have her back, and that she wanted him back. As usual, Margaret was making the best of a situation she fully comprehended and didn't wish to complicate, which would have made life more difficult for Dolf.

Under the circumstances, Theodora looked almost as relieved as Maggie did, despite her fear of Mum. That is, until Mum said: "Well, howdy, Grandma. You been over and seen your new grandkid yet?"

The count looked at her. "What are this grandmaman business?"

Theodora ignored him and shot a poisonous look at Mum, then said, directing her words solely to her escort: "This is Dolf's grandmother, Mum." Then turning to Mum, but elaborately ignoring Maggie, she said: "This is the Count Mandel-Pritolet, my *good friend*."

Maggie simply evaporated, not expecting to be introduced or acknowledged in any way. She returned to her father in the kitchen. Mum noted her departure and decided to get a little revenge for her. She said to the count: "That was Margaret. She's a genuine princess."

The count's interest picked up at once. The woman had been a little beauty, and he had been greatly drawn to a princess or two in India, especially since their fathers were rolling in gold and jewels. One never knew about princesses.

"She's a common squaw," Theodora snapped, and narrowly missed being floored by a roundhouse from Mum, who managed to restrain the urge. Theodora read her look and decided to reform for the moment.

"I reckon you want to see your daughter, finally," Mum said. "She hasn't asked why you haven't come sooner . . . maybe never noticed." That netted another poisonous look. "Go on up. First bedroom on the left, at the head of the stairs. She's got company, but I imagine you just want to look in and say hello." She ignored Theodora further, and said to the count: "Come on out in the kitchen and meet Chief Henry. You furriners are always makin' a fuss over Injuns. He's a real one. A famous chief."

The count's interest picked up since he was no exception to the norm. Besides, he read American penny dreadfuls by the stack and knew who Chief Henry was. He asked: "*The* Chief Henry?"

"The one and only original," Mum responded. "That was his daughter just scooted out of here back to the kitchen."

"Run along, my dear," the count urged Theodora, steering her toward the stairs, "I'll be fine."

Theodora didn't particularly like the idea of leaving the count with anyone as pretty as Maggie, although she'd have taken poison before she openly admitted that Dolf's wife was actually quite beautiful in an exotic way. She'd noticed plenty of men attracted to Maggie, and, of course, it was obvious whenever Dolf was with her that he loved her and hardly knew other women existed. *Why wasn't he like that with me?* she thought. *I'd never have run off with Ed Pardeau. . . .* She was really blind to the fact that he had been, and that she hadn't recognized it, or how precious it had been. She'd taken his undemonstrative nature and honesty, which placed empty flattery beyond his capability, for dullness and lack of interest.

Theodora poked her head into Amy's sick room without announcing herself and, when her daughter looked up, said: "Hello, Amy. I've been worried sick about you."

Even kind-hearted and forgiving Amy, who recognized her duty to her mother, believed actions speak louder than words, and then asked herself: *If that were true, what took you so long to come see how I was?* She dismissed that thought. "Ma, I'd like you to meet the famous writer, Doe Darling."

Theodora's face registered her surprise, and she thought—*Why is she here?*—as she advanced to accept Doe's proffered hand, saying: "I'm thrilled to meet you." As a matter of fact, bleeding heart and gossip columns such as Doe's were about all that Theodora read, other than ladies' magazines for beauty hints. To satisfy her curiosity, if possible, she asked: "What brings a famous writer like you to our little backwater?" She'd really have liked to ask: *What are you doing in the house of a mudsill like Mum, talking to my daughter who is a nobody?*

Doe sized her up instantly, and said not entirely truthfully: "I came to cover the labor trouble, but I found I have good friends here in town . . . and, of course, Amy's father is famous, and I won't get away without doing a feature piece on him." She significantly omitted referring to Dolf as this woman's ex-husband, instead referring to him as Amy's father.

Theodora smiled cattily. "Wouldn't infamous be more accurate in Dolf's case?"

Doe caught the outraged look on Amy's face, and thought—*I'll let her settle with you for that nasty remark later.*—only saying: "Famous, infamous, it's all the same with my readers. My boss, Mister Hearst, is of the opinion that Dolf is a hero, a man betrayed and unfairly treated by the world, and, of course, any article I get published on him will emphasize that theme." She watched that sink in, then added: "I'm going to leave you two for now . . . I'll see you again for sure, Amy, and I promise to bring Mister Bierce."

After she left, Theodora asked Amy: "Who is Mister Bierce?"

Amy was familiar with her mother's chronic ignorance and patiently replied: "He's just about the most famous writer in America. He writes for Mister Hearst, too."

"Why does he want to see you?" Theodora asked.

"He doesn't even know me yet, but Doe is going to bring him over, since I said I'd like to be a writer like her. Besides Pa and Mister Bierce are old friends."

"How would your father meet a famous writer?"

"Because Pa is famous, too."

That brought to Theodora's mind a picture of the fresh-faced young bumpkin in jeans she'd married over two decades before, and she experienced a genuine twinge of sadness. She had never seen anything unusual about him until it was too late. Ever the optimist, able to deceive herself in the most outrageous manner, she wondered: *Is it really too late? What will he do if something happens to that squaw?*

This brought to mind what the squaw might be doing down in the kitchen with the count, the most impressionable of men. She turned to Amy and took notice of Little Maggie for the first time. "Who is that?"

"It's Pa's adopted daughter from Alaska."

"It looks like another Indian."

"It is."

"Where's that half-breed son of his?"

Amy had had enough. "Ma, stop it! If you could just see more good in people, you'd be a lot happier." And she thought: *And maybe you'd have some rub off on you.*

"Since when have you taken to lecturing your mother?"

Amy had had enough. "If I'd started when I first recognized that you needed it, I'd have done it since I was first able to talk."

Theodora stormed out the door without even kissing her daughter or saying good bye. She heard Amy's laugh following her and heard her say to Little Maggie, but deliberately loud enough for Theodora to hear her:

181

"I guess that will fix her clock. I should have done it long ago. Wait'll I tell Pa."

That was too much for her mother. She dodged back in, eyes blazing. "I ought to slap your sassy mouth."

That was when Jim Too announced himself, sensing hostility in a person instantly from tone of voice, scent, body language. He rose, growling deep in his throat, and placed himself between Theodora and her daughter, hackles raised alarmingly, teeth bared. Panic entered Theodora's eyes. She had never understood animals and didn't like any of them. She retreated, half stumbling, turned, and almost ran from the room. She called back: "That filthy beast should be shot!"

Mum was just mounting the stairs to see how things were going, and heard and correctly gauged that remark. "If anyone does any shootin' around here, it'll be me. And I'll start with skunks, not dogs. I've put up with about all I can stomach from you for years, and it's time to take your case under advisement. If I hear another mean word out of you, I'll do what your ma should have done years ago. Now pick up that oily article in the kitchen and git the hell out of my house, and don't come back . . . ever."

Theodora was afraid to pass her on the stairs.

"I don't aim to lay a hand on you," Mum pronounced, "as long as you keep your lip buttoned." She descended to the bottom of the stairs. "Now, c'mon down and git."

Getting was going to be a little easier said than done, due to the count. In the first place, he liked looking at both Maggie and Doe, and, in the second, was fascinated with Chief Henry. By the time Theodora entered the kitchen, Mop and Persimmon had joined the chief at the table and were having coffee. The look Mop directed at Theodora was as good as a poison sign at a water hole. Persimmon read it and looked at the woman and instantly disliked her.

She said: "Come, Count, I've got some appointments."

The count wondered what appointments she had made since going upstairs, since she hadn't mentioned them before. "The chief is telling me about how his tribe fought off the U.S. Army. It's fascinating."

"How can he tell you that? He doesn't even speak English."

The count pointed at Maggie. "But she does. She's interpreting."

Theodora looked at Maggie in her usual manner, saw Mum, who had just entered the room watching her, and said: "I'll wait out in the barouche."

She left in haste, not realizing that if Chief Henry had known how she thought of his daughter, he might have scalped her.

When the count looked for her a half hour later, neither she, the barouche, nor their driver were in sight.

He stepped back in the house and said—"They're gone."—and was startled to hear Chief Henry say: " ' 'Tis a consummation devoutly to be wished.' "

Mum roared. Finally she was able to get out: "Why don't you stay a while, Count? I ain't never met a real count before, and the chief, here, has obviously taken to you. Why don't you go over to his camp after a while and see how his folks live?"

The count said: "I'd like that." To Maggie he said: "Would you ask your father if that's all right?"

## Chapter Fifteen

In the morning Dolf rode Wowakan downtown to the police station, and found the paddy wagon hitched out front. Hanratty was seated on a bench outside, smoking a two-fer, obviously waiting, Kirby beside him.

Hanratty arose, and came to the curb. "I decided to give the upstanding citizens a look at the town's free transportation with the head of the city's finest on the seat going out sleuthing."

He climbed into the front seat, and Kirby untied the team and joined him. Dolf was surprised to see Kirby take the reins. Considering his thick glasses, Dolf wondered why Hanratty let him drive, and marveled that he seemed to be able to see where he was going. Nonetheless, he kept Wowakan well to one side.

When they arrived at the previous night's bombing site, policemen were already going over the ground for clues. Curious people kept drifting up to rubberneck, then left reluctantly when ordered away by the policemen.

Hanratty called to his favorite—"Hey, Gorman!"—and motioned him over. To Dolf he said: "Gorman is one of my best men . . . you probably noticed he was the first one on the scene over at Bradley's when it blew."

Gorman informally saluted the chief with a wave.

"Howdy, boss. Look at this." He pulled a roll of thin copper wire from his back pocket.

"It figures," Hanratty said. "With Cloverwood holed up right across the way, they weren't going to set it off with a fuse . . . they had to be sure he was gone."

Dolf had been thinking the same thing and nodded his agreement with that.

"What else?" Hanratty asked.

Gorman said: "Not much. No tracks worth anything. People traipsed all over the place last night before we got here."

"I don't think you're going to find much more," Hanratty said. "You can pull the boys in, I guess. If you want to snoop around a little more, go ahead. It's up to you." To Dolf, he said: "Let's go over to the hospital and see if the poor bastard that Pookay had staked out here can talk."

*If we don't get any more out of him than we did from the others*, Dolf thought, *it'll be a waste of time, but you can never tell.*

They found Molton still heavily doped, sound asleep, and too groggy to rouse. Hanratty looked at him and uttered what Dolf thought was a strange remark coming from the unsentimental police chief: "The poor devil." He didn't even say "poor bastard".

Dolf wondered if his friend was going soft in his old age, and figured that more likely he'd always had a compassionate streak in him, but kept it well concealed for both personal and professional reasons. He grinned inwardly. *I wonder what he'd do if I told him I always knew he was an old softy.*

"We can come back later," Hanratty said. "Let's drop in at Julia Parrent's bakery. She's got a couple of tables over there for people to come by and get coffee and doughnuts anytime. You been over to see her yet?"

"Yup. She's one of the first people I went to see when I blew in. You remember her husband was killed by a dry-gulcher who thought he was getting me. She ought to hate me, by rights."

"She ain't the type. She thinks your shadow is mighty long. Besides, you straightened up her boy, last time you was here."

Dolf nodded. "He's still working out at the ranch. According to the boys, he's one of the best natural cowmen and horsemen around." He added strictly to himself: *He was sure one of the worst rustlers . . . lucky he didn't get killed running with that rough crowd.* He recalled how he'd rounded him up along with a bunch of hardcases and pretended not to recognize the boy until he identified himself. He'd hung the rest, and let the kid think he was going to hang him, too. The boy took it without showing the white feather and never peeped, too proud to beg for his life. All he'd said was: "Mister Morgette, don't tell Ma . . . ever . . . please."

At the time Dolf had been employing that peculiar posse Hanratty had mentioned the other day—a bunch of Chief Henry's braves. They'd covered all the water holes in the area and picked up a score of horse thieves who comprised a huge rustling ring. They'd tied their hands and left them sitting on their horses with ropes around their necks, fastened to sturdy tree limbs. Their taking off was completely at the discretion of their horses. Some with well-trained horses probably kept them standing still for quite a while. Regardless, as Dolf had pointed out to Chief Henry's braves, it would be the horses, not them, who were responsible for the hanging. Those reputedly humorless braves had laughed like hell over that.

Recalling another part of that episode, he'd told Chief Henry the boy's background and that he didn't see any way out of hanging him, since he'd told his posse there were to be no exceptions. The chief, noting the boy's spunk, hadn't tried to interfere, but he obviously would have spared him if it were up to him. He'd said: "This is too bad that this thing happened, what will you do?" Dolf wondered what the chief would have done if he'd gone ahead anyhow. *Most likely he'd have cut the kid down before he strangled and thought a lot less of me afterward.*

Julia Parrent spotted them coming in, and cried warmly: "Well, hello! Let me clean off a table for you." She rounded the counter, hugged Dolf, and presented her cheek for an affectionate peck.

"How about me?" Hanratty asked.

She hugged him, too, then pushed him away, saying: "I get to see you every day. Dolf shows up once in an age." She turned back to Dolf. "Why don't you stay home for good this time?"

"I'd like to. Maybe I will."

Dolf was surprised to see her son, Harvey Jr., come out of the kitchen with a coffee pot and cups to serve them. He set them on the table and offered his hand.

"Howdy, Mister Morgette," he said, smiling broadly. "Heard you was back."

Dolf noted that he'd turned into a man, with the strong grip of a rancher used to handling a rope. He looked a lot like his father had with the same, stocky, broad-shouldered build. Dolf wondered if he was a scrapper like his pa, and bet that he was. He said: "I didn't hear they canned you out at the ranch . . . how come you're in here wearin' an apron?"

"Just helpin' out Ma. I come to town to see how the gals were and to look over the new babies. Too many people over there makin' over babies already, so I ducked out."

"Why don't you sit and have some coffee with us?" Dolf suggested.

Harvey looked a little surprised, as though he thought he'd be in the way, not used to the fact that he wasn't a kid any more. He looked at Hanratty to see how he felt about it.

"Glad to have you," Mike said.

Dolf told Harvey: "I was headed out your way yesterday, but got headed off by another bombing. We had a second one last night. I suppose you heard."

Harvey nodded. "It's a hell of a note, isn't it? People maybe gettin' killed over a lousy buck a day. I'm sure glad I ain't a miner. I get the heebie-jeebies underground in the first place, but I suppose I'd do it if I needed the money bad enough."

Dolf recalled that he'd worked in the underground for a while as a young fellow, for that very reason, and could appreciate Harvey's fear. He'd also been trapped in a mine alone, and knew how that felt. The recognition of that possibility always hanging over a miner's head was at the root of fears like Harvey's, he suspected.

"You aimin' to be around long?" Harvey asked.

"As long as it takes to find out who's behind these bombings. The chief here hired me."

Harvey looked surprised. He knew, as the whole family did, that Dolf had had his belly full of law work.

Sensing what was behind Harvey's expression, Dolf answered his unspoken question: "Amy was on that train that got bombed."

"I heard," Harvey said. Something in his expression, when he said it, triggered a question in Dolf's mind. This young fellow had been living around Amy on and off for a few years, whenever she came home from school. They had had an opportunity to become very close. Consequently he wasn't surprised at Harvey's next remark: "If you fellows don't find the skunk behind that, I will. Your daughter is the finest girl I know." He uttered the words hotly, then caught himself when he noticed Dolf looking at him quizzically, and quickly added: "Don't get the wrong idea. I know she's miles above my kind and hardly knows I'm alive, but all the same. . . ."

*I'm not so sure she's miles above your kind, kid*, Dolf thought, *and she ain't the type to think so, either. Might even marry your kind if she ever gets her high-flying ideas about a career out of the way.* The thought prompted him to say: "Why don't you come over and look in on her with me before you go back?"

Harvey's voice and elated look betrayed him. "I'd sure like that."

They were interrupted by the arrival of Sheriff Mulveen. He came directly over. "I see Hanratty is tryin' to get you in the doughnut habit, Dolf. Got me into it. He could stand to get a little fatter, but I don't need any extra weight."

"Set," Hanratty invited. "What's on your mind besides gettin' fat?"

Mulveen looked at Dolf as he spilled his news. "We just heard that the Kelbo boys broke out of the pen. They caught three of 'em, but Yancey and that mad dog kid, Billy Joe, got clean away."

"When?" Hanratty asked.

"Last night."

Dolf said nothing. The Kelbos had been among the kingpins in the rustler gang he'd put out of business on his last visit to Pinebluff. He'd been the principal individual behind sending the five brothers to the pen. Before then he'd captured four of them and left them sitting on horses with ropes around their necks, tied to strong limbs overhead, just as he had the others of their gang. Luckily for them, their brother Yancey came on the scene just after Dolf departed with his posse. Yancey was able to cut them down before their horses left them swinging. They were all aware Dolf had tried to put them out of business for good and, being the feuding type, from Tennessee by way of Texas, might well think of getting even.

Everyone looked at him to comment on this development. Finally he said what he was thinking: "This is the last place they'll show up, since they went over the road from here."

Mulveen said: "They might come lookin' for you, considerin'."

"Not likely anyone outside of here knows I'm back."

"The whole world knows where you are most of the time," Hanratty said, "in this case, thanks to Doe Darling. She got it on the wire no sooner than she met you. The papers up at the capital picked it up sure as hell, so the Kelbos know you're home, all right."

Dolf shrugged. *There's plenty never left here that think they owe me something, too.* It was the reason he was seated with his back to the wall, even in a doughnut shop that belonged to one of his best friends. You never knew. Some others he might have strung up had slipped out of his net, such as Dutch Pete and the Loco Kid.

Just then Ed Kirby, who'd stabled the paddy wagon team, ducked his head in the door, saw Hanratty, and came over. "I just got this," he said, handing his boss a wire.

Hanratty glanced at it, and handed it back to Kirby. "The sheriff just told us. Thanks. Put it in the file. I'll be over in a little while."

He didn't invite Kirby to sit down, knowing it would have been a waste of breath. The man didn't seem to have an interest in the conviviality of such get-togethers, nor in treating his stomach occasionally as most people did.

Hanratty and the sheriff both left shortly after Kirby. On his way out, Hanratty said to Dolf: "Why don't you drop over and see that guy at the hospital later."

Dolf nodded. "I'll let you know if I find out anything you ought to know."

After they were alone, Harvey asked Dolf: "Who was the fellow that came in and gave Chief Hanratty that telegram?"

"Fellow named Kirby that works for the chief. Why?"

"He used to live over in Fort Belton when we did."

Dolf racked his brain to recall if he'd seen him over there, but couldn't place him. "What did he do over there?" he asked.

"I can't recall, but I know I saw him there."

"I'll ask him when I see him again. Now, let's mosey over to the house and see Amy. You got a horse over at Dawson's, I reckon."

"Two. And a buggy. But I'll walk over. See you there in maybe a half hour if that's OK."

Dolf looked up Julia in the back room, and gave her a hug and kiss. "I'll see when Mum can have you over for a meal. Maybe this coming Sunday."

As he left, he wondered why she'd never married again. *Most likely she's one of those that never will . . . a one-man woman.* He wondered if he'd remarry if he lost Maggie. He didn't think so. All the other women he might have married were married off to members of his family or to friends.

Julia Parrent watched him go to the door, moving confidently, a tall, dark figure, but not forbidding, as some thought. She went to the front window and watched him mount Wowakan, turn him into the road, and trot away.

Behind her, her son said: "He's a hell of a man, isn't he? I hope I can be half as good."

Julia replied: "You are in the ways that count. I hope you never get tangled up in the kind of trouble that turned him into a killer. God never cut him out to be one, but the Almighty moves in strange ways."

Harvey wondered about that, thinking: *If God didn't cut Dolf out to be a killer, he turned him into a first-rate one, anyhow, not that every one of them he killed didn't need it. But Ma is right . . . I sure hope I never have to kill anyone, but if it comes to a ground hog case, I ain't gonna mess around and get killed while I argufy the right of it with myself, and I guess that's how he got started. Dolf is a right sudden feller.*

Harvey's mother watched his face while he was working that out in his head. She said: "God uses us as his instruments . . . we have to figure out as best we can what He wants us to do."

"How about crooks like the Kelbos?"

"He probably gets absent-minded about their kind, which is why He had to make the ones like Dolf . . . to adjust their cases, since they aren't good enough at figuring out for themselves that we all ought to be good and upright or we'll wish we had been."


By the time Dolf got back to Mum's, the diverse gathering in the kitchen had broken up. The count and Doe Darling were with Chief Henry at his camp, and Mop and Persimmon were down at the barn, where they met him and took charge of Wowakan.

Mop was dying to tell Dolf that Mum had finally told

off his ex something fierce, but thought he'd better leave it up to Mum, if she wanted him to know.

"Find out anything uptown?" Mop asked.

"Nothing new. Mulveen got a wire that a couple of the Kelbos broke out of the pen. You might keep your eye peeled for them."

"Which ones?"

"Yancey and Billy Joe."

"The worst two. Wouldn't you jest know it? If I see 'em, I'll load 'em so full of buckshot the coroner'll need a wheelbarrow to get them out of here. Best I get old Hannah down and double charge her." Hannah was the .10-gauge, muzzle-loading shotgun he kept on hand for marauding coyotes after Mum's chickens and kitties.

After Dolf was out of hearing, Persimmon asked: "Who're the Kelbos?"

"A bunch of mean skunks that Dolf sent to the penitentiary. Should 'a' been hung. He must think they might come back here lookin' for him. Somehow I don't think they're that dumb, but most crooks are dumb or they wouldn't be crooks."

Dolf entered by the kitchen door, and yelled: "Anybody home?"

"In here," Maggie called from the sitting room.

He went down the hall to join them and was surprised to find Amy, propped up in a big armchair. She smiled at him as he crossed the room and gave her a kiss. "Don't ask," she said. "I'm feeling fine. Doc said I could get up whenever I felt good enough to move around. I got here on my own legs, too. He's supposed to be over to eat with us at noon, and I want to surprise him."

Dolf crossed the room and stood behind Maggie's rocker, hands on the back and rocked her gently. "You may not remember me," he said. "I'm your husband. If we don't get some kind of break on this bombing business, I'm going to take a vacation and go fishing."

That brought a smile to his wife's face. "Promise?" she asked.

"Promise."

They were interrupted by the arrival of Doc, who breezed in the front door like a member of the household, heard them talking, and popped in, carrying his professional black satchel. "First things first," he said, crossing to Amy, sticking a thermometer in her mouth, and pressing his stethoscope to her chest. After listening a while, he said: "No signs of pneumonia, which is good." He pulled out his turnip watch, took her wrist, and counted her pulse rate. "I wish mine was that low," he said, but didn't say what it was. Then he took out the thermometer, read it, and swabbed it with alcohol before putting it back in its sheath in his case. "Absolutely normal," he said to no one in particular among the group that had been silently watching. "Now, what am I being fed for dinner?"

Mum said: "Chief Henry brought over a fresh-killed puppy . . . how about that?"

Maggie protested laughingly: "He did not! I made him stop eating dog."

"I don't mind dog," Doc said.

"Since we ain't really got it," Mum said, "how about pork chops, then, or fried chicken? Or beef steak? Or trout? Or ham? Or canned beans?"

"Fix whatever you want to. I'll eat it."

Mum left for the kitchen, Maggie trailing along to help. Little Maggie hustled in from outside and over to Dolf, putting up her arms to be lifted into his lap.

"Hello, honey," he said. The shiny gleam in her eyes prompted him to ask: "What have you been doing?"

"Me and Jim Too were hunting bears," she said seriously.

"I'd be pretty careful about that," Dolf said. "You might find one. What would you do then?"

"Bring it home."

"It might not want to come. It might want to eat you."

"Not me," she said. "Somebody else, maybe. Maybe Henry." She brightened up over that idea as though the thought of her brother being eaten by a bear appealed to her.

"If you really see a bear," Dolf said, "you'd better keep quiet and sneak away. Especially if it has little ones with it. They can be dangerous . . . a mamma bear will think you might hurt its babies and come after you."

"Uhn-uh," Maggie said confidently. "I'd pet its babies and it would know I loved them."

Dolf looked over at Doc. "Let's pray she never gets to try out her idea."

Doc shrugged. "You can never tell."

"I'd bet on her," Amy said.

"Good," Little Maggie said, sounding very much

adult. "I love you, Amy, and now it's time to sit on your lap."

Dolf deposited her next to Amy in the big chair. "How about down here?" he suggested.

"Lap," Little Maggie said, and crawled up.

"Are you strong enough?" Dolf asked Amy.

"Of course, I'm strong enough, as long as she's on the side where I don't have a bruised rib."

Doc asked: "Where's Doe? I understood she came out here."

"She and the count went over to the chief's camp," Amy answered. "They said not to wait lunch on them, so there's no telling when they'll be back."

A thought crossed Doc's mind, and he laughed, explaining: "With her they might end up in Singapore, and we won't see 'em for months."

Dolf asked Amy: "If I ain't bein' snoopy, just what part of France did your ma pick this one up in?"

"Oh, she didn't pick him up in France. He picked us up at the junction. We never saw him before. He had a French accent, and, since me and Ma were learning French this summer, she spoke to him in French, or what passes for it, I guess. Then we struck up a conversation in English, and were getting to be great friends when the train wreck happened."

"Is he staying out to the ranch?"

"I don't think so. Ma didn't say, but why would he be?"

Dolf shrugged, thinking: *I sure jumped to the wrong conclusion this time.*

"He's staying at the Cosmopolitan," Doc put in,

"right next door to me, as a matter of fact. I'm teaching him the American game of draw poker in the evenings when I ain't settin' bones."

His remark changed the subject so that Dolf felt he didn't need to admit to his daughter that he'd misjudged her mother. "How's he coming on his poker lessons?" he asked.

"Prime. So far he's into me and Bierce and some of the other boys for a couple hundred bucks."

"What does he do for a living?"

"Sponges off his pa, when he's not at sea. Get this. He's an admiral. Also a mining engineer, which is why he's up here. His old man owns a big chunk of the mine Bradley runs, if I got it right."

"Does Bradley know that?"

"Not yet. I think he came up here to snoop for the old man and figure out what all the trouble is about. Maybe I shouldn't have said anything, so keep it under your hat. He was pretty oiled and there was just the two of us when he let that slip, then asked me not to tell anyone."

"You two must be getting pretty thick."

"Maybe. But he had had quite a bit to drink. French admirals are like that."

Dolf got up to answer a knock at the front door, and found young Harvey Parrent standing outside, looking like he was ready to run. As soon as he saw Dolf, he said: "You sure I ain't hornin' in on a family affair?"

"Sure, I'm sure. C'mon in. Amy's right down here. She'll be glad to see you." He led the way into the sitting room.

Judging from the look on his daughter's face, Dolf

decided maybe she wasn't so glad to see Harvey.

"Pa!" she wailed. "You should have given me time to get prettied up." She laughed and made the best of it, blushing a little.

Harvey ducked back out as soon as he heard her words. From the hall he hollered: "I'm sorry. I guess I'd best be leaving!"

Amy yelled back: "Don't leave! Just wait a minute till I get presentable."

Doc threw back his head and laughed. Dolf looked confused. He thought Amy looked scrumptious the way she was, and she did. He recalled how Harvey had sounded, the intense little break in his voice when he mentioned Amy. *Um-hum, there's something in the wind here, or I miss my guess.* He took the precaution of seeing that Harvey obeyed Amy's request not to leave, and caught him halfway down the driveway on his way back to town.

He called after him: "Come on back! I guess that was my fault."

"No way," Harvey said. "She ain't seen me in over a year and sure doesn't want to see me now from the sound of it, I reckon."

"You heard her say not to leave, didn't you?" Dolf asked.

Harvey shook his head. "All I heard was her givin' you 'what fer' for bringin' me around . . . it sounded like to me."

"She just said to give her time to get presentable, whatever that means. I thought she looked pretty good."

"She always looks beautiful. But I'd best not go back. Like I said, I don't want her thinkin' I'm gettin' ideas where she's concerned. I know how far above me an educated gal like her is, and know how to stay in my place. I'm just sorry as all get out she was hurt, and I wanted to tell her so." He might have added: *Besides I just like to look at her.*

Dolf put his hand on Harvey's shoulder and gave him a steady look. "If you think you're below anyone in this world, you need a good talkin' to. Amy doesn't think like that. And you don't know much about gals. Don't you know why she squawked so loud when you come in unexpected?"

"Uh-uhn. I don't guess I do."

"It's not because she thinks you're beneath her. It's because she likes you a whole lot and wanted time to pretty up special before she let you see her."

Harvey's mouth was open, his eyes disbelieving. "I kinda doubt that, but, if she wants to see me, I'll come back up for just a minute."

"You'll come back up and eat with us, or I'll have to take your case in hand, kid. Mum is fixin' us all something to eat. C'mon."

Harvey blushed deeply when Dolf took him back in to see Amy. By then she'd called Margaret to get Little Maggie out of the way, and Doc had disappeared into the kitchen.

"Howdy, Miss Amy," he said. "I'm sorry to come bargin' in, but I wanted to say how sorry I am you got hurt."

She smiled at him, and he felt like the sun had come

up for the second time, and his heart did something that tickled him and caused a little shiver of a sort he'd never encountered before. His knees were weak all of a sudden, and he wished he could sit down. He took a chair gratefully when she said: "Why don't you sit down. What's going on out at the ranch and how is my horse?"

Dolf tiptoed out. *She sure knows what to get him talking about to settle him down. I remember how I felt the first time I came courtin' a gal I thought a whole heap about.*

## Chapter Sixteen

The Kelbos broke out of the pen with outside help. In this case from an unusual source, Dutch Pete, a legendary Western badman who'd indirectly got them in the pen in the first place. Under many aliases Pete had operated for years from Texas to Canada. He'd never once looked out through bars himself, although some of his associates, such as the Kelbos, had had that misfortune, but usually only if they crossed him. Yancey Kelbo had done something stupid that aroused Pete's ire and ended up in the slammer as a result. It hadn't been what Pete had intended in his case; he'd actually hoped to get Yancey killed.

Yancey hadn't planned to cross Dutch Pete, but true to form hadn't thought out what he was doing and had double-crossed his own gang for a price, thinking no one would ever find out. Pete and several followers were hiding out in a camp in the hills. For a Wells Fargo reward, Yancey had tipped off the law regarding the whereabouts of that camp. This indiscretion had backfired. Dolf Morgette, then a U.S. deputy marshal, had led a posse financed by Wells Fargo that quietly surrounded the camp at night. At first light, when he called for the surrender of the men present, some elected to shoot it out, and, among those killed, was Old Man Kelbo, Yancey's father, which he sure hadn't planned. Dutch Pete, not far away and riding toward his camp, heard the firing, and got away. It was some time later before he deduced who had put the finger on them.

Dutch Pete had been one of the moving forces in the large horse-stealing racket Dolf had broken up. For a few years since then, he'd been lying low, posing as an honest ranch foreman in New Mexico. He was a first-rate cattleman, since that had been his trade before taking up the owlhoot trail. The pickings were so good in his rôle as ranch foreman that he'd stayed even after the Idaho heat had died down. With him were the Loco Kid and two hardcases he'd recruited just before Dolf had wiped out the Idaho operation, Phil Cranston and Dusty Rhodes. They'd found rustling in the Magdalena area to their liking, and that had supplemented their salaries by enough to keep them on the job. They'd sweetened the pot with an occasional train, stage, or bank hold-up. Under Dutch Pete's tutelage, they'd all learned to pull off jobs without being suspected. This was simplified by the fact that so many others of the same persuasion worked that part of the country, so that lawmen had a hard time selecting suspects if they weren't positively identified committing the crimes.

A letter from an old associate in Canada reached Dutch Pete one day and set him to thinking about resuming operations up north. It had been the most profitable deal he'd ever been involved in. Undoubtedly it was the biggest horse-stealing operation in the West, until Dolf had broken its back. Quite simply it consisted of running stolen horses down the back trails from Canada to Utah and Arizona and selling them, then rustling others there and running them back north for sale in Canada, the Dakotas, and Montana in addition to Idaho. Plenty of new ranch operations wanted cheap horses, and a lot of old-timers looked the other way about bills of sale as long as the horses were from far away. Dutch Pete had even peddled horses to town fire departments, sheriffs, schoolteachers, and occasionally the U.S. cavalry when the right purchasing officer was willing to do business.

Hiram Smith's ranch in Canada had been their northern base of operations. The letter Dutch Pete was reading was from Hiram. He wrote:

Dear Old Friend,
   The time is ripe I think to start up again and test the water. Things look pretty good to me. For one thing I heard Morgette has gone to Alaska for good.
   I got a letter from John Tobin over in Sioux City where he's been working—imagine him working—in a packing house at that. The Kelbos managed to have a letter to him smuggled out of the pen. They wanted him to help them bust out. And here's the

part that's really interesting. They claim they stashed their whole roll somewhere out around their old ranch under a fence post, or at least that's what they say. They're willing to divvy for help getting out. If the Kelbo boys got the old man's dough, too, they must have around fifty thousand—maybe twice that. That much sugar is worth going after if we never make a nickel from the old game. Of course, I figure something will happen to the Kelbos after they lead somebody to the loot. That's a little out of my line, but I thought it might look good to you. You might remember your old pal for putting you onto it.

Tobin wrote me and told me what was in the Kelbo letter. He doesn't want any part of Idaho again, and I can't say that I blame him. You may recall that Morgette turned him loose on foot with a dozen or so of Chief Henry's braves after him. They ran him for ten miles or so before they gave up.

Anyhow, Tobin is a good man for our old game, and, if you want him and would like to try to talk him into coming back, his address is: Box 12, Sioux City, Iowa.

Let me know what you aim to do.

As ever,
Hiram

This letter hit Dutch Pete about the time he was getting an itchy foot. He had a good deal on a ranch, with a cabin to himself as foreman and the pick of the horse string, even a steady girl over in Alma, but he was game to move on. The old freedom was calling. Naturally he didn't show the letter to anyone, including the boys he'd brought with him, but waited to talk it over the next time they rode into town together for a little toot.

He stopped his horse in the middle of a meadow where they could be sure no one was listening. Pete broke out a pint of whisky and passed it around.

"I been thinkin'," he said.

"Oh, oh," the Loco Kid put in. "When the boss starts thinkin', we're in for it."

They all laughed. "No job this time," Pete said. "I been thinkin' about headin' back to Idaho. The heat's died down. The old game is waitin' for us. Next time we won't get greedy."

"Yeah," the Kid said, "especially on Morgette range, right?"

"That notion crossed my mind, too, although old Dolf is in Alaska for good, from what I hear."

"He'd better be."

Pete gave him a look and growled: "I ain't scared of him."

The kid held his tongue, reading the warning. He had his own rep as a shootist, but didn't want to cross swords with the boss. He'd done well under Pete and liked the life.

Phil Cranston chipped in: "I wouldn't mind a change of scenery. That's why I left Ohio . . . to see the country. The damned farm wasn't for me, or the fat milkmaids around there, either. How about you, Dusty?"

"Whatever you guys decide, suits me. I'd like a little cooler weather as far as that goes."

"It gets plenty cool up there, especially in the winter," the Kid said.

"Don't I remember. But this ain't winter."

"I aim to get as many as I can of the old crowd back together," Dutch Pete said. "There ain't too many left. We can break the Kelbos out of the can up in Boise, I reckon."

He expected that would get a rise out of the Loco Kid for sure, and wasn't disappointed. The Kid said: "They ain't apt to be grateful to you even if you do. We got 'em in there, sort of."

He referred to the fact that the Kelbos had expected them to back a gun play against the Morgettes, but instead they'd been miles away, splitting the breeze out of the country when the showdown came off. Rather than doing up the Morgettes, the Kelbos had all been captured and jailed.

"We can lie our way out of that. Ain't nobody better at hoss stealin' than old Yancey . . . most likely that's because he's had more practice at it than most. His brothers ain't no slouches, either."

"I don't trust that young kid, Billy Joe," the Loco Kid said. "He's crazier than I am."

That got another general laugh.

"We can maybe arrange an accident for him. But the rest are pure gold for what we aim to do."

This conversation led directly to the escape of the Kelbo boys from the Idaho state penitentiary a few weeks later.

The news story covering that event read:

## BREAKOUT AT PENITENTIARY
## FIVE KELBO BROTHERS BREAK OUT, THREE RECAPTURED

Last night at lock down it was discovered that the five desperate Kelbo brothers were not present. At first it was thought they were hiding on the prison premises, but a thorough search indicated that they had probably gone over the wall. It is not known how that was possible without being detected since alert guards are on duty day and night.

An immediate search was started and continued in the a.m. with bloodhounds enlisted in the chase. Tracks were found where horses had obviously been left waiting for the Kelbos, since their tracks led there directly, but the horses either broke loose or were turned loose by someone, so that the escapees had to proceed on foot. All five horses were found grazing in the neighborhood. Three brothers, Lute, Jud, and Rafe, were quickly recaptured after daylight, but the most dangerous two, Yancey, the leader, and the youngest brother, Billy Joe, are still missing at the time this is being written.

Readers will recall that the five Kelbo brothers were captured in a brazen showdown with law officers right in the town of Pinebluff where they had come to settle accounts with the notorious Dolf Morgette, his brothers, and associate Doc Hennessey, himself a notorious gunman from the days of the Pinebluff War. They were captured and subsequently tried and sent to the penitentiary for a long list of crimes, principal being attempted murder at the time of their arrest, but also including cattle and horse stealing, bank robbery, extortion, stage robbery, and assorted other crimes too numerous to list. They were all given long terms in the pen.

The circumstances of their escape point conclusively to outside help, especially the five horses that were left for them. Officers are on the trail of the two remaining fugitives, and it is impossible for them to escape. News of their arrest is expected momentarily.

In the unlikely event that they are not apprehended and go back to their old stamping ground, they are in for a surprise. We understand from a recent dispatch from Pinebluff by the famous Doe Darling that Dolf Morgette is home visiting the families of his brother and son, both of whom are expecting blessed events in the near future. The Kelbos' likely reception by this noted gunman, and sometime lawman, can be imagined. We hear he has taken a temporary job on the Pinebluff police force to investigate the recent bombings there.

Yancey and Billy Joe, hearing the bloodhounds on their trail, swam, walked, and stumbled for miles in the river. They emerged exhausted, beyond the point where their pursuers expected it was reasonable for them to have traveled. Nearby, they stopped at a farm and hid in a haystack for two days, alternately roasting and freezing, and getting hungrier every hour. They had watched the farmhouse carefully and were satisfied that a single man operated it. The third morning they emerged before daylight and managed to milk a cow, which diminished their immediate hunger pangs, then watched their chance to enter the house of the bachelor hoe man and helped themselves to breakfast while he milked the rest of his cows. When he returned before they were finished, they held his own Winchester on him. After eating, they appropriated some of his clothes, then forced him to harness his work team to a wagon, left him tied and gagged, and drove away.

Yancey had read the above newspaper article about their escape while they ate breakfast. "Well, gaw damn," he complained, "that bastard Morgette is up at Pinebluff. Well, we're goin' up there, anyhow. Give us a chance to even up an old score, maybe. And this way we won't have to cut in anybody when we dig up our dough . . . Christ knows where Dutch Pete got to. Some of his crowd might have turned loose them horses their own selves so's we'd get caught. I wouldn't put it past the Loco Kid." He realized it didn't make sense for Dutch Pete to pull such a stunt if he expected to be cut in on their money, but you never knew about the Loco Kid. He was like Billy Joe.

"Suppose," Billy Joe said, "Dutch Pete and his crowd set up a watch on our old place. I would. They'll be down on us like a duck on a June bug."

"Have to wait 'em out. If old Billy Blackenridge is

still around, he'll hide us out. He hates Dutch Pete's guts. While we were up in the can at Pinebluff, waitin' for our trial, he told me Dutch Pete dropped in and scared the shit out of him. I mean really scared the shit out of him, so he had to clean his pants out. I sure wouldn't tell anybody if I got that scared."

Billy Joe just shook his head. He never got scared. The idea of being scared meant nothing to him; he couldn't imagine it. He knew his brothers were scared a lot, just like most people, and he pitied them. He remembered how they'd prayed for their horses to stand still when Morgette left them tied under trees with a rope around their necks, how they'd begged Yancey to come cut them down quickly when he stumbled across them. Billy Joe just figured he'd wake up some place else if he got killed.

Since he'd been to prison, he'd started reading the Bible and thought maybe where you woke up was what they called heaven, and it made sense to him because he'd always known there was such a place. It was why he was never scared. However, it never occurred to him that, if it were true, killing someone to get even with them sent them to the good place and really did them no harm. It was beyond his reasoning ability to conclude that, under these circumstances, it was senseless to shoot people to get even. He always had someone in mind to get even with. Right then he was planning to get even with Dolf Morgette for having him sent to the penitentiary. The part that had graveled him most was how Dolf had arrested him. Even though he'd emptied his pistol at Morgette, Dolf had grabbed him, contemptuously turned him over his knee, and spanked him rather than shot him like a man deserved. Besides that, he was sure Morgette had killed his father, or at least was responsible for getting him killed. His pa was the only person he'd ever respected. (He was totally incapable of realizing that he had respected his father, if it came down to putting it into words, or that his respect was because his father was the meanest, rottenest person he'd ever known. He just knew he had to get even because Dolf had no right to kill his old man.)

Yancey and Billy Joe ditched the wagon and rode the plow horses bareback for two days through rough terrain where trailing them would be slow going. They hoped no one was after them, since the farmer they'd tied and gagged might not be found for a few days until someone missed him, but they didn't count on it. They sneaked into a ranch house and stole some provisions, more clothes and blankets, and would have stolen better horses if there had been any around the place. Billy Joe stole a Winchester and shells, so that they were both armed. When they figured it was safe, they rode back to the railroad at a water stop, planning to catch a ride on a freight train.

They watched from the hills above it to make sure no people were there. Satisfied the coast was clear, Yancey said: "Best we shoot the hosses up here out of sight, so no one finds them and maybe figures out which way we went."

Billy Joe gave him a look that scared him. "We ain't shootin' these good old plugs," he said. "They carried us up here with nuthin' to eat but grass, and we owe 'em."

Yancey quickly said: "OK. I guess that makes sense."

"Yer damn' right it makes sense. I'd shoot you before I'd shoot these old boys."

From his look, Yancey was convinced that was so. "All right. I guess I wouldn't have done it my own self when it came right down to it." Billy Joe didn't believe him, but let it go so long as the horses were allowed to live.

All told, even making good time at last on a freight train, it took a week from the time of their breakout for the two Kelbo boys to make it to the junction. They dropped off as the train slowed and dodged into the timber. This was country where they were known.

"What now?" Billy Joe asked.

"We hoof it to Pinebluff and sneak in at night. I aim to go over to Billy Blackenridge's cabin, if he still lives there. He'll hide us out for a while, or at least bring truck up to a camp where we can hide out while we get together an outfit and work over to the old ranch."

"What then?"

"We'll watch the place to make sure Dutch Pete isn't around. Then we dig up our pile and head back to Texas."

"Not before I get a shot at Morgette," Billy Joe growled. "He killed Pa."

"We ain't mortal certain about that," Yancey said. What he wanted to say was: *Who gives a damn? You're out of your mind if you brace Morgette.* But he knew it would only make his brother more determined and might even cause him to turn on him. *The young fool has got crazier since he's been readin' the Bible. I wouldn't put it past him to bump me off and think he was doin' me a favor.*

"It don't signify," Billy Joe said. "If Morgette didn't pull the trigger himself, he was behind whoever did. Besides, he sent us up the river. I'm gonna get him if it's the last thing I do."

*Lots of people said that*, Yancey thought. *Well, good luck, kid.* He didn't give a damn which way things came out. He planned to go back to Texas, settle down, go straight except for maybe a little rustling from neighbors he didn't like, and live out his days in peace.

## Chapter Seventeen

Mum's house was dark and quiet. The only regular sound was the grandfather clock tolling the hours and sounding its melodious single *bong* once each half hour. Little Maggie awakened her mother, asking for a glass of water. They kept a lamp burning low in her room, the connecting door open since the child was in a strange house. Her brother was with his grandfather over in his camp. Margaret reflected how different it was at night in an Indian camp. Her people had adopted such conveniences as kerosene lanterns, but, when she was a child, the only light in a teepee came from the fire. When it burned down, everything was pitch dark. Some families had matches and candles when they were close to a trader, but most didn't.

She got Little Maggie settled back down, and stayed with her until she went back to sleep. When she got back into bed, she snuggled up to Dolf's broad back and put her arm across him, feeling his comforting warmth. He stirred and responded to her embrace by pushing against her, but continued to snore lightly. Some wives claimed to hate their husband's snoring, but she took it as a comfortable assurance that he was still alive and with her. She wondered how long their life together would last. Whenever they came back to Pinebluff, the old dread returned—the thought that some enemy might take him unawares and the news would be carried to her that he was dead. It was a dismal thought, but she couldn't stop it from recurring no matter how hard she tried to blot it out by thinking of something cheerful.

In the distance a dog barked, followed by another, then a chorus of them, some probably from the Indian encampment. She would have felt more comfortable there, and certainly safer, but Mum would have a fit if they chose to stay there when they were in town.

Outside the window an owl hooted, and was answered by another farther away. After that the night fell into deep silence. A sense of foreboding pervaded her mind. She felt like shaking Dolf awake and asking: *Why do you keep bringing me back to this place where I have no peace of mind, where your old enemies are everywhere, lusting for revenge, and where you make new enemies almost everyday by doing other people's dirty jobs for them?*

She'd heard that the Kelbos had escaped, and, despite

assurances that this was the last place they'd come, she knew in her Indian heart that it was not so. She was sure this was the first place they'd come, but she didn't know why, only knew that her premonitions almost always came true. The newspapers were speculating that the Kelbos had had outside help in their escape. Undoubtedly the outside help were more of Dolf's old enemies who would come here with the vengeful Kelbo brothers. They couldn't tell who those others might be, wouldn't know till they struck.

She heard their dog, Jim Too, growling, and she jumped, then tensed up. He was down the hall in Amy's room. She knew he wouldn't growl unless something was nearby that didn't belong there. She nudged Dolf.

Low voiced, he said: "I'm awake. I heard him, too." Dolf always awakened immediately at any threatening sound. She knew the pistol he kept under his pillow would be in his hand, ready. He whispered: "Probably something outside. He's in a strange place and likely not sure about some of the nighttime sounds. If anything gets in the house, he'll come fetch me."

He got up and moved to the hall door, which was open to let the breeze flow through their room. She could see him dimly in the lamplight that filtered in from Little Maggie's room and remembered feeling this same numb dread as a child, when her father would get up, alerted that enemies might be in camp on a horse-stealing raid. Sometimes they were, and pandemonium would break loose when the men of her tribe ran out, crouching low to skylight the raiders and shoot them. It was a tricky business, making sure they weren't shooting a friend. They knew that the raiders would be running away as soon as they knew they'd been detected, and never ran after them because any running man would be taken for the enemy and shot at.

They only pursued after daybreak, tracking the horses if any were stolen. Sometimes they would return with the horses and a few scalps. Sometimes one of their number would return draped across a horse, dead, and there would be mourning. She couldn't help thinking: *How relieved I was when the old fighting days were over. I thought I'd never have to feel terrified and helpless again, and now I feel the same way. I don't want to be a mourner someday when they bring Dolf back, dangling from a horse. I want to get away from this dreadful place as soon as we can and never come back.*

She could barely restrain herself from screaming the words at Dolf, but she was her father's daughter and would never do such a thing. If Dolf had to stay here because he was who he was, and do a job, she would never utter a word of complaint and would back him in whatever he did, kill for him if need be. She'd done it before and knew she would again if it came down to it. She kept her own .41-caliber pistol in the drawer of the bedside table, or under her pillow, ready, on nights when Dolf was gone or came home late. If he went out now, searching the house in the dark, she would be right behind him, pistol in hand.

After a long while, he returned to the bed. Jim Too hadn't growled again, so it was undoubtedly a false alarm, something passing outside, perhaps a deer or elk, even a bear, maybe a loose horse or milk cow that had escaped its enclosure.

"Nothing to worry about, I guess." Dolf returned his pistol to its accustomed place, and got under the blankets.

She snuggled next to him. She couldn't help saying: "Why don't we go back with Father for a few days when he leaves?"

He read her mind and said: "I might just do that, if things stay quiet here. But we have to wait till Amy's well enough to go out to the ranch. I want her where it's safer than in town."

Margaret thought: *From what I heard going on between them, I'll bet you'll have to hog-tie her to get her back with her mother.* She didn't mention that, but suggested: "She can come with us. It would do her good. I can nurse her if she needs it."

"We'll see. I'd like that, and I think Amy would, too," he said. "I'm as anxious to get away as you are. Besides, your father will scalp me if I fool around and don't go fishing with him."

She couldn't restrain a small laugh at her next thought, and said: "At the rate we're going, you may end up fishing through the ice."

"Maybe. If it comes down to it, we'll stay here for the winter."

*I'd as soon die*, she thought, *if you mean in town. I'd love to spend a winter with Father, sleeping under buffalo robes, getting up to crisp dawn, and building up a fire to get a meal for you men and our kids. Father would love to sit around in the cozy teepee and tell the kids old-time stories, and I'd like to hear them again myself.* She decided to take a hand in this game and enlist her father in her scheme. *If the Kelbos disappear mysteriously, at least I won't have to worry about them.*

The Kelbos were very much on some other minds. The following morning, the city council held a special session to question Chief Hanratty on his plans. The council, in Hanratty's view, was a mixed bag of good and bad. The current president was Tom Miller, also president of Alby Gould's local bank and a good, solid man with a lot of common sense. He was the bright spot. The worst of the bunch was Collis Crowder, who had proven unco-operative in Dolf's investigation of the wagon bombing. A holdover from the old days was Emil Griffenstein, basically a businessman with his own interests uppermost in mind. Nick Bradley filled out the current membership, because Hal Green, who had been a member, was barred from holding any other government office since he'd become lieutenant governor. His empty slot soon would be filled by a pending election. Will Alexander was running and expected to be elected, although Crowder objected that he wasn't a resident. Will was present at this meeting as an interested observer. Hal Green was there as a member of the press and had brought Doe Darling along.

Crowder asked: "Who is she?" What he meant was: *Who let a damned woman in?*

"She's working for me as a reporter," Hal responded.

Crowder said: "I move we have a closed session."

He'd also have liked to exclude Will and Hal, on general principles.

Ben Miller reminded him: "I haven't called this session to order yet, so you'll have to hold that motion."

As soon as the meeting was called to order, Crowder repeated the motion and was voted down. Bradley knew all too well who Doe was and had no intention of antagonizing a representative of a large newspaper, even if it was published in California. Besides, her stories were "paragraphed" all over the globe. The others were curious about this big name reporter and willing to risk what she wrote about them.

When Ambrose Bierce showed up later and was introduced, Crowder made the same motion regarding him and was voted down. Bradley had even less taste for getting on the bad side of this nationally known poison pen. The rest felt about him like they did Doe Darling. They would like to see their names in a large city daily.

Miller turned to Hanratty. "I guess what we all want to know is where we stand on catching our bombers."

"Nowhere," Hanratty admitted bluntly. "I'm working on it day and night. I've got all my boys on it, the sheriff is working on it, and we have our ears to the ground."

"Which means?" Miller prompted.

"I've got a lot of informal contacts. If we had some bigger rewards out, it would help. In a camp full of starving miners anybody might sing if there's enough money in it."

"We've got rewards out," Bradley said.

Will nodded, since he'd put up $1,000 personally on

the bombing at his place, and the state had matched it.

"Obviously not big enough, or we'd have had someone take the bait," Hanratty said. "Either that or the guys behind the bombings don't need the money." He looked at Bradley as he said that. The latter ignored the look and the remark, although everyone there got the implication.

"So, we're nowhere," Miller said.

Crowder chipped in: "Maybe we need some new blood in the matter."

His dislike of Hanratty was widely known. The chief gave him a cold eye. He said: "If this august body would like my resignation, I'll be only too glad to oblige." At the same time he thought: *Under the circumstances, you'll play hell finding a replacement unless you recruit one from some insane asylum.*

The same idea occurred to the others, with the exception of Crowder who was the type to bite off his nose to spite his face.

"We don't want that, Mike," Miller said, not asking anyone else for an opinion. His own was that they weren't apt to get anyone better than Hanratty. His experience on the Barbary Coast was just what was needed in a situation of this kind. He changed the subject, saying: "We'd better be thinking about what we're going to do if the local situation blows up and we have a shooting war on our hands."

Bradley quickly said: "That's not apt to happen. The miners will come to their senses and settle when they get hungry enough."

Will spoke up, interjecting: "If me and Alby Gould

weren't bankrolling soup kitchens, the miners would have come to their senses long before now, but not to go back to work. And we got a line of credit for them in the stores."

"All commendable Christian spirit," Bradley said, "but it just prolongs a settlement."

Will snapped: "It prolongs getting your god-damn' mine blown up. You ought to be chipping in with the rest of us until your board in New York wakes up."

"That'll be the day," Bradley snapped back. Then he realized how that sounded, and added: "I mean it'll be the day when we chip in."

Miller pounded his gavel. "Will, I hate to point it out, but you aren't supposed to be putting in your oar till we ask for questions."

Crowder nodded his warm agreement with that. Will did most of his business with merchants who weren't such skinflints. Crowder said: "On the subject of why we're here, we might ask the chief what plans he has to protect lives and property in case of riots. What's to prevent the miners from coming into our places and taking what they want?"

Miller looked at Hanratty. The chief said: "If it comes down to that, we'll do the best we can, but my force isn't big enough to handle the kind of mob we might have on our hands. If we stand in their way, we'll die game and maybe take a few with us, all for nothing."

There were no suggestions that the force be enlarged.

Griffenstein, a thrifty Jew, put in his first suggestion, looking at Hal Green as he said: "I think we need to bring in troops before the lid blows off." He looked around for support.

"How about that, Hal?" Miller said.

"If it comes to it, I suppose there's no way to avoid it." His own view was that troops always took the side of big money, which was to say usually the wrong side. It was also simply a way to get the whole country to pay for a local injustice.

"Why should we avoid it?" Crowder asked.

"Just what I was going to say," Bradley put in. "If my Pinkertons move in, the miners are apt to do anything. Americans never fire on their own Army." Then he realized what he'd said, and added: "I mean my company. Pinkertons never do."

Miller couldn't let the comment about not firing on the Army pass. He said: "Oh? You must have missed hearing about the Homestead strike?"

"That was different," Bradley said. "A bunch of foreign socialist agitators were behind that. Anarchists."

Miller laughed. "A foreign agitator, all right . . . a Scotchman by the name of Carnegie was behind that, through his cat's paw, Henry Clay Frick."

Bradley exploded: "The company men didn't shoot at the Army!"

"No, but they set them up like a bunch of clay pigeons where they shouldn't have been."

"You mean where they should have been," Bradley retorted.

"Tell it to President Harrison. You'll play hell getting troops in here under this administration, especially in an election year."

Miller sighed. "This isn't getting us anywhere. We found out from the chief what we wanted to know. He's working on the bombings, and I don't see where anyone else could do any more, and there isn't much any of us can do about riots, except pray. I think we owe a vote of thanks to Will and Alby for their part in trying to keep the lid on that. By the way, Chief, do you have any idea where Cloverwood could have got to? He might be a big help in keeping the miners in hand, if we can talk some sense into him."

Hanratty looked innocent. "I'm lookin' for him. If he turns up, this council will be the first to hear about it if you want to reason with him."

"Good. Good. He's got a lot of influence, if he'll use it."

Bradley snorted. "If I'm any judge, he used his influence to blow off the back of my building, to say nothing of blowing up the Pinkerton camp." He wisely didn't mention the bombing of Will's front gate, which everyone suspected he'd engineered.

Miller shrugged. "No argument about him being a prime suspect. But we'll have to prove it. Unless someone squeals on him, in case he is behind those bombings, I'll bet we never hang it on him."

Bradley snorted again, remembering his hat that Cloverwood had trampled. "Hanging *him* would be more like it."

"One other thing, Chief," Miller said, as though Bradley hadn't said anything. "The Kelbos have escaped, as we all know. They caused a lot of trouble up here before we sent them over the road. They may be back looking for some of us. Do you have any ideas about what we might do about that ahead of time?"

"Happens I do. I think there should be a good-size reward out for them and we ought to have posters hung all over the county with their ugly phizzes on them."

"I'll drink to that," Will butted in. "I'll put up a thousand. How about you Hal . . . will you print up a bunch of Reward posters?"

"Glad to," Hal said. "We know why they'd come back here. For revenge on the community. And with Dolf Morgette in town, they'd go for him first of all."

"Who cares?" Crowder asked.

"I do, for one," Hal said. "He's been my friend for years."

"Amen," Will added. "This community owes him a lot, and that doesn't include a grave."

Crowder looked sour, but said no more.

Hanratty said: "Dolf can take care of himself, or at least he thinks he can. But we all need friends. They'll try to get him from behind, naturally. And he ain't bulletproof. Most likely they'll try it at night, too. Their kind always do."

Hal laughed. "Not always," he said, remembering the last time. "But I'm sure they will this time." Everyone knew what he meant—the last time the Kelbos had staged a showdown in broad daylight, expecting heavy reinforcements that failed to show up as promised. The Kelbos had been scared half out of their wits and had thrown down their pistols, except for Billy Joe, who everyone knew was at least half cracked.

In that inconclusive manner, the meeting adjourned.

As they were splitting up, Miller motioned Bradley to him. "Mister Gould and Will would like you to stay here for a business meeting."

"What kind of a business meeting?"

Miller said: "Ask Will."

Will had overheard them. "I'll tell you when we're alone. But if you want to settle this business, we have an idea how we might be able to do it privately."

Bradley definitely looked interested. He was on the hot seat with the big powers in his company who knew nothing of the real situation and expected the impossible of him.

Before she left, Doe Darling approached Bradley. "I wonder if I could get an interview with you when you're not busy?"

Bradley had an eye for ladies, particularly ones this pretty. "You certainly may. Do you know where my temporary office is?"

"I'll find it," she said. "May I bring Mister Bierce with me?"

Bradley started to make a face, then thought of the potential propaganda coup if he could swing both of these news people to sympathy for his side in this affair. "Why not?"

## Chapter Eighteen

The only creature on the face of the earth that Ransom Shephardson Thompson had ever treated with compassion was his younger half-brother. It was a fact that even puzzled their mother. In every other respect, Ransom took after his father who had been an antebellum Southern planter, an arrogant and demanding, completely self-centered individual who exactly fit the stereotype of his kind later popularized by writers.

His Mississippi holdings of over five thousand acres had been inherited. When he died young, thrown from a green Thoroughbred, his wife Amanda, who had never been allowed to learn much about the business, found herself in dire need to learn quickly. Her husband's attorney, John Findlay, had attempted to wrest as much of the estate from her as he could. As it turned out that was exactly none.

Amanda found her own attorney, Anthony Kirby, a self-made product of the cotton-raising frontier that had moved West in the early 1800s. He was twenty years her senior, an upright man who she came to regard almost as a father. He took her case as much to see justice done as to make his fee. In the end he overcame the obstacles that Findlay threw in his path by killing him in a duel. An individual of contrasts, he was also a bookish, gentle person if allowed to go his own way.

When the case was settled, the widowed Kirby honorably courted and won the hand of his much younger client. Amanda learned to love him as she'd never loved Thompson, and never looked at another man after Colonel Kirby was killed at Vicksburg during the Civil War. She was left to raise Kirby's son, Edward, then fifteen years old, and try to keep the plantation running to put food in their mouths.

Her first born, now Lieutenant Ransom Thompson,

returned from the war a local hero, having fought with Forrest's various commands for three years. He had followed the fortunes of his idol, Forrest, from the time they escaped from Fort Donelson by precariously threading their horses through the flooded, icy bottoms of the Tennessee River.

Ransom wasn't cut out for Reconstruction and was little help for Amanda as she tried to salvage her plantation with the help of a half dozen loyal former slaves who worked for their board. He was more inclined to go carousing in Memphis, visiting with his old commander, and eventually got into shooting trouble there and fled to Texas. She was able to forgive him for running true to form for his class, although she'd never fully understood him or felt the warmth for him that she did for his rather helpless younger half-brother. However, she wasn't able to forgive him for dragging his younger brother to Texas with him. She had had her heart set on making enough money to send Edward to law school. This final blow may have broken her heart. In any case she died within a year, leaving the portion of her land that she'd salvaged to the blacks who had served her so loyally. She was only forty-six when she died.

Ed Kirby kept a photograph of her on his desk in Hanratty's office. He would have liked to keep a photo of his brother Ransom there, except that it would have been an embarrassment to his plan to avenge his brother's death. As Shootin' Shep Thompson, Kirby's older half-brother had run the underworld in Fort Belton, Montana. Ed had been his nearly invisible right-hand man, keeping accounts and doing his office work, which had been considerable, since Shep had his hand into almost everything that would make money, much of it illegal. His main enterprises had been several saloons. Eventually he was killed there in a gunfight with Dolf Morgette, the town marshal at that time. Money had been even on the outcome, in case it ever came to a showdown. It did when Shooting Shep tried to whipsaw Dolf, assisted by Rudy Dwan who operated the saloon in which the fight had taken place.

The affair started when Dwan picked a planned fight with Ben Parrent and was whipping the boy unmercifully when his older brother, Harvey, a hard, burly homesteader had taken over and proceeded to clean Dwan's plow. Shootin' Shep stepped in to interfere, expecting Dolf to arrive and settle the trouble and, when he did, tried the sneak shot that got him killed.

Afterward, Ed had one ambition, which was to get even. In his twisted mind, he'd come to believe that Dolf, rather than Shep, had sought an unfair advantage and ended up winning a gunfight that should have gone the other way.

Since Dolf's arrival home in Pinebluff, Kirby had hidden in ambush in several spots, every night, in hope of getting in a sneak shot at him as he moved around town. He discovered that Dolf had an aggravating habit of never going the same way twice. Finally Ed had sneaked up on Mum's place one night, hoping to spot Dolf inside and pick him off through a window. He discovered that Mum always kept the shades drawn after dark. He'd watched in frustration as the lamps had been extinguished one after another, and everyone had obviously gone to bed. As he left, he stumbled into a wooden sawbuck, which had been the noise at which Jim Too had growled.

The next morning, while Chief Hanratty was down at the council meeting, Kirby sat at his desk and mulled over his problem. He concluded that he needed help in putting Dolf out of the way. What if Dolf returned to Alaska and stayed for several years, perhaps never came back to Pinebluff? The thought of going to Alaska on the revenge trail didn't appeal to Ed, who was far from being the outdoor type. If it had, he'd have done it before then. He definitely was not athletic. He could barely stay on a horse, although he'd tried to learn for years.

His main problem was that he lacked the money to hire the killer he obviously needed. The alternative was to find someone who he could convince that Dolf was out for them. He'd tested the water with Pookay, in hope of recruiting someone to rake his chestnuts for him, but didn't see how he could persuade him that Dolf was much of an immediate threat to his welfare.

Then the recollection of Big Bill down in his cell set him to thinking what he might be able to do with him. He regularly took Big Bill his meals, since Hanratty trusted his assistant as much as he ever trusted anyone. After considerable thought regarding an approach, he unlocked the stairway door, locked it behind him, and carried a lamp down the stairs. Big Bill was sound asleep on his cot. Kirby rattled the keys and woke him up.

"What the hell do you want?" he asked Kirby.

"How'd you like to get out of there while you're still able?" Kirby asked.

"What does that mean?"

"A little bird told me you might not be around much longer."

Big Bill eyed him suspiciously. "Why would the likes of you be telling me that?"

Kirby ignored the question and asked: "Do you have any idea how many people around here Dolf Morgette made disappear the last time he was home?"

Big Bill had heard plenty of rumors about the bodies found hanging in the surrounding mountains. Skeletons were still being found, and people would say: "Some more of Dolf's work." He waited for Kirby to continue. Obviously he had a proposition to make. Everyone had an axe to grind, Cloverwood had learned. Finally, when Kirby remained silent, he asked: "What's your proposition?"

Kirby said: "You've got a lot of hardcases in your crowd. If you thought Morgette was out to get you, most likely you've got one or two that you'd send after him."

"What have you got against Morgette?"

Without thinking as carefully as he should have, Kirby blurted out: "He killed my brother." Then he realized he might have put himself in Cloverwood's power and quickly clammed up. Finally he said: "If I let you out of here before Hanratty comes back, are you willing to help me get Morgette?"

Cloverwood would have enlisted in the Army if it

would have freed him. He had his work to do. Whether his foremost motive was self-aggrandizement or not, he saw his mission in life as organizing the working man to gain him a decent bargaining position with the bosses, to help him earn a living wage.

Big Bill recognized that, as far as this had gone, he had no alternative. After what Kirby had just confessed to him, turning him down would be signing his own death warrant. Kirby couldn't risk the possibility that Cloverwood might squeal on him. Big Bill had noted the six-shooter in the other's waistband. Obviously Kirby had figured out that he had to kill Big Bill if he didn't go along with him, and he'd come prepared to do it. It would be easy to make it look like a jail break, and Kirby would be a hero.

Cloverwood said: "I'll be damn' glad to help you." He wanted to make it sound convincing. "What's your proposition?"

When Hanratty returned to the jail, he was surprised to find the office empty. After Kirby didn't show up for more than an hour, he began to worry. By this time his assistant should be taking Cloverwood his noon meal. He looked around for a note that might explain Kirby's unaccustomed absence. Then he looked over the key rack to see if the key to the basement, which also held the key to Cloverwood's cell, was hanging in its place. It wasn't. He went to the basement door and found it still locked. Now thoroughly alerted, he got the ring of master keys from the safe, lit a bull's-eye lantern, shifted his six-shooter into a handy position, and went down to the basement cell-block.

Kirby's voice reached him as he was still coming down the stairs. "Is that you, Chief?"

"It's me all right. Where are you?"

"Locked in."

"What happened?"

"Some bird came in and pulled a gun on me. I don't know how anyone knew where Cloverwood was, but he made me take him straight down here. They locked me in and left."

Hanratty considered the people who knew he had Cloverwood on ice. Not a one would have let the cat out of the bag. "Some of Cloverwood's crowd made a lucky guess. This place ain't exactly a secret. I've had a few other hardcases down here. What did the guy look like that busted him out?"

By now he had Kirby out of the cell and they were headed back upstairs, Kirby leading. He was glad the chief couldn't see his face, in case he wasn't telling a convincing lie. He'd seen several men with Cloverwood from time to time and picked one of them to describe.

"George Elm," Hanratty growled. "Wait'll I get my hands on him." He thought: *Elm, of all people, should have known better. I can send him back up the river.* But it never occurred to him to doubt Kirby, who had not impressed him as overly bright and certainly not capable of this degree of deception.

Cloverwood, a very clever man, had no intention of playing along with Kirby. Suppose, now that he was free, someone took a shot at Dolf Morgette, which everyone familiar with his past would consider a prime possibility, especially in Pinebluff? Suppose someone pulled off another bombing? Down in a cell, he wouldn't have been a suspect; free he'd be a prime suspect in either case. He must move quickly to forestall that possibility. He had to keep out of sight, and so his first move was to make it the nearest place of hiding he could reach, a cabin in a gulch within a half mile of town. If anyone recognized him—and his was a conspicuous and well-known figure—it was a chance he had to take.

He considered sending an emissary to Hanratty, but decided that might tip off Kirby. Instead, he sent a man to look up Dolf Morgette. The man found him at Mum's and asked to talk privately with him. Dolf took him outside, and they sat on the porch.

"Big Bill Cloverwood has to talk to you. He busted out of jail and wants to arrange a meeting with you somewhere."

This was totally unexpected news. Dolf asked: "What's on his mind?"

"He wouldn't tell me, except that I should tell you it was important, especially for you. And he said you should keep this quiet just now, even from Hanratty."

Dolf considered the possibility that Big Bill would set up an ambush, but dismissed the notion. He didn't have sufficient motive, although Dolf recognized that the union leader was leery of him because of Amy's injury in the train wreck. Besides, he knew the organizer wanted to be free to continue with his unionizing of the miners. "Did he say where he wanted to talk?"

"Anywhere. And he said to be sure that you didn't let any of this slip out, especially around Hanratty's office cop, Ed Kirby."

That intrigued Dolf. "Let me think it over for a minute." He took out a cigar and got it going to suit him. While he did, he puzzled over all the angles to this. He could see why Big Bill might want to talk and persuade him to be an intermediary to make his peace with the law. He couldn't see what possible reason there was for keeping the whole thing a secret, especially from Kirby. Finally he said: "Bring Cloverwood here. It's as good a place as any, and he can get almost all the way here in the timber. I imagine he'd just as soon not be seen."

The man said: "He's worried you'll run him in again. He'd like you to promise not to because he said it could be a matter of life or death to you."

Dolf almost laughed. This was beginning to sound like the penny dreadful stories that he'd read as a boy. But he had more to gain than lose by hearing Cloverwood out. "Tell him to come along. I won't run him back in. When does he want to come?"

"As soon as possible."

"How long will that take?"

"Maybe an hour."

"I'll be waiting here on the porch."

He went in and found Margaret and told her what he would be doing. "Why don't you take Little Maggie over to your father's camp for a while."

"Are you sure you'll be safe?"

He grinned, gave her a squeeze, and kissed her lightly. "As safe as I ever am," he said truthfully.

She thought: *And I know how safe that is.* Her worry showing, she only said: "Come on over as soon as you can."

He knew that was shorthand for: *Let me know you're safe as soon as your meeting is over.* He went inside and had a cup of coffee with Mum and Amy, who was now getting around slowly under her own power.

Mop wandered in, but didn't stay. As he was leaving, he said: "That kid Persimmon is a real horseman. Our hosses all love him. He can handle a team, too. Good as most men already."

"Good," Dolf said. "We'll put him on permanent . . . I'll pay the tab. What's he worth?"

Mop shrugged, afraid to delve into an affair that also involved Mum. He looked at her for permission to speak up.

She said: "Pay the kid whatever you want . . . how about twenty a month and board for starters? I'll put up half."

"We'd better break it real easy to Persimmon," Mop said. "He thinks a quarter is big money. How about we put half of it down at the bank and get him in the saving habit young?"

After Mop left, Dolf said: "I'm gonna have a little confidential confab out on the front porch with a fellow I'm expecting to come up. Police business, mostly. I'm going out there and wait for him."

"What fellow, if it's any of my business?" Mum asked. What she really wanted to know was if she ought to be behind the window curtains with her shotgun.

"His name is Cloverwood. He's a union organizer." Then he winked at Amy and added: "And just now a jail breaker and fugitive."

Mum gave him a severe look. "He ought to fit in good with us Morgettes. I recall helping you bust out of jail, or what amounted to it, a time or two."

Cloverwood came alone, riding a plug. He dismounted and said: "The best I could get in a hurry. Belongs to the guy I sent up to talk to you." He tied the horse to the porch railing by one rein.

"Come up and sit," Dolf invited. There was a quality in Cloverwood that he liked—possibly his directness and beyond that his championing of the little fellow went a long way with Dolf. He offered the union man a cigar, which Big Bill gratefully accepted, noting it was a lot better product than Hanratty's two-fers.

He bit off the end, spit it out, and leaned over the match Dolf lit for him. "Thanks," he said. "Hanratty didn't even give me a two-fer down in that rat hole. Grub wasn't too bad, though, but that's because he relieved me of my roll and said he was sending out for it and paying from that." He paused, reflectively, then said: "You know, Hanratty's a tough son-of-a-bitch, but underneath he's a hell of a good guy."

Dolf waited for him to get down to business.

Finally Big Bill said: "The reason I said not to mention my coming over here, especially to that little rat, Kirby, was that he let me out of that dungeon provided I promised to have you done up for him."

"Why? What's he got against me?"

"Claims you killed his brother."

That set off a bell in Dolf's mind. Young Harvey Parrent had told him that Kirby was a man he'd seen around Fort Belton. But the man he'd killed there was not a Kirby; it was Shootin' Shep Thompson. If Thompson was Kirby's brother, they sure didn't have a family resemblance. Shep had been a big, florid blond, handsome in a flashy way. Kirby was dark, short, stocky, and definitely homely, and the thick glasses didn't help. Nonetheless, it had to have been Thompson, unless Kirby had lied to Cloverwood. The latter was obviously curious, waiting for Dolf to tell him why he'd killed Kirby's brother, if he felt inclined.

"I had to kill a fellow name Shootin' Shep Thompson over at Fort Belton," Dolf explained, "when I was marshal, but no Kirby."

Cloverwood's mouth opened. "I remember Thompson. It made the papers all over the country."

Dolf nodded. "Shep and his partner, Rudy Dwan, thought I kept too tight a lid on the town. They ran the rackets. Tried to whipsaw me." He didn't have to tell how that had come out.

"Anyhow," Cloverwood said, "I went along with Kirby's proposition. He had me where I could hardly tell him to go to hell. He impresses me as the kind that would have shot me down and claimed I'd tried to break out."

"That was good thinking. You're likely right. Kirby knew, if you'd squealed to Hanratty, the town would be watching Kirby's funeral pretty soon, if I know Mike. I wonder what Kirby told him, or maybe Hanratty doesn't know yet that you're gone."

"What're you planning to do about me?"

"Nothing," Dolf said. "Thanks for doing the square thing. If you'd like a good horse to pull out on, in case you have to run for it, I'll lend you one."

"I'll take you up on that."

Dolf led the way across the yard toward the barn. Hanratty's man, Gorman, on a roving patrol that the police chief had started just in case it might turn up something, passed by on the road and saw Cloverwood with Dolf. It was hard to miss the figure of the big union man, especially his trademark checkered pants and green vest. Gorman made no special note of it, since he was unaware that Hanratty had been holding Cloverwood incommunicado. He did wonder at seeing this unlikely pair together, but thought it must have something to do with Dolf's investigation of the bombings.

Cloverwood said: "I'd like to get square with all you guys, so I can have time to get the workers organized to fight that little prick, Bradley."

"You could start by telling me what you know about the bombing over at Will Alexander's. I don't really give a damn except about that one, and the one that took out the bridge and wrecked the train my daughter was on. I don't reckon you want to be sweated on that."

Cloverwood drew a deep breath and started in. "I ain't gonna lie to you about that bridge, Dolf. I had it done. If I'd known your girl was on the train, or any women, you probably know me well enough to know I wouldn't have done it. And I'd cut my arm off to get your girl well overnight. I hope she's coming along OK."

"Up and around," Dolf said. "She's over in the house."

"That's good," Bill said. "I'd like to go over and own up and apologize all to hell, if you think it would do any good."

"She's a square-shooter," Dolf said. "She might like that."

"I sure would."

"How about the bombing over at Will's?"

"Your guess is as good as mine."

"How about the job on Bradley's building?"

"So help me Christ, we didn't have a thing to do with it, and I can't find out who did. I half figured Will might be evening the score."

Dolf turned that over in his mind and smiled inwardly. The same thought had occurred to him.

"How about the wagon down at the Pink camp?"

"Nobody will believe me, but I don't know a damn' thing about that one, either. Like I said to one of my boys, we might have a loony shadow bomber on our hands."

Gorman dropped into Hanratty's office, and flopped in a chair as he often did. They had become good friends.

"How's it goin'?" Hanratty asked.

"Lots of exercise and fresh air. Of course, the horse gets most of the exercise."

"No suspicious, bearded anarchists lurking with bombs tucked under their coats?"

"Mostly cows. I did see Cloverwood over having a confab with Morgette."

"You what?"

"Cloverwood and Morgette were walkin' across the yard together, jawing about something."

Kirby sat upright and looked like he'd like to bolt through the door, then quickly looked to see if either of the other two were watching him, and was relieved to see that they weren't.

When Hanratty did look his way, he said: "Kirby, hitch up the paddy wagon. I think we ought to take a run out there."

Kirby recovered quickly and managed an innocent look, then said: "Why don't I call up Morgette for you first, and ask him if Cloverwood is still there?"

"Just do what I say!" Hanratty snapped. "I don't want him to know I'm comin'. I don't want either one to know I'm comin'."

"Why not take my horse?" Gorman suggested. "Get you there a helluva lot quicker."

"OK," Hanratty said. "You can take off for the rest of the day. I'll send the horse over to Dawson's when I'm through with him." To Kirby, he said: "Hold things down here. I shouldn't be too long. Morgette probably arrested him and is giving him the third degree." Being a cop, with cop's brains, the thought occurred to Hanratty that Dolf may have had something to do with seeing that Cloverwood was busted out. He thought he knew Dolf pretty well, but he might have something up his sleeve, since Cloverwood had almost got his daughter, Amy, killed. That was why he wanted to slip over to Mum's unannounced.

Gorman wondered why Dolf would arrest Cloverwood and what the excitement was about, but had learned not to grill his chief. He was glad to be free to get a cold beer.

As Hanratty loped down the road, many eyes followed the chief, since he seldom rode a horse, and he seemed to be in a fair hurry. He was thinking: *Dolf may have sieved the son-of-a-bitch by now.* That touched his funny bone. *I wanted the son-of-a-bitch out of town, didn't I?*

Kirby watched Hanratty leave and made sure Gorman was out of sight. He had no intention of being around when the chief got back, especially since he suspected that Dolf would be with him if Cloverwood had spilled the beans.

He didn't even go to his room, but removed a six-shooter from his desk drawer, crammed a handful of cartridges in his pocket, and shoved the pistol under his belt. He opened the safe and removed the bankroll that he kept there. He started out, then came back and shoved his picture of his mother inside his shirt. After a last look around, he practically trotted down to Dawson's to rent a horse, attracting the notice of a few passers-by who wondered what important police business he was on.

Hank H. saddled and bridled a horse for Kirby and, like the others who'd noted him hustling down the street to the stable, wondered what his hurry was, or for that matter what police business was so urgent it impelled the little man to ride a horse. Hank tolerantly watched Kirby's two attempts to mount and was almost moved to give him a boost, but thought it might make him angry. Nonetheless, he couldn't suppress a grin when Kirby swayed in the saddle as he turned the horse. The hostler thought: *He'll fall off on his ass unless he's damn' lucky.*

## Chapter Nineteen

Big Bill mounted the horse Dolf had loaned to him, and looked down. "I'll keep in touch. I'll be back and apologize to the girl later . . . a promise. But I think I'd better pull my freight right now." He extended his hand, and Dolf shook it warmly. Cloverwood left, leading the horse he'd ridden in behind him. He turned just before entering the timber and waved.

*He's a damn' good man when you take him all around*, Dolf thought, as he sat on the bench by the barn and relaxed.

Persimmon came around the building, leading Wowakan, saw Dolf. "Your horse let me get on him." He was grinning broadly.

"I ain't surprised," Dolf said. "He's pretty much a one-man horse, but he likes you. Just be careful. He's quick and he's fast and strong. Be sure you can hold him. He wouldn't hurt you on purpose, but you've got to ride him every second."

They were interrupted by the approach of Hanratty at a high lope. He saw Dolf and Persimmon and turned over to them, pulled up, and dismounted.

"I heard Cloverwood was over here," he said. "Where is he?"

"I let him go," Dolf said. Noting Hanratty's outraged expression, he added: "Before you fly off the handle, Mike, wait'll you hear what he told me, and you'll know why I didn't pull him in. Besides, I'm sure I can get him to come in any time we need him. Let's go over to the house." When he was out of earshot of Persimmon, he said: "Cloverwood was let out of that cell by your man Kirby."

"What? What the hell for?"

"If I got it right, I reckon he thought Big Bill might help him kill me."

"I wouldn't believe Cloverwood on a stack of Bibles. Why would Kirby want you out of the way?"

"I believe Cloverwood, in this case. I suspect your man's name isn't Kirby. I had to kill his brother over in Fort Belton."

Hanratty knew of that shooting. "Shootin' Shep was his brother?"

"Or maybe half-brother, if his name really is Kirby."

"I'll be go to hell! Let's go down and grab the little son-of-a-bitch before he runs for it." Then he paused, thinking what had transpired in his office. "Never mind. He won't be there." He told Dolf what had happened. "I wondered why he didn't want to drive me out here in the paddy wagon. By now he's probably splitting the breeze for parts unknown."

"If he's as set on gettin' me as Cloverwood said, I wouldn't count on him goin' too far."

Hanratty nodded. "You'll have to be careful from now on." Then he realized what he'd just said, and added: "More careful, I mean."

Dolf told Hanratty what Cloverwood had told him about the bombings. They were interrupted by the arrival of Will Alexander in his buggy. Hanratty said: "Speak of the devil."

Will dropped his hitching weight, then came up on the porch. "Howdy Dolf . . . Chief," he said. "I'm glad you're here, Mike. You'll want to know how Alby and I made out with Bradley. There's a chance we can put a stop to the trouble that's brewing." He took a chair, and let out a sigh. "What a little schemer that bastard Bradley is." He paused, considering where to start. "In a nutshell, first of all, we offered to buy out Bradley's mine. He said he'd wire New York and see how the big bugs felt about it. He wants to hold onto his job, so we can't be sure he actually sent the wire, but he said he would. Then he made us promise to keep him on as manager if he helped us persuade them to do it, so I guess he sent the wire."

"Did you promise to keep him?" Hanratty asked.

"Sure." Will grinned. "I'd have promised him whatever he wanted. And keep the promise about like he would. We can fire him later, if the deal goes through. Anyhow, Alby decided to go back to New York himself. He's sending a wire to his cousin and getting him right on it back there. His cousin is Jay Gould, by the way. By now Alby's probably on the Bullet, headed East.

It'll take him the best part of a week. If we can hold the lid on that long, this whole thing will blow over."

*We'd better get word to the miners before someone goes off half-cocked*, Dolf thought.

As though he were reading Dolf's mind, Will said to Hanratty: "Maybe Cloverwood will help us out if you let him out of the can."

"He's already out," Hanratty said. "Busted out."

"How?" Will was surprised and showed it.

Hanratty brought him up to date on what had been going on while he and Alby were meeting with Bradley.

"Do you suppose we can get hold of Big Bill?" Will asked.

"Probably no later than tomorrow night," Dolf said. "I have a notion he might even be over tonight."

"How's that?" Will asked.

"Just a hunch. He said he'd keep in touch. I think he meant real soon. He wanted to get out of sight quick, but he wants to apologize to Amy for almost getting her killed."

"I'm surprised he admitted that," Will said. "Did you sweat it out of him?"

"Nope. He owned up like a man, even though he wasn't sure I wouldn't let him have it after he did. From what he'd probably heard about me, maybe he half expected it and wanted it over with."

"I doubt that," Hanratty said. "He figured you ain't that kind, which you ain't."

"You should have plugged him," Will said.

"I don't think so. And it's a good thing I didn't. He's the key to keeping things quiet here till Alby can close a deal, if he can. What do you think the chances are, Will?"

"Maybe fifty-fifty. We're willing to pay a premium price, and, if Bradley goes along with us, he may be able to convince them that, if they keep stalling, their mine won't be worth much."

"Suppose they just see the light and raise wages?"

"You don't know their kind. You could hang one from a church steeple on a rope and threaten to cut it, if they didn't shell out, and they'd make you cut the rope rather than do the right thing if it cost them a few pennies."

*He's right*, Dolf thought, *I don't know their kind . . . and don't want to.*

While they were still talking, Doc pulled up in the old light delivery wagon he used for house calls, Doe Darling beside him. Dolf wondered where he'd kept it while he was gone to Alaska. Someone was sitting on the tailgate, legs dangling, and got down when they stopped. They were surprised to see Ambrose Bierce.

Doc said: "Come to check up on the patient. What're you birds cooking up?"

Will looked at the others and said: "I don't see any reason not to bring this crowd up to date on what's been going on." He looked to Dolf, then Hanratty and, when they nodded affirmatively, said: "You fill them in, Dolf."

When he finished, Dolf looked at Doc and said: "If I'm not mistaken, Doc may be willing, under the circumstances, to tell you something about our visiting count that could help out a lot when it comes to buying the mine."

Doc frowned for a few seconds, and then said: "Why the hell not? I promised his nibs I'd keep his secret, but it seems he's here under cover representing his old man who owns a substantial piece of Bradley's mine."

"Maybe we can convince him that they should just pay an honest wage," Will said. "And if that doesn't work, it shouldn't be too hard to convince him his mine could be blown sky-high. In that case, he and his old man might persuade the boys back East to sell."

Bierce spoke up: "I wouldn't bet on it."

They all looked at him, waiting for his reasoning.

He went on: "I thought that fellow picked up poker pretty quick for a furriner, and I got to studying him and remembered where I'd seen him before. He's changed a little in fifteen years, but he was a gold brick man back in Deadwood. He was known then as Kid Pritchard. He was already an old hand at the con game then. Of course, he didn't have the fancy French mustache and goatee or wear a silk hat, but he had that phony accent."

"Amy says he can speak French, but that don't prove anything," Dolf added.

Hanratty said: "If what Bierce says is true, I probably got a flyer on him . . . I'll have to look through them. If he's what you say he is, I'll put him down where Cloverwood was roosting and let him reflect on his sins."

"I think," Dolf said, "we ought to give him some rope and see what he's really up to."

Doe Darling said: "Oh, yes. Please do. This is wonderful. What a story this is going to make. I won't break it till you say so, but it will beat the daily grist we've been putting out."

"Hold on with that 'I' stuff," Bierce interrupted. "You wouldn't even know who *he* is if it wasn't for old camera eye here."

"You know I meant *we*." She sounded aggrieved.

Hanratty said: "How about using your phone, Dolf. I just remembered there's no one minding the store, not that it makes a damn."

As he left, Doc said: "Let's give old Pritolet all the rope he wants, like Dolf said. I think we should have our usual poker lesson tonight. Come on down, Dolf, and look this bird over."

"I might just do that." The idea was particularly appealing since his son had reported on his mother's maneuverings to interest the count in her. Unlike the others after a rich ranch owner, the count was playing coy, pretending to be rich himself. Now that Dolf knew who he was, it was obvious what his game was. He would probably reluctantly accept Theodora's proposal of marriage, then reveal how his papa had disinherited him and cut him off with no allowance due to his marrying beneath him. He would then graciously allow her to support him and drag him around the world to ornament her cultural excursions.

Will said: "It'll be interesting to see what he tries to get out of us besides pickings at the poker games. Most likely, if Doc didn't spill the beans, he'd find some other way to see we found out who he was supposed to be, and make sure we knew his old man only paid him peanuts. Then, when we offered him a bribe to help us settle the union trouble, and after talking a lot about his honor, he'd take our dough and slope. We'll have to play along with that line and see what he offers us. Doc, why don't you ask him if you can tell us who he is because you think he ought to help us buy the mine?"

"Good idea. Now, I've got to go in and see Amy."

"I'm coming with you," Doe said. "I brought her some tablets and pencils to start her on her writing career."

Dolf eyed her. "Your idea or hers?"

"Both," Doe said, giving him a look he couldn't quite fathom. As she turned, she kept her eyes on him, thinking: *I'd give up writing for the broom and mop for a man like you.*

After everyone had gone, Dolf walked over to the Indian encampment and found Margaret.

She looked relieved to see him. "What happened?" she asked.

He told her the full story. There were no secrets between them. She said: "I hope it all blows over. You can get your fishing trip in, and we can all go back to Alaska. Why don't we take Persimmon with us?"

Dolf had considered the same thing. "If he wants to come," he said.

She laughed. "*If* he wants to come? That's funny. Do fish swim? Of course, he wants to come. He thinks the sun rises and sets on you."

"If he does come, we'll have to bring *our* horse along this time."

"*Our?* Which horse is that?"

"Wowakan."

• • •

After supper, Margaret was not pleased to hear Dolf announce: "I'm gonna mosey down and join the boys in a few hands of poker. I want to look over our count who's a no count."

Mum said: "He's still mighty interesting. There's more in him than you might think."

"Father thought so, too," Margaret put in. "He's pretty hard to fool."

"If you two say so. Anyhow, time will tell. I guess I'll walk and get some exercise. If Big Bill Cloverwood shows up, tell him to ring me up down at the Grand."

He was almost at the Grand, when the bullet whistled past, followed quickly by the report of a heavy-caliber pistol. Dolf saw the flash from the corner of his eye and expected the sounds before he heard them, and was in motion before the shooter had fired a second time. A third followed as he ducked into the alleyway beside the Grand. His .45 was in his hand before the second shot, but he didn't stop to fire back. He'd learned that your best chance was to present a rapidly moving target except in daylight when you could see your attacker. Both of the last two shots went far wide, since he couldn't hear the slugs whine past, proving his strategy was sound. He heard them hit, one thudding in the board wall of a building and the other shattering its window. From the dark alley he peeked out and saw no one across the street to fire back at. Two men were running for cover, but he was sure neither had been the shooter.

He stayed under cover until Hanratty's night man on

that beat showed up. By then quite a number of people had got up their nerve to come out and see what the shooting had been about. Doc and Will were among them, not that either would have hesitated to come out if they'd known Dolf was in trouble.

Dolf told the policeman: "Someone took a few shots at me." He answered a few routine questions, then suggested: "Let's go inside if you want to get some more information, just in case that jasper would like to try again. He might be a bum shot and get the wrong man."

Before the policeman finished his interrogation, Hanratty himself came on the scene, pushing in through the crowd that was still gathered outside the Grand.

"I hear someone took a few shots at you," he said.

Dolf and the policeman told him the story. Hanratty sent the cop back to his patrol, and looked at Dolf quizzically. He said: "If you didn't have so many friends, we'd probably know who to suspect. Probably Kirby. Too early for the Kelbos to be back, I'd guess. What do you aim to do now?"

"Play poker for a while."

Hanratty grinned. "Under the circumstances I might take a hand or two *meself*."

Doc, standing by listening, said: "Good. I like to win graft money better than any other kind."

"What makes you think you're gonna win?" Hanratty asked. "And are you suggesting that the old man here has his hand out?"

"Heaven forbid. I never knew an Irishman with that much sense. Let's get with it."

Less than that had earned a lead pill from Hanratty,

coming from the wrong party—in this case he merely grinned. Dolf thought: *If I ever saw two of a kind, these sure are.*

Doc led the way to the private poker tables in a room behind the main club room. "I've got a reserved seat for Dolf here in the corner," he said.

The count showed up last. Waiting for him were Doc, Dolf, Hanratty, Bierce, and Will Alexander. They had played a few warm-up hands and had the room well fogged with cigar smoke. Seeing Will, who'd come at Dolf's request to sound out the phony count, Pritolet said: "Ah, as you *Americains* say, 'new blood'."

"Old blood is more like it," Will commented. He didn't get up but accepted Pritolet's extended hand. "I've been skinned by this whole crowd a time or two before."

This was the first time Dolf had really looked Pritolet over since he'd written him off as a fairly harmless gold-digger. Under his mustache and beard was a strong face and a firm, protruding jaw. His hair was still mostly black, his eyes, sparkly most of the time, revealing good humor. Dolf could see what Chief Henry might have seen in him. Pritolet was also well set up, perhaps six feet tall and broad shouldered, carrying no excess weight and standing erect. *Wouldn't it be funny if he really was a count when Bierce met him in Deadwood,* Dolf thought, *one of those European younger sons out scattering wild oats and playing badman? Theodora could do worse than marry this one, even if he doesn't have a cent.*

Dolf played conservative poker, not drawing unless he had something to draw to, a percentage system by which he got to look at the most cards for the least money and got a view of the waters ahead without venturing on rough seas with a leaky boat. As a result, he seldom lost very much, and sometimes won quite a bit. His idea of a poker face was to act natural all the time and avoid gestures that gave you away. He knew that all good poker players learned as much from watching the other players as they did from their cards. Of course, they played straight five-card draw poker, so the only cards they saw were their own hands.

They broke up after midnight, early for a high-stakes poker game, but this was a friendly game with a pot limit, and Hanratty wanted to leave for bed, as did Will.

Bierce said—"We can still play after the old fellows leave."—which earned him the look from Mike Hanratty that he'd aimed to fetch with the remark.

"I've got some business to talk over with Will and the count, before Will leaves," Doc said.

"In that case," Bierce said, "I have some business in the bar. Care to come, Dolf?"

Dolf eyed Doc to see if he wanted him to listen in and, getting a nod, said: "I'd better stay here." Even if he hadn't been invited to the confab, he wanted to walk as far as Will's place with him, since Will was almost as much a target in this town as Dolf himself. From Will's place to Mum's, the streets were dark and irregular; they'd been cow paths not long before, and there were short cuts across lots so that it was unlikely he'd be ambushed again.

"I want a few words with the count alone," Doc said, "then we'll see where we go from there, if anywhere."

Dolf and Will left the table, and went into the bar with Bierce.

In a short while, Doc came for them. "He's game to deal," Doc said. "This should be interesting."

Dolf voiced his speculation of a few hours before, saying: "Just because this guy was Kid Pritchard in Deadwood, how can we be sure he wasn't one of those wild, titled rich kids having a fling?"

Nearby Bierce said: "I thought of that. I can say for sure he was Kid Pritchard, but can't say he isn't really a count, though I'd be careful dealing with him. Whatever he is, he doesn't look . . . or act . . . like anyone's fool."

With that, the three returned to the table where Pritolet was waiting.

Will opened the conversation by telling Pritolet why Alby had gone to New York. "We're trying to head off serious trouble that might make your pa's mine worthless."

"We have thought of that," Pritolet said. "It's the main reason I am here."

Dolf, watching and listening closely, thought: *If this guy is a fake, he's one hell of an actor. The way he said "we", right off, like he'd really talked to his father, would almost convince anyone, and he didn't fumble around for words. Of course, real con men don't.*

Will wondered what other reasons might have

brought Pritolet to their town, since he'd said the mine was the main reason. Will dismissed the idea of asking him—at least just then. He said: "Good. Then maybe you'll help swing a sale to us. We're offering more than a fair price. The possibility of your mine being blown up is no joke. A few more days of fooling around, and the miners are going to take matters in their own hands. They'll shoot up the Pinkertons, and blow up the mines, and pull out. They're starving to death, especially the married ones with families, and they don't have anything more to lose."

Pritolet nodded. He didn't beat around the bush, but said: "I'll send a wire to Papa."

They all thought it would be best not to press him about what the wire would say, in case he *really* was a count, and there *really* would be a wire. Dolf knew that Hanratty probably saw most of the significant wires that came or went from Pinebluff, so he had no doubt he'd find out if such a wire was sent and its contents, if it wasn't in code.

The meeting broke up after that, and Dolf said: "I'll walk by your place with you, Will."

*En route*, Will asked: "What do you think? Is he a count or a no count?"

Dolf chuckled. "If he's a fake, he's the best actor I've ever seen."

"My idea, too."

## Chapter Twenty

The next couple of days passed quietly, but the whole community was on edge, waiting for another shoe to drop. Dolf stopped to pick up his mail and found he'd received several letters, one from Iowa. He thought: *Who the heck do I know in Iowa?*

He opened it first, and looked down at the signature, surprised to see John Tobin, thinking: *Chief Henry told me Tobin finally outran his braves ... the old boy probably told them to run slow.* He was recalling the scene where he'd taken the noose from around young Harvey Parrent's neck and learned that Tobin, also there about to be swung off, was the only one of the gang that had treated the kid squarely and that he'd tried to talk him into going straight. Under the circumstances, he could hardly have done less than give Tobin a chance for his life. His chance had depended on whether he could outrun Chief Henry's braves on foot. Dolf had had occasion to learn before then that Tobin could run some, since he'd once eluded another posse by streaking away on foot and hiding in the brush. Dolf's good turn was just about to pay off.

The letter read:

Dear Dolf,
  I read in the papers that you're back in Pinebluff. Keep your eyes open. The enclosed letter from Yancey Kelbo will tell you why ... you'll know by

the time you get this, whether it's something to worry about or not.

There was more, but Dolf read Yancey's letter first. It was the letter that Kelbo had had smuggled out of prison to Tobin, and it read:

Dear John,
    I got a proposition for you. We need help busting out of here and can pay damned well for it. I got your address from Hiram Smith, but I don't trust him too much. Anyhow, we have a bundle hid back at the old ranch in Pinebluff and will cut you in for a big piece of it if you get us out of here. If you agree, just send us a letter and tell us how things are going and use the words in it somewhere . . . "I sure miss Idaho" . . . and I'll know you buy our proposition.
    If you can't do it, or don't want to risk it, I guess we'll have to try Smith and you can give him the word, but don't tell him what I said about him. We'll just have to trust him. He usually can get in touch with some boys that are game for that sort of racket.
    You wouldn't like it here. You don't know how lucky you are.
Your old friend,<br>Yancey

*Tobin must have meant I'd know whether to worry about this or not*, Dolf thought, *because I'd hear by now whether the Kelbos had pulled a break. Well, they did, so now we can be sure the Kelbos will be coming back here and not going somewhere else.*

He turned to the rest of Tobin's letter:

Smith wrote me that he was going to try to get Dutch Pete and the Loco Kid and some of their gang who were laying low down in New Mexico to come up and bust out the Kelbos. So, if you hear they make a break, you'll know how they managed it and keep your eyes open for that whole bunch. They're sure to come up there. I heard Yancey say once he'd trust a fence post bank better than one in town, so I guess he wasn't kidding. Be funny if someone stole all the old posts around their ranch after they pulled out and they couldn't find the loot. Is anyone living out there?

I almost forgot—Smith said he thought it was time to start up the old racket again, so be on the look-out. He wanted me to come back, but I've got a good job here, like my boss who's a good man, and aim to go straight. Please don't tip off anyone here about my past because the people I work for don't know.

I guess maybe this will help pay off what I owe you. Look out for yourself.

Sincerely,<br>John Tobin

*I guess the Bible was right about throwing bread on the water*, Dolf thought. *Tobin wasn't even sure the*

*Kelbos had busted out yet, or ever would bust out, but wrote me anyhow to make sure he warned me in time. He ran a hell of a risk all around. He probably still ain't sure I won't have him arrested. I'll have to drop him a line and let him know it's OK, just in case. I don't think there was much love lost between him and any of that gang. He was the best of the bunch.*

He walked over to Hanratty's office and, not finding him there, went down to Julia Parrent's bakery and hit pay dirt. He joined the chief of police at a table.

Julia called from in back: "Whoever's out there, just pour yourself some coffee, I'll be out in a minute."

Dolf got his coffee, and rejoined Hanratty, saying: "I got some interesting news in the mail."

Hanratty eyed him. "Good, I hope."

Dolf handed him Tobin's letter with its contents, and watched Hanratty's face working as he read it.

When he finished, Hanratty said: "We'll show this to Mulveen if it's OK with you. Simp Parsons is his deputy up at the junction, and he can be on the look-out if any of 'em show up. And he knows 'em all by sight, so we're lucky he's there."

Dolf nodded his agreement. "I'll look Tobe up as soon as I leave."

"You won't have to. This is our morning exercise . . . I'm waitin' for him."

Before Sheriff Tobe Mulveen showed up, Julia bustled out, saw Dolf, and hurried to the table. He got up, and gave her a hug, and kissed her cheek. He didn't notice her blush and, if he had, would have thought it was charming in a mature woman.

"What do you want with your coffee?" she asked, pulling back and patting her hair.

"Just a doughnut . . . any kind is OK, but a Bismarck if you have it." Bismarck was the name in that country for the jelly-filled doughnuts that were Dolf's favorites.

"I've got a fresh batch, still warm. That's what kept me in back."

Mulveen, coming in, heard her, and asked: "Fresh batch of what?"

"Bismarcks," she said.

"I'll take four."

She knew he was serious. He sometimes ate six.

"Ahhhh . . . ," he said, settling into a chair that creaked under his weight. "What's new, if anything?"

Dolf handed him the letters.

He labored his way through them, moving his lips, and paid no attention to the arrival of his doughnuts and coffee.

*He may be a big eater*, Dolf thought, *but he's a lawman first.*

"I'll be go to hell!" the sheriff exploded. "The old crowd. Maybe we can finish the job this time. I'll ring up Simp and have him on the look-out."

*They'd have to be dumber than I think they are to come in on a passenger train*, Dolf thought, *and, if they hop off a freight, it'll be on the slow grade before it hits town.* He thought of suggesting to Mulveen that they put somebody on look-out there, but was afraid he might hurt his feelings. Besides, he wasn't sure Mulveen had enough men to spare. Mulveen finished his doughnuts, and hurried away.

Hanratty said: "I guess I'd better get back to the office, too. Lots of paperwork, now that little son-of-a-bitch Kirby lit out. I got Gorman workin' with me, but he's about as good at paper as I am. You don't happen to know somebody good at paperwork."

"How about Bierce? It'll keep him out of the saloons," Dolf suggested, smiling.

Hanratty laughed. "His prices are probably a little rich for me. Maybe I'll ask Doe." He sighed.

Julia called from behind the counter: "Before you leave, Dolf, I'd like to chat with you!"

"I'll have another doughnut in that case. And how about a warm up?"

She joined him after Hanratty left. "I hope no one comes in. I need a breather."

"I'll bet your feet are killing you by the time you close."

"And everything else. But it's a good living. Nobody ever said life was going to be a bed of roses." She gazed out the window, watching people pass. "I get a girl or two to help every once in a while. Marie didn't show up this morning. She's the best one I've had yet, so I'm a little worried. I hope she isn't sick."

Dolf recognized that Julia probably had something special on her mind and waited, sipping his coffee.

Finally she said: "Harvey has been mooning around lately. I finally asked him what was ailing him. He said nothing was, but he talks about Amy all the time. He's so innocent, he doesn't know he's in love with your daughter."

Dolf snorted. "I kinda read the signs myself."

Julia watched him closely as she asked: "How would he suit you as a son-in-law?"

Dolf knew she was watching him and looked her directly in the eyes as he replied: "He'd suit me first-rate. He's a chip off the old block, and there wasn't a finer man anywhere than Harvey, Senior."

He saw the hurt look of remembrance capture her eyes and knew she wasn't entirely over it, probably never would be; good women were like that. Nonetheless, he thought she deserved another good man to take care of her and hoped one would come along someday. Impulsively he took her hand and squeezed it gently. "I didn't want to make you feel bad, but I couldn't help saying the truth."

Tears welled in her eyes, and she brushed them away. "Sometimes I can still hear his voice or feel him touch me. Do you believe dead people come back, Dolf?"

"Maybe some of them . . . if they want to help bad enough. I believe we go somewhere . . . or, at least, the people worth it do. I don't know about heaven, but I don't figure there's any hell except just dying forever if a person wasn't worth much."

She wasn't surprised to learn that he had this philosophical side and was comforted by his words. "Bless you," she said. "I feel a lot better." She looked up toward the ceiling—"Are you there, Harvey?"—and actually managed a little laugh.

Getting into her mood, Dolf waved at the ceiling. "Hi, Harvey."

Julia went to the door with him when he left. He gave her another affectionate peck. She said: "God bless you,

Dolf. Take care of yourself." She watched his tall, retreating figure stalk away as she saw her girl, Marie, pass him, coming to work, and noted the look she gave him. *Lord, have mercy on all of us*, Julia thought. *There isn't enough of him to go around. I thought when Harvey went, I'd never get married again, but if one showed up like him . . . or if he lost Maggie, God forbid.*

Dolf had ridden Wowakan downtown to keep up their bond and give the animal some exercise, and he walked up the street to the hitching rail where he'd left him tethered. He constantly looked to right and left as he rode through town, conscious that even in broad daylight someone might take a shot at him if he were desperate enough. He had Kirby figured as slightly cracked as he reconsidered how sinister he'd always appeared, glowering over his glasses occasionally, then turning obsessively back to his work; it was all part of his overall unsociable conduct.

He took the long circuit around and gave the horse a little run before returning to Mum's. He turned Wowakan over to Persimmon and noted how the boy's eyes glowed when he patted the horse's nose before leading him away, talking to him gently. "What a nice big boy. I'll give you a brushing and a treat, and you can have some water then. Would you like that?" He looked at the horse as though expecting an answer. Wowakan followed, bobbing his head and brushing his nose gently on Persimmon's shoulder.

*He's talking to the boy, all right*, Dolf thought, *you just have to know how to read his face and know why he's making those little rolling noises.* He looked for Maggie, wanting to tell her the latest news, and found she was over at her father's camp, which didn't surprise him. He'd have preferred not to worry her about the Kelbos and Dutch Pete, who would undoubtedly come back into the country, too, but he knew that, if he didn't tell her, she'd find out anyhow and reproach him for keeping her in the dark.

He walked over and saw her in Chief Henry's lodge, the sides rolled up to let in the breeze, seated cross-legged on a buffalo robe, with a darning basket on her lap. He entered, and settled himself against a roll of robes in his favorite relaxing position.

"Where are the chief and kids?" he asked.

"Lord knows. He takes them around and shows them off like a rooster bragging about an egg he didn't lay. I've never seen him so happy since before Mother died." She put her darning aside, and slid over beside Dolf and leaned on his shoulder, snuggling close. After he was silent for a long while, she said: "Something is bothering you." When he hesitated, she said: "Out with it, Morgette. This is your trusted mate."

He couldn't help but grin. Reluctantly he pulled out Tobin's letter, and handed it over, waiting for her reaction.

"What are you going to do?" she asked.

He told her of the precautions that Mulveen was taking.

"They'll slip by the junction at night," she said. "Probably steal horses and hide out. They'll find out you're here, if they don't already know, and come after you if they can sneak in. You'll have to be sure that Doc and Matt and Junior know. They might come after them, too. There's not much else you can do but be on guard. They know the country and will be able to hide."

"There's something else I aim to do," he said.

"What?"

"Resign and go fishing, if Will and Alby manage to buy themselves Bradley's mine. They won't need me any more. By the way, how are the girls and their new babies? I've hardly had a chance to look in on them. Are Matt and Junior still over there?"

"They're in and out. The girls noticed you haven't exactly been a frequent visitor and are both mad at you. They're all going back to the ranch tomorrow."

"I guess the ladies are up and around then."

"Of course. They're tough like my people. When we were on our long run from the Army years ago, some of the women had babies in the bushes, then caught up with everyone else. Sometimes their men were with them, sometimes they were alone because their men had been killed. Maybe they had a horse, but toward the end there weren't many horses left. They got up, and caught up, leaving a trail of blood. It's a wonder wolves or bears didn't get some of them."

Dolf pictured this misery and suffering, imagining how hopeless and terrified its victims must have felt, yet had gone on, clinging desperately to life. He hated to think about it. The Morgettes had always shared with the Indians, whose land they occupied. When the Indians were hungry, which was pretty often, especially in the late winter, they gladly gave them cattle. Perhaps if they hadn't, they'd have stolen them anyhow. They stole plenty from those who treated them badly. *If Uncle Sam had kept his promises when he put these poor brave people on reservations*, Dolf thought, *there never would have been any more trouble.* He broke his unhappy chain of thought. "I'll go over and see the girls this afternoon. You'd better come along to keep me out of trouble."

He knew such a remark was more apt to keep her away, but couldn't resist teasing her. She said: "You'll have to do the best you can. I have some things to talk over with Father, first. I may come over later. The babies are both darlings."

Dolf had something he wanted to talk over with his brother's wife, Diana Alexander Morgette. He wanted her father, Will Alexander, along when he did. They hadn't told her that Pookay, who had once got her kidnapped, was the head of the Pinkertons in town, and he doubted she'd read a paper and learned of it, or been told by anyone. He and Will had decided not to prosecute the sneaky detective, but only because it suited their immediate ends. But Dolf thought it was only fair to Diana to let her know what they'd done and decide for herself whether she approved or not.

If not, he wasn't sure what course Will would pursue. Probably have Pookay arrested to wait for an extradition for kidnapping. With Will's influence in California, and Hal Green as lieutenant governor here, there was little doubt but what he'd be taken back. He could imagine Hanratty's enthusiastic co-operation in putting Pookay down in his dungeon, but more likely he'd go to Mulveen's county jail, if he were arrested. There was also the possibility that Pinkerton influence could delay an extradition and obtain bail while it was in litigation. Pookay on the loose could be dangerous if for no other reason than his proven bad judgment. *In that case*, Dolf thought, *Obie is just as apt to sic some of his hardcases on Will, or even me.* Nonetheless, he felt they should tell Diana the truth.

## Chapter Twenty-One

Billy Blackenridge was just getting ready to turn in when Yancey Kelbo snooped in his window to see if he was alone. Satisfied the coast was clear, he tried the door and, finding it locked, knocked. Billy didn't usually get visitors at any time, much less at bedtime. He jumped at the sound. The bombings had him on edge, and, worse yet, he'd had a visitor a couple of days before that had aggravated his nervousness: Dutch Pete.

Pete was sure the Kelbos would eventually make it to Pinebluff and, like him, would know the most likely refuge would be Billy's place. Everyone knew he'd do almost anything for money. Besides, he'd practically been a member of the old gang. Pete wanted to be prepared to intercept Yancey and Billy Joe as soon as possible, and force them out of their money cache. He knew that they wouldn't be anxious to see him, even though he'd helped them get out of the pen. In the first place there was the matter of his collecting payment from them for that job. Since he'd double-crossed them a few years back and left them high and dry in a showdown with the Morgettes, he was sure they'd like to get even and equally certain they didn't trust him. Why should they?

Pete had once scared Billy so badly that he'd dirtied his pants, and he was still frightened out of his wits of the outlaw. When Dutch Pete had visited him the other night, Billy was sure the outlaw had reconsidered his old grudge and was there to shoot him. He almost kissed Pete's hand when he found out that he harbored no such idea. They'd talked over old times, had a few pulls on Billy's bottle, and then Pete had got down to business.

He had said: "I need a favor."

"Anything at all," Billy had answered anxiously. "Just say the word."

"You've probably heard by now that the Kelbos have busted out of the pen." When Billy had nodded affirmatively, he went on: "I believe they're headed here."

"To my place?" Billy had asked.

"Maybe, but I meant to Pinebluff. Anyhow, if they do come to you, I want you to get in touch with me. It's important I get in touch with 'em. But don't let on I've been here or that you aim to contact me. If you do, the Kelbos might kill you on general principles."

Pete had known that wasn't true, but, if Billy thought so, he could be more certain the slippery jailer would obey his wishes. He had said: "If they show up, they'll want some supplies, or maybe even want to hide here for a day or so. I'll check up every night, or have someone come by. If the coast is clear, we'll come in and talk. If the Kelbos are here, we'll hang around till you go to work in the a.m., then have a little confab with them. I know you don't want to get hurt, in case they ain't exactly glad to see us and it goes to smoke."

Pete had had no intention of looking out for Billy's hide, but he didn't want to scare him so that he would go to the sheriff and maybe stay down at the jail till the coast was clear. He needed Billy here as a magnet.

This prior meeting was in Billy's mind when he let Yancey in. He hoped his guilty feelings didn't show on his face. "Hi, Yancey," he said. "It's been a few years. I heard you busted out, and wondered if you was headed this way. Have you et?"

"Nope, and I'm starving. Billy Joe is outside with me. We could both use some grub."

Billy said: "I just got beans and sidemeat, and coffee . . . and bread, of course."

It sounded good to Yancey, who'd have eaten a fried rattlesnake if he could get one. He called in Billy Joe, and they cut several slices of bread and wolfed them down while Billy heated up some grub. "You got anything to drink?" Yancey asked.

Billy got a fresh quart out of his cupboard. He kept booze even when rations were a little skimpy. As the years had passed, his phantom fears of almost every possible kind of threat to his neck had grown, and he leaned on whisky for courage. He watched Yancey and Billy both lower the level of the bottle substantially and hoped they'd move on before they killed the bottle. Besides, they might get ugly if they were drunk.

They cleaned their plates without talking, then

Yancey asked: "You got the makin's?"

"I don't smoke," Billy said. "I guess I could go out and get some tobacco and papers."

Yancey wasn't used to Billy having money or he'd have sent him out for some steaks. He considered that and said: "Someone is apt to get the idea you got company if you do. The law is lookin' for us. Best we do without smokes for now. We're gonna stay here for the night." He touched the rifle he'd leaned against the table when he sat down, to emphasize the fact that he wasn't going to accept no for an answer, and continued: "In the morning, we want you to get us some grub, and we'll borrow some blankets and make a camp in the hills. I'll pay you in a few days. We've got to wait on somebody a while." What he actually meant was they had to wait until the possibility of Dutch Pete's watching their old ranch had died. It might take a month before Pete was convinced they'd headed home to Texas instead of coming here. They'd have to pull a stick-up of some sort for a grubstake.

They were totally off guard, when Dutch Pete and his men burst through the door. Pete's trusted three were with him—the Loco Kid, Phil Cranston, and Dusty Rhodes, pistols drawn. Pete motioned at the window. "I got a few more outside, so don't try anything."

Yancey quickly sized up the odds and looked to make sure his crazy brother didn't make a stupid move. Billy Joe merely said: "Howdy, Pete. Kid." Yancey was pleased to see his brother act so casually and wondered if it was calculated or simply because he really didn't know, or care, what was going on.

"We thought we might have to wait around for you to show up," Yancey said.

"I'll bet," Dutch Pete replied. "I'll just bet."

Yancey's pulse quickened. He knew they were in a tight spot, maybe a fight for their lives from that moment forward. Their only chance would be to escape from Pete's gang. He was sure they weren't apt to let them live after they led them to their money cache. They had to stall, pretend they couldn't find the right location, and hope they'd get a chance to make a break before that wore thin. If they stalled too long, Pete would probably rub them out regardless, and shrug off the loss. His heart sank when Pete said: "We'll just take them rifles for safe keeping for now." He wasn't even making a pretense of the old camaraderie. They were definitely no longer members of the old gang.

Pete had their hands tied behind them before he took them away and, as an added precaution, had tied them together with a rope. "If you two try to run, you'd better both go around the same side of all the trees you come to," he said, and guffawed. "If you're nice, when this is all over, we might only turn you in for the rewards on you." He didn't say any more, since he figured what Blackenridge didn't know wouldn't hurt any of them. He was sure Billy was afraid to blab deliberately, in the manner that had earned him his nickname, Billy Blab, but he wasn't smart and might let something out unintentionally. For all of his bluster, Dutch Pete had no stomach for having Dolf Morgette on his trail.

The idea of being turned over to the law sounded

good to Yancey; going back to the pen, sorry as it was, was better than dying.

By plain bad luck, Doe Darling stumbled onto the Kelbos being taken back to their old ranch by Dutch Pete. She'd hired a driver and guide to take her around the Quarter Lien district in which Pinebluff was located. She wanted a feel for the locale, as she put it, and it was now even considered reasonably safe to visit the struck mines being held by the miners, since news of Will's and Alby's purchase offer had been publicized by them in the hope of postponing violence. A good feeling was in the air at the thought of the trouble blowing over and life returning to normal for the strikers. They were all in debt, but at least they could work their way out and have a chance to eat regularly in the meantime.

Just before she'd left town on her ill-fated tour, she'd filed an interview with one of the miner's wives and put it on the wire. She knew it would be picked up by most of the nation's newspapers so long as they could plead that they were only copying something from another paper. Doe had written:

> I asked a typical miner's wife, Mrs. McKelvey, what she thought about the trouble, and she said: "It's all the fault of Mr. Bradley and his kind. Mr. McKelvey was willing to work a ten-hour day, and a six-day week, as long as he got four dollars for a shift. When they cut it to three, everybody but Bradley's kind, in their big offices back East, knew

you can't live on that out here. My man has worked in the mines all over, and, when they were still run by the fellows who made the original mineral strikes, there was never any trouble. When they sold out to big money from wherever, that's when the trouble all started, every time. You can't even begin to ask *them* skinflints why they can't pay as much as the little owners did before them. If those big bugs ever need more money, it's because they bought bigger mansions and yachts than they could afford. Most of them never had a callus on their hands in their lives. They got their money from their daddies who did."

I asked Mrs. McKelvey what kind of men the miners were, since everyone I've met in the cities thinks of miners as coarse roughnecks. She said: "The miners are no different than the farmers, like my father. They're decent, hard-working men, and all they want is a chance to support their families. It's the single fellows who give us a bad name. Some of them are heedless boys, like cowboys. They spend a lot of time in saloons when times are good, and are game to get into fights with anybody who wants one, and sometimes get into shootings, which naturally get reported in all the papers. But even most of them aren't that way. Lots of them are saving money to go into business or buy a little farm or ranch."

What do you think of Mr. Alexander and Mr. Gould who are trying to buy out the striking mines and put them on the old scale and even cut work back to an eight hour day and a five day week? Mrs. McKelvey asked: "What would you think of a couple of angels that dropped out of the sky when you were down and out and needed help the worst way? We worship them. We hope they succeed. Most of the men would stay here and work for them their whole lives and never cause a bit of trouble. It would be like heaven on earth. We pray for them and what they're doing every day. They're the ones who have put up most of the money so we can get stuff on tick at the stores, or we'd have starved before now."

I interviewed a lot of other wives and got the same story. It was a different tale when I talked to Mr. Bradley, manager of the Magnate, which is the biggest mine on strike and owned by outside capital. Mr. Bradley is obviously what is called a "dude" out West, a well-barbered man, wearing expensive clothing. He is a flatterer, commenting on my smart outfit and comely appearance. [This was vintage Doe Darling, who always managed to get in a comment on her own good looks.] I asked him what his view was of the local trouble. He started by saying: "Times are hard, and I don't think the miners appreciate this. When we have to tighten our belts to stay in business, it's only fair for them to do their share."

I asked him how much he'd been making before the strike and how big a cut he'd taken, since they expected the miners to take a 25% reduction in pay. He looked uncomfortable and said: "That's beside the point. If I gave up my whole pay check, it would be a drop in the bucket."

Before I interviewed him, I took the trouble of looking up salaries of well-known executives in the United States in a recent business publication and learned that Mr. Bradley had made $25,000 last year, and had received a large bonus at Christmas and a 15% salary increase for this year. The president of Magnate, back East, is making three times that, and he's into a lot of other companies, so that's not all he makes. I thought it best not to mention that to Mr. Bradley just then, in the interest of keeping the interview going. When I asked him about the miners and their complaints, he said: "They've been improvident. Most of them throw their money away in saloons and let their families go hungry, then come home drunk and beat their wives and kids when they complain that they want something to eat."

"What percentage of the men are that kind?" I asked.

"Most of them," was the reply.

I asked: "Do you associate closely with a lot of them off the job, I mean like visiting them when they're sick or checking on how they have to live, their cabins and that sort of thing? Have you ever eaten a meal with them, or invited one of them into your home?"

He didn't exactly say yes and he didn't say no, he simply smiled crookedly, looked closely at me, and asked: "Would you?"

In reply I said: "I have."

Bradley and others of his type need to reflect where their soul will be going someday—if they have one. It is certain they have no consciences.

Doe knew that Willy Hearst would publish that sort of thing—one of the few newspaper publishers who would. He had enough money so he couldn't be hurt by advertising boycotts, and his dislike of Collis P. Huntington and the Southern and Central Pacific railroads was proverbial and inclined him to hate the rich as a class. (Doe had refrained from looking into whether Hearst treated his workers like Bradley did in Hearst's Homestake Mine at Deadwood.)

She was feeling especially good, riding with Persimmon and Hank H. in a two-seated buggy, with a picnic lunch beside Persimmon on the back seat. Her chattering over everything and anything alerted Dutch Pete's crew to their approach, and he and his men were well off the road in the trees, waiting to see what the commotion was about before allowing themselves to be seen. They all knew Hank H. from their time in Pinebluff some years before, and decided to stop the buggy and have a little fun. A pretty woman was always a magnet, too.

When they spotted her, Pete said: "I wonder who the gal is?"

They circled and came into the road ahead of the buggy. Hank H. pulled in the team. Doe, sensing that trouble might be brewing from the rough look of the men, asked: "Do you know them?"

They were close enough that Hank, even with his near-sightedness, recognized Dutch Pete and the Loco Kid as well as the Kelbos. He said, low-voiced: "Outlaws. Two of them are the Kelbo boys that broke out of the pen last week."

"What are they doing here?"

Hank shrugged. "Search me."

Persimmon felt his stomach tighten at the word "outlaws". He was an avid reader of penny dreadfuls and had an exaggerated idea of just how bad outlaws were—a notion that they were sub-human brutes in most cases.

Hank spoke first. "Howdy, Pete. How long you been back?"

Pete said: "Long enough. What have we got here?"

Hank had the wit to think he might get out of trouble by trading on Doe's reputation. "An important newspaper lady . . . maybe you've heard of Doe Darling?"

Pete looked surprised. Almost everyone had. He removed his hat and made a mock bow the best he could in the saddle. "An honor," he said. "Did you come out here to interview us, maybe?" He guffawed, looking at his men for approval.

She rose to the occasion. "No, I didn't. But now that we're all here, I'm game, if you are."

Pete thought that over and seriously considered it, especially for what he might gain by it, besides publicity, and rejected the idea. "Naw. We ain't got time. We've apprehended some famous jailbirds and are taking them in for the rewards."

Doe was taken by surprise by a churlish-appearing

outlaw using the word "apprehended" rather than "caught", or maybe "ketched".

Pete had spotted the picnic basket on the rear seat, quickly circled over, and snatched it out. Persimmon grabbed for it, but was too late, and was probably lucky he didn't get into a tug of war with Dutch Pete.

"I'll just take this along to remember you by, Miss Darling," he said, and spurred his horse away, yelling: "C'mon, boys!"

Doe watched them disappear into the trees, the Kelbos' horses being led by the others, their hands bound to their saddle horns.

"So much for Robin Hood," she said to no one in particular.

Hank H. said: "You're lucky they only took the lunch." He wasn't certain how well a woman would have fared with the two Kelbos, just out of prison, and was thankful they hadn't met them alone. He wondered why they were tied up? He couldn't believe that Dutch Pete was holding two members of his old gang simply for the rewards out on them.

"That takes care of our picnic," Doe said. "Let's go back to town. I'll buy dinner at the Grand." She wanted to report what they'd just seen to the authorities, and also file another story for the *Examiner*. This wasn't quite as good as meeting the James boys would have been before Jesse was murdered, but she didn't meet desperadoes every day, especially in their natural habitat.

## Chapter Twenty-Two

Several people had congregated in Hanratty's office quite by chance. They were pulled together by a mutual feeling that things were drifting, and they felt uncomfortable as a result. Hal Green had to return to the capital in a few days and had stopped by to discuss the possibility that the situation would worsen and the militia be called in. Will Alexander was there to report on the telegram he'd received from Alby about the negotiations to buy the Magnate—although the situation wasn't encouraging, it wasn't hopeless, yet. He thought he should give Hanratty a little encouragement that his bailiwick might not suddenly explode. Dolf walked in on the meeting, because he worked there, at least nominally. Gorman was there, struggling to master the typewriter with fingers too big for the keys and swearing under his breath occasionally. Ambrose Bierce came in because his nose for news had led him there.

Hal was just saying: "The governor has alerted all the militia companies except our local one, which he thinks can't be depended on, and I sure agree with him there."

"They could be depended on all right," Hanratty said. "To run Pookay and his riff-raff out of town and kill a few while they were at it."

An unexpected visitor glanced in, saw the group, and rapped on the frame of the office door. Hanratty looked up and exclaimed: "As I live and breathe, Wyatt Earp! What the hell brings you here . . . we ain't got a race track."

Wyatt grinned. "I got a job offer from Pinkerton."

Dolf got out of his chair, and shook hands with his old friend, thinking: *I'll bet Josie ran him out, and he's taking a little trip to let things cool down.* He said to Hal Green, who he was sure had never met Wyatt: "This is my old friend, Wyatt Earp. I reckon you've heard of him."

The two shook hands. "I've heard a lot about you," Hal said. "It's a pleasure."

Wyatt nodded, sizing Hal up as he did everyone, and deciding he'd do to tie to in a pinch. He knew Hal was lieutenant governor, and didn't like politicians as a class, but this looked like a different breed to him.

Hanratty interrupted: "You said you got a 'job offer', but you didn't say you took 'em up on it?" It was a question.

"I didn't sign on, even though I didn't know that little piss ant, Pookay, was in charge. But I might have come up anyhow. I still own some claims across the mountain that I might develop, or maybe sell."

"We got a hell of a mess on our hands here," Hanratty said. He sketched in the situation in broad terms. He concluded with: "How'd you like a job on the force?" He was only half serious.

"If you need help, I'll be in town," Wyatt said.

Hanratty would have bet a bunch that Earp was up in his bailiwick on business for Wells Fargo.

Just then Doc Hennessey arrived, in the company of Count Pritolet, to whom he'd taken a great liking, whether he was a con man or the real McCoy. They were on a first name basis, Doc calling him Hank.

"Drag in some chairs from across the hall," Hanratty said, "there ain't no limit to this party. We're mostly hangin' crêpe."

Dolf introduced Doc and the count to Wyatt. "I always wanted you and Doc to meet each other." He didn't say why and didn't think he had to. Here were two men with fight sticking out all over them, and such men usually appreciated one another.

"Heard a lot about you," Doc said.

Wyatt nodded. "I guess I can say the same. Read about you, too. You and this big galoot over here," he said, pointing to Dolf, "were in the papers a lot when I was still down in Dodge City."

Hanratty interrupted. "While we're all here, it might be a good time to figure out what we all know about the bombings we've been having . . . maybe somebody knows something the others don't. You, too, Wyatt. Now that you're here, you might like to hear the lowdown. Let's start with you, Dolf."

Dolf considered for a few seconds. "I reckon everyone here knows by now that Big Bill fessed up to bombing that railroad bridge." He looked at Hanratty as he went on: "We don't know any more than we did about the bombing over at Will's. We haven't got a clue who did the other two . . . on the Pinkertons' camp or Bradley's building. So I guess you might say we're nowhere. Only *we* know about the letter I got about the Kelbos." He explained the implications of that. "I reckon we'd best put a watch on the old Kelbo ranch, since they've had time to get up here by now. Mulveen's deputy, Simp Parsons, is watching the trains up at the junction, but even the Kelbos wouldn't be dumb enough to come in openly. In any case, we'll be hearing about them pretty soon, unless I miss my guess."

The words were hardly out of his mouth, when Doe Darling burst through the door, out of breath. She had tried to contact Dolf at Mum's by phone as soon as she returned to town, discovered he was with Chief Hanratty, and rushed down the half block to get hold of him personally. She was startled to see the assemblage in the office, but babbled her news to everyone in general.

"I just got stuck up by a fellow named Dutch Pete, and he had your Kelbo boys with him."

"Dutch Pete!" Hanratty exploded. "I must have a dozen Wanted dodgers on him." He turned to Dolf. "Nine to one he busted the Kelbos out. They had outside help."

"He had them tied to their horses," Doe said. "Hank H. said he couldn't figure why, but he said it looked like they were headed toward the old Kelbo Ranch."

"How long ago?"

"A couple of hours by now."

Hanratty said: "Gorman, ring up Mulveen. Tell him I'd like him to drop over here *pronto*. We've got to round up some horses for a posse. Dawson probably has enough. How many of you guys are game to go after those birds?"

He didn't get a single dissenter.

"I can get you at least a couple recruits," Dolf advised. "My brother and son are still in town. They've got their own horses and a few extras, since they've got buggies. I've got a few down at Mum's. I'll get them up here while you guys are getting your outfits together."

Hanratty said: "Let's all try to get back here within a half hour."

The assembling posse in front of the police station attracted a crowd of curious gawkers. Some called: "What's goin' on, Chief?"

Hanratty ignored them. He was amused to see the count show up in cowboy outfit with two huge, fancy LeMatt nine-shot pistols strapped around him. He didn't laugh at the guns, though; he knew the nine-shot cylinders revolved around a shotgun barrel. The count was also carrying some kind of bolt-action European rifle. He'd have had the same respect for it if he knew the rifle shot a six-inch group at five hundred yards under no-wind conditions.

Mulveen, as sheriff, was in charge. He addressed the assembly: "Raise yer right hands and consider yourself sworn in as a posse. Now let's hit the trail."

Following him were Hanratty, Dolf, Will, Doc, Wyatt Earp, the count, Hal, Bierce, Matt and Junior Morgette, and Deputy Sheriff Simp Parsons, who'd got in on the train for a confab with Mulveen just a few minutes before Hanratty had phoned.Doe Darling had begged to come along and been flatly turned down.

As soon as the men were all outside, she got on the phone to Dawson's to summon Hank H. back with her buggy. Gorman, who'd been left to watch the office much to his disgust, listened to Doe's end of the conversation, divined her purpose, and merely grinned. He had a notion to play hookey and go with her. When

Hank H. arrived, Persimmon was still with him.

"Where to?" Hank asked.

"Back out where we were this morning." Hank looked doubtful. Doe said: "It'll be safe enough. The sheriff just headed out there with a big posse. They think they'll find those men out at the old Kelbo Ranch. How much farther is that from where we turned around?"

"Maybe a couple of miles. I got a fresh team, so we could make it in an hour, if that's what you want to know."

"Good," she said. "Let's keep 'em in their collars."

In the back seat, Persimmon wore a constant grin from ear to ear. He'd never had so much excitement with anyone as he'd had with Doe that morning. He'd almost wronged his pants when he thought he'd have to fight it out with Dutch Pete over the lunch basket, but he wouldn't have missed it for anything. He decided he'd die for Doe if he had to. It wasn't due to his youth and inexperience, either, since lots of mature men had felt the same way about her.

Dutch Pete's gang, with their prisoners, stopped to eat Doe Darling's lunch before proceeding to the old Kelbo place. Pete examined the contents of the basket. "Fustrate. Lots of sandwiches, boiled eggs, even cake, and lookee here . . . a bottle of champagne. That gal travels first class."

The Kelbo boys watched the food disappear, and Yancey asked: "How about us?"

Pete said: "Up till you find that pile of yours and

divvy, you boys won't be eatin', I don't reckon. If you don't play along, you may not be eatin' at all . . . you'll be too busy playin' a harp."

They found the ranch buildings tumbling down and the area grown up in brush and weeds. Yancey scanned the area to see if the old corrals were still standing. As they drew closer, it was obvious that the area had recently been occupied by a large band of unshod horses. The weeds were trampled down, and fresh droppings were everywhere. Yancey heard Dutch Pete, who was riding in the lead, exclaim: "Well, god damn, look at this!"

Yancey was anxious to see what had brought that out of him, and one look caused his heart to sink. Most of the corral poles had been dug out, and one significantly large hole indicated why they hadn't needed to dig out any more.

Pete scrutinized Yancey closely, asking: "You boys didn't happen to let slip that you had something buried up here, did you? Or send somebody up for it without tellin' your old pals?"

Yancey looked dumbfounded. "If I'd sent someone," he said, "there'd only be one hole." The thought of Hiram Smith flashed into his mind. He saw that as a possible blessing in disguise, a way to stay alive a while longer. He'd been mortally certain that Dutch Pete intended to kill them as soon as he had their money. Yancey looked around and saw where something had been removed from one of the holes—the key hole, the one closest to a large cottonwood. The loot was undoubtedly gone. *This could only be the work of Tobin or Smith*, he thought to himself, *or someone they tipped off*.

Pete said: "What've you got to say about this? I oughta shoot you on general principles."

Sensing an opportunity to get an edge, Yancey said: "Not if you want to run down who I think got away with the dough."

"And who is that?"

"It wouldn't be too smart of me to say, now, would it?"

Pete glared and put his hand on his pistol, and for a moment Yancey thought he might have gone too far and his heart rose in his throat.

"You think Smith got it?" Pete asked.

"He might have"—Yancey gulped—"but I don't think it's in his line. I can think of a better suspect. I know what you have in mind for us, and I'll turn the whole bundle over, if you just turn us loose and let us head home to Texas."

Pete asked the Loco Kid: "What do you think?"

"These jaspers ain't no use to us dead."

"What's your proposition, Yancey?"

"Turn us loose and give us back our guns. Two of you can come with us while we go after that dough and get it back. That way we have a fightin' chance if you decide to double-cross us."

Pete gave a nasty laugh. "Why don't I just cart you in to the law in town and collect the reward? It's better'n nothing, and that way you go back in the can for being a real prick."

Even that sounded better to Yancey than being shot

on the spot. He shrugged his shoulders. "I guess you could do that. But there must be at least a hundred thousand in it the other way."

Pete's eyes gleamed as he speculated on what he could do with that kind of money. After he ditched the rest of the gang, he could live like a king in South America. "OK," he said. "Cut them loose and give them back their guns."

They had just completed this transaction when Dusty Rhodes said: "Somebody is comin'." A lone rider was approaching. "Looks like an Injun," he said. "What the hell would one o' them be doin' off the reservation and riding up to the likes of us bold as you please? Maybe loco."

They all watched the small, blanketed figure draw nearer, riding a large Appaloosa.

Margaret Morgette had carried the news of the Kelbos' impending return to her father, saying: "I'm tired of people like them hounding Dolf."

"What can I do?"

Margaret recalled her father's posse that had assisted Dolf in rounding up that vile crew the last time. "We have men who know what the Kelbos look like, don't we?"

Chief Henry nodded, divining what she was suggesting. "Many of us know those badmen," he said.

"Then, if you will, I'd like you to put some men on look-out so we know as soon as the Kelbos are in this country."

As a consequence, Chief Henry knew of the arrival of

the Kelbos before anyone else. He had had them trailed and spied on wherever they went, and he knew as soon as Dutch Pete had captured them. From that time forward, Dutch Pete's gang was under constant surveillance. While that was in progress, Margaret had another group of men pursue the other part of her plan—to search for the post-hole bank of the Kelbos' out at their old ranch. They had hit pay dirt only a couple of hours before Dutch Pete arrived on the scene.

That morning, messengers had come to Chief Henry and informed him that his quarry was moving toward the old Kelbo Ranch. Margaret was in camp with him when the news arrived, and they both departed with another contingent of Chief Henry's old, experienced warriors. They watched from hiding as the outlaws discovered that the money was gone and heard their angry argument.

"Are you sure that they are completely surrounded?" Margaret asked.

"Yes. None of them can escape. What do you want me to do now?"

"I speak their language. Let me go and tell them to surrender."

"No. That would not be safe."

"I'll carry my six-shooter in my hand under a blanket. You and the many men can cover me and shoot as soon as anyone makes a threatening move. I know that Dolf would like to capture these men. This is the only way we can do that."

The chief wondered why she hadn't brought Dolf along, if that were the case, or told him what she planned to do. He decided that she thought these men would put up a fight for sure if Dolf showed himself, fearful he'd hang them as he had the rest of their gang a few years before. He didn't know that Margaret's true reason was that she had plans for the treasure that Dolf would not have agreed to. He would have returned it to the people from whom it had been stolen, particularly the bank. These white men didn't need more money as Margaret saw it. She intended to start a secret fund to feed her tribe when the crooked whites in Washington didn't appropriate the promised money, as they often failed to do.

Margaret steadily rode toward Dutch Pete. When only a few feet away, she shook the blanket from her head. "Do you know me?"

Yancey Kelbo did for sure and exploded: "It's Dolf Morgette's squaw!"

She gave him a cutting look—how typical not to acknowledge that she was Dolf's wife—then directed her gaze back to Dutch Pete and announced: "My father's braves have you completely surrounded. If you surrender your guns, you will be taken to town and get fair trials."

Dutch Pete looked around, saw no one other than Margaret, and decided she must be running an insane bluff. He reached for his pistol, which was his final mistake in a long, crooked life. A .41 slug from Margaret's pistol tore into his abdomen. He jerked forward and gasped—"I've got it."—fear and agony showing on his contorted face. He tried to lift his pistol, but more shots tore into him, Chief Henry's being first, since he'd had a rifle trained on him from the moment Margaret had started forward. Her horse, trained for war and buffalo hunting, stood solidly, used to the sound of shots, but Pete's horse reared and threw his dying body to the ground.

Yancey swung up the rifle he'd just had returned to him, and Margaret cut him down. His brother yelled—"I'll get you for this!"—but was knocked out of his saddle before Margaret could turn her pistol on him. She dropped low on the far side of her horse, and kicked him into a run to get out of the possible line of any further fire.

The rest of the gang hung steel to their mounts and tried to make it to the heavy timber. Margaret heard gunfire receding for a minute or two as the overmatched whites tried to cope with old warriors at their chosen type of warfare. Their big domestic horses were no match in rough ground for the swift Indian horses that had been trained for war and buffalo hunting.

When Mulveen's posse reached this scene, they found the bodies of Dutch Pete and Yancey first, and Dolf wondered if they had shot it out and killed one another. Gradually, as they read the signs and circled, they found the other bodies, left where they'd been killed.

"Pretty clear what happened here," Mulveen pronounced after his posse had reassembled. He rose to one of his finest moments. Even he had correctly read the story told by so many unshod horses. Indians had pulled off this mass killing and had done the community a great service—and he was aware who the only Indians were who might have done it. The only Indians in the area in such numbers were Chief Henry's tribe. Mulveen said, straight-faced: "This looks to me like the Kelbos and Dutch Pete shot it out over something."

"I reckon," Will Alexander agreed. "They call it a falling out among thieves. Happens all the time, especially over divvying up a lot of money."

Dolf hadn't missed the significance of the holes around the fence posts and wondered if whoever had made them had found the Kelbo stash, and what had happened to it. He decided not to mention it if no one else did. He made a mental note to cross-examine Margaret as soon as possible. Chief Henry had undoubtedly learned of what was apt to happen here from her. Or perhaps she'd only alerted him to be on guard, and his men had detected the Kelbos and trailed them. It would be just like her to do something like this to guard him because she was always certain he wasn't able to protect himself without her help. *Maybe she's right*, he thought. *She sure bailed me out a time or two. And a man should accept all the help he can get and be grateful for it.*

Rushing out to the Kelbo Ranch in her buggy, Doe and party ran into Margaret and Chief Henry coming toward town on the road. Hank H. pulled up.

Doe recognized them and showed her surprise. "What are you two doing out here?"

Margaret said: "Father and I often take long rides together. Isn't it a wonderful day for it? And I might ask what you're doing out here?"

Doe debated not telling her why she was there, then figured Margaret would hear the truth, anyhow. She told her the entire story of what had been transpiring since morning.

Margaret slyly suggested: "If that's so, it probably isn't safe for you to go any farther."

Doe laughed. "And miss a story like this?"

"Be careful," Margaret cautioned. "We'd go with you, but our people must be careful not to interfere in white man business. It always gets them in trouble." She knew, of course, that Doe was in little or no danger.

As she and her father rode on, Hank H., who was wilderness-wise, said to Doe: "Out riding, my foot. Did you see all them Injuns back in the trees? I may be half blind, but I can see well enough to make out that many. They been up to something."

"Maybe hunting," Doe guessed.

Hank H. didn't think that was likely, but said nothing further.

They continued to the Kelbo Ranch, and Doe got what she considered the scoop of the century. Then she remembered that Bierce had been riding with the posse, and that he could beat her back to town since he was riding and she had a slow buggy. She looked around for Bierce among the assembled men, and finally asked Dolf: "Have you seen Ambrose Bierce?"

"He said he reckoned he'd head back to town," Dolf responded, "since we didn't need him. If I remember right, he told the sheriff he wasn't used to riding any more and needed a nap."

He correctly read Doe's expression and grinned inwardly behind a poker face.

## Chapter Twenty-Three

Hal Green's newspaper reported the shootings as follows:

> The drama that recently had its first act down at the state pen with the escape of the notorious Kelbo brothers played out its last act yesterday at the abandoned Kelbo Ranch some ten miles south of Pinebluff. It will be recalled that the Kelbos were a brotherhood of Texans, who, with their father, were known unfavorably in every Western community in which they ever lived, and there were many of those from Texas, New Mexico, and Arizona, through Utah and Idaho. Old Man Kelbo was killed in a mysterious gang shoot-out in Pinebluff's hinterlands a few years back, and today, in a remarkably similar bloodletting, two of his sons were killed: Yancey and Billy Joe. Both sets of killings bear the earmarks of shoot-outs among gang members, probably over a division of spoils, which is usually the case in such situations.
>
> There is another possible angle in the recent example, which is that the Kelbo boys held a long grudge against at least some of the others who were found dead with them. When they were cap-

tured and sent to prison some years back, during their stay in jail before trial, they repeatedly boasted how they would have successfully shot it out with their captors if members of their own gang, who had promised to be on hand, had not abandoned them at the last minute. They also bragged how they would have killed the Morgette brothers and Doc Hennessey, who met them in a showdown at Packard and Underwater's Corral (now Dawson's). Two of those accused by the Kelbos of deserting them in that fight, both well and unfavorably known in this community, were Dutch Pete and the Loco Kid. They were found dead today by Sheriff Mulveen's posse, along with the Kelbo boys. There were four other bodies, as yet unidentified, found shot to death at the scene, presumably supporters of either the Kelbos or Dutch Pete. It is possible that others were present and escaped.

This gang killing is one of the bloodiest encounters of its kind that the turbulent West has ever seen, and the excitement here has, for the moment, taken all minds off of our troubles in the struck mines. People on the streets are talking about nothing else. . . .

The story continued with a description of the evidence that someone had been digging around all the fence posts of the old Kelbo Ranch corral, obviously searching for buried loot, which may or may not have been discovered. The possibility that a substantial treasure was still to be found started a local gold rush that Hal recognized would soon obliterate all signs of what had actually happened at the killing site.

The true circumstances of the killings as unmistakably evidenced by the many tracks of unshod horses prompted Dolf to look up Margaret as soon as he could detach himself from the posse. He found her at Mum's, sipping tea and chatting with Mum and Amy.

"Thank goodness you're back," she said, sounding natural and looking perfectly innocent. "Did you find anybody?"

He told them about the experience of the posse and related the plausible story that appeared later in the news item above. As he did, he watched Margaret and thought he could see the edges of a gleam of mischief in her eyes, perhaps prompted by her knowledge that he was telling a whopper. On the other hand, he knew that Chief Henry was capable of having pulled off the job without telling anyone, including his daughter. He decided to leave it up to Margaret and the chief to tell him the straight story if they wished.

He changed the subject. "I hate to run off again, but I promised Will Alexander to go over and talk with him and Hal about what we're going to do if Alby isn't able to buy the Magnate mine."

Margaret's humorous mood evaporated at the thought of his walking the streets of Pinebluff again, at night, vulnerable to hidden assassins. She recalled that once before, in Juneau, Alaska, she'd covered his back and prevented his possible murder by sneaking up on a potential dry-gulcher and slugging him with her father's old coup stick. She also recalled that Mum had once prevented the killing of Dolf and Matt when they were incarcerated in the local hoosegow by filling Yancey Kelbo's pants with birdshot. He'd been creeping up a ladder to a window in the second-story cell-block with the obvious intention of murdering Dolf and Matt.

After Dolf left and Amy had gone up to bed early, tuckered out, Margaret related her plan to Mum. "Mop can take care of Little Maggie," she concluded. She called him from his room, and Persimmon, who had been reading a penny dreadful, came out with him. She debated whether or not to tell them what she and Mum were actually up to and decided it was best to lay their cards on the table.

When she had finished, Mop said: "Why not take your little girl over to your pa's and we'll all go? Me and Persimmon both know the back alleys of this burg like the palms of our hands."

"How about giving me a six-shooter?" Persimmon said. "I know how to use one."

Mum scotched that notion. "I don't doubt it, young man, but in this case all we need from you is a good set of lungs."

Persimmon looked crestfallen, especially since his juices had just been pumped up by the adventures of the James gang in the pages of his book. "I'll take my slingshot," he said. "I'm aces with a slingshot."

It was full dark when the little cavalcade rode uptown in Mum's light wagon, Mop driving. They hitched it on the back street near Crowder's, and spread out on foot.

Will, Hal, and Dolf were talking in low voices over after-dinner cigars in the Grand's dining room. The count was hosting his own small party nearby, consisting of Doe, Bierce, and Doc. Dolf noted Doe's casting her eyes their way several times and bet her nose for news would prompt her to come over and horn in. He won his bet.

She walked over casually. "Good evening. You three look like you're hatching the kind of mischief that makes page one. Can I sit down?"

Will regarded her with good humor. She was one of his favorite people, considered by both him and his wife, Clemmy, as a second daughter. He glanced at Dolf and Hal and said: "I don't think it can do any harm if she knows how things are coming along back East, either."

"I'm all ears," she said.

*Aren't you always, little lady?* Dolf thought. *And that isn't all.* He wasn't blind to her charms for men, either.

"In a nutshell," Will said, "things aren't going too good. The Magnate mine people are running true to form. They aren't exactly against selling, but they want about twice what it's worth. Their kind are always that way. If we could just make them see that their mine isn't apt to be worth anything if they keep stalling, they'd sell in a minute."

Doe rejoined the count's table and sat down in a chair across from Bierce, whereas she'd been next to him when she left. When the others appeared not to be watching, she made a quick motion with her head, signaling that she'd like to see him alone.

In a while he arose and stretched. "I'm gonna walk off dinner and stretch my weary old legs. If you gentlemen don't mind, I'm going to take my charming colleague here along . . . you fellows have monopolized her long enough. Are you game, Doe?"

"If these two will excuse us," Doe said. "Besides, I have some newspaper talk on my mind that would only bore these two."

"I know when I've been invited out," Doc said. "See you later. Me and the count have an appointment with the pasteboards."

The count rose and bowed to Doe as she left.

Once out of hearing, Doe told Bierce: "I've got a great idea. I got it from something Will said."

"Let's talk while we walk," Bierce suggested.

Once on the sidewalk, he prepared and lit a cigar while she waited, then said: "Shoot. Are we going to jail for whatever you're planning?"

She laughed. "I don't think so."

"That's a comfort. I wouldn't like Hanratty's jail . . . I've inspected the dungeon he had Big Bill in, and it's not my idea of luxury."

"As you know, I interviewed Bradley," she began, and dug down in her bag and pulled out a small pamphlet and held it out. "I sort of borrowed this. I don't think he's missed it yet."

"What is it?"

"His company's telegraph code book, I think."

"And what do you propose we do with it?"

She told him about Will's misgivings regarding the purchase of the Magnate and his idea of what would break the stalemate. The result of the meeting was a coded message to Bradley's superiors that read:

IMMEDIATE ATTENTION COLON MINERS HAVE JUST BLOWN UP THE MAGNATE STOP DAMAGE EXTENSIVE ENOUGH TO PUT IT OUT OF BUSINESS COMPLETELY STOP ESTIMATE AT LEAST A YEAR INTERRUPTION OF OPERATION AND MAYBE A MILLION IN EXPENSE STOP RECOMMEND IMMEDIATE SALE ON BEST TERMS YOU CAN GET END
BRADLEY

Bierce filed the wire, and got an inquiring look from the operator, who knew his identity, but assumed it was a coded message on behalf of his newspaper who must have some connection with the Magnate's big bugs back East.

Dolf left the Grand by the side door, accompanied by Will, who he planned to see home. They emerged from the alley onto the street. They had walked perhaps fifty feet when a figure emerged from the alley, a rifle half raised in his hands.

The rifleman yelled: "Turn around, Morgette!"

Recognizing the situation in a flash, Dolf pushed Will away hard, and leaped to one side, jerking his six-shooter and spinning to face toward the voice. There was good shooting light from reflected business windows, and he saw the raised rifle, then the muzzle flame, and recognized Kirby behind the gun. The bullet whizzed by close enough to hear. *Missed,* he thought. *I can't miss at this range.*

But, even under the circumstances, he shot only to put the man out of business, rather than kill him. His heavy .45 slug cut one of Kirby's legs from under him. He fell, still trying to work the gun, and, in a snarling voice that reached Dolf, said: "If I wasn't almost blind, I'd have got you."

Obviously in shock, but moved by animal determination, he worked the lever lying on his side and tried to swing toward Dolf, who kept him covered, not wishing to shoot again if he could avoid it, especially since Kirby had given him fair warning. He rapidly started toward the downed man, planning to kick the gun out of his hand. As he moved forward, a small figure ran from the alley, and sprang through the air onto Kirby's rifle, trying to wrest it away. Their bodies were entangled on the ground when Mike Hanratty erupted from the door of the Grand, took in the scene in a flash, and ran toward the struggling bodies. A lusty kick of his size fourteen boot to Kirby's head put him out of action.

Hanratty looked toward Dolf. "You hit?"

"Nope," Dolf said as he came up and looked down at Kirby's inert form. He shook his head. "The poor bastard must be almost blind . . . but he's got guts." He reloaded and holstered his six-shooter.

Doc led the charge of others from the Grand and went to Kirby, briefly examined him, and said to himself—

"Gotta get a tourniquet on this."—and pulled out his handkerchief.

Dolf had picked up Persimmon from where he landed on Kirby and looked him over. "I guess I owe you one," he said.

Mum and Margaret came out of the alley briefly, were unnoticed in the excitement of a converging crowd, and stepped back. "They ain't gonna need us now," Mum observed. "If I'd been a few seconds sooner, I'd have loaded him with buckshot. C'mon, best Dolf never finds out we was here."

Mop joined them, coming from across the street. While he was driving them home, Mum said: "I wonder how long it will be before that one out there is out of the pen and makes another try. Dolf is too softhearted."

*She's right*, Maggie thought, *but I wouldn't love him the way I do, if he was any other way. I guess I'm stuck with him.* She'd barely been able to restrain herself from running to him, but knew it wouldn't have been the thing to do. *He'll be home and tell me about it, and I can hug him then.*

"Ain't that kid a caution?" Mum said.

"Should I go back and get him?" Mop asked.

"I don't think so. He'll want to be with Dolf. And Dolf'll want him with him, under the circumstances."

Before morning an urgent wire reached Will Alexander, which the operator hired a messenger to carry out to his house. It read:

WILL ALEXANDER FROM GOULD

SUDDEN SURPRISING CHANGE OF HEART HERE STOP WE JUST BOUGHT OURSELVES A MINE STOP DID SOMETHING HAPPEN THERE TO CHANGE MINDS STOP DETAILS TO FOLLOW END

Will wondered if maybe the count was the real McCoy and had sent off a wire that had swung the deal. He decided that, if he had and wanted them to know about it, he'd tell them when he was ready.

This news shared the front page with the story of the night's shooting in front of the Grand. Dolf slept late and finally came down to breakfast where he read what Hal had written under the headline:

### SHOOTING AND MINE PURCHASE RIVALS FOR NEWS

The two stories shared side-by-side columns on the front page.

Later that day, Dolf was discharged at a routine preliminary hearing regarding his shooting of Kirby. After he was discharged, Dolf took Hanratty aside. "I reckon you can spare me for a while. There likely won't be any more bombings. As for solving the three, we may never get to the bottom of them. Like Big Bill said, maybe we got a shadow bomber on our hands."

"I don't give a damn if we ever solve them," Hanratty said. Then, pausing, with a distant look, he said: "I reckon you're goin' fishin'. I wish I could."

"Why not?" Dolf asked. "Gorman can hold down a soft job like you got."

Hanratty ignored the jibe, if he heard it, and didn't change expression. "You sweet talkin' devil, Dolf. You talked me into playin' hookey. When are *we* leavin'?"

"First thing in the a.m. Get your possibles together and come out to Mum's for breakfast. We'll pull out from there. All you need is personal stuff and a bedroll."

## Chapter Twenty-Four

Margaret had named the lake to which they were going Emerald. She and Dolf, on their first vacation there, had climbed to the top of the snow-covered peak and sat side-by-side on a rocky promontory, looking down at their distant camp. The lake had shrunk to a small oval. They could see deeply into it until it finally clouded in its depths to an opaque emerald green. Margaret explained the name for the lake to Chief Henry, and he accepted it, carefully pronouncing the word: "Em-er-ald. Em-er-ald. I like the sound of it."

Early the morning of their projected departure for this vacation excursion to Emerald Lake, Dolf and Mum were seated at the kitchen table where Mop and Persimmon had eaten breakfast. Dolf called to them after they were outside: "Persimmon, it didn't slip your mind that you're supposed to go camping with me, did it?"

The boy popped back in, grinning. "I reckon you're kidding, Mister Dolf?" It was the only name his mouth could form to address his hero, and he was to use nothing else for a lifetime.

Dolf was holding off on eating breakfast, waiting for Doc, Hanratty, and an as yet undetermined number of others to show up for a breakfast party. Margaret was upstairs getting Little Maggie washed and dressed. Dolf wondered if the count would accept his camping invitation, sent by way of Doc. He was sure that Doe Darling and Bierce were coming. Doc had called and told him they'd both been enthusiastic over the prospect.

After Persimmon left, Mum noted that Dolf seemed to be deep in thought. Finally she asked: "What's on your mind? You've been pretty quiet."

"I've thought a lot about it," he responded, "but can't decide what we're going to do about Amy while we're gone."

"I hate to miss a trip up there, but I guess I'll have to stay with her. Or maybe she could go out to the ranch and stay with her mother for a few days."

An aggrieved voice interrupted: "*Who* can stay with *whose* mother?" Amy had made it downstairs without help, and poked her head in the door. "Mother, my foot! Doc told me she's taken a room at the Grand and is chasing the count."

"No kidding?" Dolf said. He was surprised Doc hadn't told him. "How is she making out?"

"Not too good, I guess." Amy giggled. "Ma never changes. Do you suppose she'll ever grow up?"

*I'd sooner see her drop dead*, Mum thought.

Dolf said: "Some ways your Ma is more growed up than most of us."

304

"Name one," Amy challenged.

"She knows her mind, which is more than most folks do."

Amy nodded. "She does that. And she's made up her mind she wants another husband if she can't have you back. You know she said to me on the train coming out here . . . 'I made an awful mistake by betraying your father.' Can you imagine her using the word betraying?"

*Or admitting a mistake*, Dolf thought. He had trouble remembering how desperately he'd once loved her.

This was the first frank talk he and Amy had ever had on the subject of Theodora. For once Mum kept out of it, too fascinated to butt in. But she thought: *Of course, that idjit woman wants Dolf back . . . I never seen a woman that didn't look at him once and want him. What a fool she was, and I'm glad she'll go to her grave knowing it.* She looked at Dolf now and noted that, for all he'd been through, he still didn't look old, had only a bit of iron gray over his ears and at the temples which lent his appearance a distinguished touch. He had the most regular profile she'd ever seen, nose straight and only a trifle long, with a wide, firm mouth under his black sweeping mustache, and a very strong chin, almost to the point of massiveness, which was the only slight deviation from absolute perfection. His large, wide-set, dark blue eyes were normally shining and friendly, and, when he smiled or laughed, they fairly sparked, his chin dimple deepened, and the corners of his eyes crinkled. However, if angered, which was seldom, his face turned to granite, and his eyes turned almost black.

He laughed now and looked almost like a boy. "I got poisoned at that spring once, Amy, and that was enough. I got you two kids out of it, and God knows I'm glad of that."

Amy went to him, and hugged him awkwardly, since she was still stiff and he was sitting down. He took her shoulders and held her away from him, looking at her, eyes glowing. "You were the cutest little girl I ever saw . . . and now you're sure the prettiest girl I ever saw."

Maggie joined them, carrying her daughter, and said: "You told me *I* was the prettiest."

"You ain't a girl any more," Dolf said. "But you're sure pretty."

Mum said: "You wiggled off that hook pretty slick. You're a real Morgette. Take after your granddad McKenzie." She beamed at them all.

"Anyhow, back to the subject," Amy said. "I'm going with you. Doc said I was in good enough shape, and I feel a lot stronger."

"I never thought you weren't," Margaret said. "You can ride in a travois and be more comfortable than in bed."

"If the dang' horse don't run away," Mum said.

"Father has horses that have pulled them all their lives. Most of them are more apt to balk than run away. Besides, I'll lead this one myself."

They were interrupted by the arrival of a large contingent from town, and Dolf was happy to see the count with them. Mum had stretched out the dining room table to its full length, set for an army. Those who weren't going camping came as a sort of seeing-off party, and, since Matt and Junior had delayed their departure to join Mulveen's posse the day before, they were still in town and came with their wives and the new babies.

"We'll put them in on a bed," Mum said of the babies, "where we can hear 'em squalling if they need something." Then recalling how that was, she looked pensive and added: "And, if they don't, too."

Doc, the count, Bierce, and Doe came in a hack from the hotel, and jumped out, lifting out their luggage afterward. Hanratty and his meager camping outfit were delivered by the paddy wagon. Will Alexander had Dawson's large surrey deliver the crowd from his place—himself and Clemmy, Matt and Diana and William, their new baby, Junior and Catherine with newborn Margaret (a name Junior was sure would cause his mother a conniption); accompanying them was a surprise arrival, Harvey Parrent. Dolf hadn't known he was still in town and was glad to see him. He intended to insist that he come along up to Emerald Lake for what he considered an excellent reason—he was mortally certain Harvey was in love with Amy, and he'd rather see Amy become a ranch wife than a globe-trotter with high-flying ambitions like Doe Darling. Besides, although she wasn't apt to recognize the symptoms, he thought his daughter felt something deeper than mere affection for young Harvey.

A little later, Chief Henry rode over with his grandson who was mounted on a high Appaloosa that had been on earth quite a number of years and stood steady as a rock when little Henry reined it in. The hollows above its wise eyes also pronounced that it was long in the tooth. Dolf smiled as he watched his son slide off without help from anyone, lead the animal onto a good patch of lawn grass, and pat its nose, which was all he could reach easily. He heard him say with authority: "You stay there." Whether it was obedient or not, it was a fair bet it wouldn't stray far until it had eaten down the entire lawn. Jim Too was with them, since he'd decided that Amy didn't need protection any longer and had gone to Chief Henry's camp to look up his young charge. He was sure that Henry required supervision most of the time. Besides, there was the challenge of again whipping all the dogs in the Indian village that had forgotten their last lesson, and the new ones that had never met him. His plan was then to lead them like a wolf pack.

The cavalcade was impressive by the time it was joined by several close friends of Chief Henry, and their wives, families who were too old to have young children. The chief was no fonder of noisy kids than he had been a few years before, although he would never admit it.

Including extra mounts and pack horses, the column numbered around two hundred horses. They wound slowly upward through fragrant balsam, columbines, and dazzling blue lupine. The trip required two days. Late afternoon the second day, they set up camp in the usual grassy meadow below a towering, gray mountain peak. Elk were so unused to seeing humans that they only moved to the far end of the park and continued grazing.

Persimmon took it all in with awe. He'd never had his own horse, and Dolf had given him a .22 rifle to carry. "In case of an Injun attack," Dolf had told him, tongue-in-cheek. Persimmon looked perplexed for an instant, then brightened. "Aw, yer funnin' me again."

Persimmon looked around at this paradise, where aspen and willow hemmed the lake and long webs of spruce and lodgepole pine ascended to timberline. Squinting at the mountain seemed to turn it into a rugged face that gazed down like a giant. He thought: *If it's a giant, he's old with all that white hair, and his nose is running*, since the giant was completely covered with snow at the very top that melted and formed little streams that rushed down the descending cañons, then joined the creek that ran into Emerald Lake and out the far side. He reflected how he'd learned from a geography book in school that it rushed down eventually to the Mustang River, through its cañon into bigger rivers, and finally to the sea. He wondered if ever a drop of water made the circuit and came back as rain, blowing in from the Pacific.

Dolf and Maggie made a place for him in their teepee, his own buffalo robe bed near the rolled up tent skirts from which he would be able to see the stars at night. Dolf told him: "Those robes might look like they'd be too hot to sleep in just now, but it gets cold up here at night . . . a lot colder than down lower. Might have ice on the wash basins."

Margaret watched Dolf wander off by himself after dinner. She had expected it. Her father noticed and nodded slightly to her, as though to say: *I, too, expected it.* He thought: *My son is a great warrior and must talk with his medicine, especially in places like this.*

Dolf, walking silently as a wolf, Jim Too beside him, came unexpectedly upon two people seated on a log, facing the lake below. He recognized them as Harvey and Amy, close together, watching the moon rise over the shoulder of the mountain.

He heard Amy exclaim: "Oh, it's so beautiful! No other part of the world can be this beautiful."

He retreated quietly, feeling guilty over having overheard even that innocent remark. Jim Too sniffed toward the pair on the log, then followed.

Harvey felt as though he was in heaven. He'd never before touched more than her hand, and now she leaned her shoulder against him. Its warmth and the strength he felt in her small body surprised him. She smelled of scented soap. He wanted to turn and bury his head in her long hair and hold her tenderly, but wouldn't have done it for the world, being absolutely sure she'd resent it, perhaps slap his face for being fresh.

Therefore, he was astounded when she said: "Harvey, have you ever kissed a girl?"

He felt himself blushing deeply and was glad it was dark.

Finally she said: "Well? You can tell me."

He realized she was giggling, and he felt like giggling himself but finally got up his courage and stammered:

"I never kissed anyone but Ma . . . and that was only on her cheek."

They were silent for a long while. She admitted: "I never kissed a boy. When I was younger, Ma told me I'd have a baby if I let a boy kiss me. Isn't that silly?"

He thought about that seriously, since he knew where kissing was supposed to lead, and figured her ma may have given her better advice than she knew. He didn't know what to say so remained silent.

At last she said: "I'd like to be kissed. Would you like to kiss me?"

He felt he'd like to be somewhere else, not that he didn't want to kiss her, in fact it was what he wanted to do most of anything in the world, but he didn't know how. Finally, sensing that she'd be offended if he didn't say or do something, he confessed his problem.

She giggled. "Let's try it. I heard one of our cowboys say once . . . 'There ain't no wrong way.'" She turned her face to him and invited him to get his first practice.

He'd never dreamed she was so straightforward and earthy. He trembled, frightened that he might botch it and she'd laugh, but determined to try if it killed him. His first attempt was pretty clumsy.

"It's hard in the position we're in," she said. "Let's get up and face each other and you can hold me. I won't break. Just don't squeeze too hard."

He hadn't thought of squeezing at all. He was almost afraid to touch all of her, but thought: *I'm in this pickle now and have to get out. I hope she doesn't laugh.*

Tentatively he drew her close and put his arms around

her shoulders. She pressed closer; he could feel her whole body against him and was suddenly terribly embarrassed by an awful possibility. When he tried to pull away, she held on, tilting her head back and presenting her lips. He conquered his apprehension and tried again and was a little more successful, wondering at how soft and warm and yielding her mouth was, even when she pressed it against him. She sighed, and he could hear her breathing a little faster. Then he started to feel what he was afraid might happen and pushed her away.

She asked: "What's the matter, don't you like to do it?"

"I liked it real well, Miss Amy," he confessed." I just think we ought to take a little breather. Let's walk or something."

Being a ranch girl, raised around earthy people, she figured out his problem. "Come back here," she said. "Being natural is nothing to be ashamed of." She wanted to feel him and know she was responsible for arousing him.

And he wanted nothing more than to return and hold her; finally, slowly, he moved back against her. She pushed hard against him, and he knew she must feel everything, but she didn't pull back. Instead, she pressed harder. Finally she pulled her lips away and took a deep breath, followed by several more. He was breathing as heavily as she was.

"Was that so bad?" she asked, wiggling against him again wickedly.

"It's wonderful," he admitted. "And I hope you know

I can't help myself." Then, softly: "I love you Miss Amy. I love you something fierce. I want to marry you and take care of you always, Amy." It was the first time he used only the name Amy.

His proposal brought her to her senses. "We're too young to know our minds yet. Or at least I am. I'm going away with Miss Darling and see the world and learn to write . . . maybe I'll be famous someday, like her."

He felt a terrible lump rise in his throat at the thought of separating, perhaps never seeing her again, especially after this night. *If she felt like me*, he thought, *she wouldn't say that. She was just having some fun with me.* He felt the tears in his eyes and hoped she didn't notice in the moonlight. He tried to turn away, but she saw them. "Please don't feel bad. I'll be back here someday. I'm just too young to be thinking about babies and housework and drudgery, and I don't want to look like ranch women do by the time they're forty. Some of their horses look better, and I know they're happier."

Harvey's heart got a lift from that. *Sometime,* maybe, was a lot better than never. "I wouldn't let you be a drudge," Harvey said. "And I won't touch another woman till you come back." He felt tears coming again as he vowed: "If you don't never come back, there won't be anybody for me." It was all he could manage to say because of the lump in his throat.

*Dear God, what did I do?* she thought. *I like him better than any man, but I'm just too young.* The passion she'd experienced, the first time ever, had ebbed. She took his hand. "Let's just walk a while. It's so beautiful."

Dolf saw them outlined against the lake a little later, holding each other close, and wondered if they were as happy as he hoped they were. He never felt half so carefree as he did in this spot. Later that night, after he was sure everyone in the lodge was asleep, he drew Margaret close, kissing her over and over, and they quietly made love. Completely relaxed afterward, he slept like a baby.

Several days of hunting and fishing passed peacefully, with good talk and lots of coffee and smoking after supper. Doc, the count, and Hanratty had their private firewater sessions around their own campfire, usually joined by Bierce. Dolf sometimes sat with them companionably, but seldom took a drink.

On their last day of bliss, Doc asked Dolf: "Do you happen to know what the date is?"

"Nope," Dolf said. "And I don't give a hang." He didn't especially think anything of the circle of his many friends congregating, smiles on their faces.

"You reckon we'll have much more of that bomb trouble?" Doc inquired innocently.

"I'd bet we don't. Unless that shadow bomber gets in some more work."

"I'll bet you a double eagle the son-of-a-gun does," Doc said. "Wouldn't surprise me if he came up here and made trouble."

"It would me," Dolf said. "Or anywhere else, either, come to think of it. I'll take that bet just for the heck of it."

Doc shook his hand, savoring Dolf's startled expression as a huge explosion shook the hillside down the valley, setting loose a small avalanche. Dolf looked stunned for a moment, then, noting Doc's grin, said: "You set that up, you devil."

He grabbed Doc and threw him over his shoulder, easily keeping him there despite his struggles.

Doc yelled: "Don't be a poor sport. I tried to tell you it was the Fourth of July."

Dolf waded out into the lake until it was up to his boot tops, then threw Doc as far as he could propel him. When Doc came up sputtering, Dolf said: "Happy Independence Day."

## Epilogue

The happiest person at the departure of Dolf and Margaret for Alaska was Persimmon. They had adopted him, and he was going to America's Ice Box to see polar bears and perpetual snow—or so he thought. Mum had decided to stay in Pinebluff for a while and come north with Doc, who was going south to see his family and old friends, planning to head north before freeze up.

At the train, Harvey Parrent came to see Amy off. They stood to one side, talking urgently. Theodora started toward them, and Dolf reached out and held her arm. "Leave them be," he said in the voice she'd learned would tolerate no nonsense.

She gave him a dirty look. "I want to say good bye to

the count. Turn me loose."

Dolf watched them and grinned when the count shook hands formally with her, and also earned a dirty look.

At the call of "All Aboard", Dolf saw Harvey and Amy kiss and hold each other tightly, then Amy turned, head down, and went swiftly to the train, ignoring her mother's outstretched hand. He felt an infinite sorrow for Amy at the sight of her streaming tears and prayed that life would treat her kindly in the end.

He remembered the desolate days and nights he'd spent in prison knowing that the woman he loved had deserted him. This wasn't exactly the same, but he was sure he knew how terrible Harvey was feeling. In an attempt to cheer him up, he went over and shook his hand. The young man was trying to control himself and not cry in public, his lower lip was quivering, and he looked completely dejected. Dolf had never seen a more heart-broken man, even in prison where you could hear grown men sobbing in the dark. Dolf said: "She'll be back. You can count on it."

Harvey said in a choked voice: "I hope so. God, how I hope so."

Then he spun and walked away rapidly, wiping at his eyes. Dolf watched his heaving back until he disappeared inside the depot.

Bierce, the count, and Doe Darling were all on the same train as the Morgettes. A night passed, and Amy's eyes, though swollen, were presentable enough that she didn't avoid the others. Doe had Amy in charge, assuring her: "You'll get the hang of news writing. And editors are all men. They'll be putty in the hands of a beautiful young woman like you."

Amy protested: "If I can't get by on my writing, I don't want to do it."

Bierce, overhearing, said: "Best give both a try. Doe can't write for shucks, but male editors made her famous."

Doe took a swing at him with her purse, and he ducked, chuckling. Then she fished into it, pulled something out, and said: "Take a look at this if you'd like to know how I got famous."

Bierce looked. "I'll be damned!"

It was the count in his uniform as a French Admiral, with an official caption below stating his name and title. "I got it from the Sureté in Paris," she said, naming the famous French police agency.

After breakfast in the dining car, Dolf told Margaret: "I'll see you in our compartment in a little while."

She suspected that he wanted to have some peace away from the young children while he smoked and devoted some quiet moments to his thoughts, as he often did. Instead, Dolf started back toward the observation car to smoke his cigar, and motioned Persimmon to follow. He knew it would do the boy a lot of good to spend some time alone with him.

They sat, companionably side-by-side, in heavy wicker chairs. After a long while, Persimmon asked: "Will you tell me about some of your famous law cases someday?"

Dolf grinned. "Sure. But I didn't do so well on the shadow bomber, did I? It looks like that one will always be a mystery."

Persimmon was quiet a long while, and finally asked: "Will you keep it a secret if I tell you who he is?"

Dolf scrutinized the boy's face closely to see if he was serious. Finally he said: "OK. You're on, as long as he never hurts anybody somewhere else. He sure didn't do much damage in Pinebluff, except maybe scaring some Pinkertons, and making a few people deaf. Who was it?"

"Hank H."

"Are you sure?"

"Sure, I'm sure. I signaled him from the top of a building across from Bradley's when it was clear to cut that one loose without hurting anybody. He put a little too much dynamite in it, though."

Dolf tried to hide his surprise, but didn't quite manage. "How about the one down at the Pinkertons'? He might have killed someone with that one."

Persimmon said: "Yeah, but he didn't intend to. He set it off with a clock timer for two a.m. He forgot that two o'clock comes twice a day, he told me. So it went off at two in the afternoon, and he was as surprised as anyone. You know he ain't quite right upstairs?"

"Why did he do it, do you know?"

"He said mine owners brought in Pinks and killed his pa years ago. And he said he didn't much care about Bradley giving me only a dollar when Pa was killed. He was madder about that, maybe, and said . . . 'I wonder if he could spare it?' It was better'n nothing. I was really hungry. I made it last a week."

Dolf was quiet a long while, puffing reflectively on his cigar. He noticed that Persimmon was beginning to look apprehensive.

The boy asked: "You ain't gonna go back on your word are you, Mister Dolf?"

Dolf reached out and squeezed the boy's shoulder. "How the heck could I do that? You'd go to jail as an accessory. Would I do that to my pard who saved my life?"

Persimmon beamed, but he was close to tears.

Dolf puffed his cigar and made it a point to look over the retreating scenery for a long while until he was sure Persimmon was OK. *There are enough tears in the world without going out of our way to cause any more*, he thought.

**Center Point Publishing**
600 Brooks Road • PO Box 1
Thorndike ME 04986-0001 USA


(207) 568-3717


US & Canada:
1 800 929-9108